Maddox Files:
Blurred Lines

R. J. Davies

Cover design by Pennina-Lynn Cobb of Penny C. Designs

http://www.rjdavies.ca

ISBN: 978-0-9939503-6-0

ACKNOWLEDGMENTS

To my fans who have enjoyed Maddox Files Back to Business and Dice Maddox Series, thank you for being a Dice Maddox supporter! Thank you for picking up "Maddox Files: Back to Business" and now this one "Maddox Files: Blurred Lines", your love and support is greatly appreciated. Thank you!

To my family for your support, a special thanks to Denziel Mornix (Denziel the Best) I greatly appreciate your patience and for being my cheerleader when I needed it. You are my muse and the wind beneath my wings, thank you!

A special thank you to my beta readers Diane Davies (my mom and one of my biggest fans), Agnes Cristina Prachthauser, Penny Cobb, Diana Fleetwood and Nikki Shaw, thank you for your feedback.

Pennina-Lynn Cobb of Penny C. Designs, I greatly appreciate your commitment, skills and expertise in designing my book covers and logo, you truly captured my vision through the logo and the book cover designs. Thank you!

Warmest thanks and best wishes to you all,

R. J. Davies

CHAPTER ONE

There was just something so good about closing a case. Since she got back into the private investigating business again, it has been busy ... extremely busy. Dice Maddox was not complaining. It still haunted her, her first case back, which was an odd case. It had ended in a weird mystery. Ryan Winters he had recovered and returned to work, but he wasn't the same. He had visited her a few times and she noticed he had changed. When she had first met him he was a confirmed bachelor and he tried picking her up at a restaurant. He hired her because a woman entered his life claiming to be his wife. She died in a shooting he fully recovered physically after trying to shield his mysterious wife from the shooter. Mentally ... he looked haunted. Her friend Ty warned her there were some things in this world that people didn't want to know about. Once you knew, there was just no way to undo what you knew.

Sighing she looked around her office it was just her here alone. People were coming and going all day and she just got a break. It had been a month since she closed her first case. In that month she managed to regain her sanctuary of her condo back ... when she went home it felt like going home. Chris kept popping in to check on her; she felt that they were better friends than a couple. Since she found out he had cheated on her they broke off their engagement but at the same time managed to still talk to each other.

Then there was Sean Larke ... handsome ... single and someone she could see spending time with. They use to go running together until a couple of weeks ago and he became busy and didn't have time for her. She wanted to keep her life free and relax. He wanted to be more than just friends. Tessa hinted the other day at lunch he was seeing someone else, but she didn't think it was serious yet. Dice didn't need that kind of distraction at this time. Her main focus was working and rebuilding a career and business she could be proud of.

When she opened the doors she didn't expect the success that she had gotten since then. It was busy non-stop. Wives wanting their husbands followed, background checks for new employees, searching for missing people.

Closing the electronic file on her last case, she decided today she was going to skip the Red Dragon customary stop for a celebratory drink. The Red Dragon was a bar that was just a few doors down from her office. The owner a Welshman named Gary Yates who was also a friend. The Red Dragon inspired by the Welsh flag. It was a great meeting place and she had found Sean frequently visited the place but that was because he also knew the owner and he had remodeled the bar after Gary took over about eight years ago.

Shutting down her computer, she gave her office the once over then turned off the lights. Heading out, the days were longer so the sun was still up at 7 pm. Locking up, she looked up and down the street, inhaling a deep breath and holding it for a few seconds then letting it out she looked back at her office sign. "Maddox Investigations" ... that was one of the nicest signs in town. Grinning from ear to ear, she felt very proud. Heading over to her car, she got in and pulled out.

She decided to stop at the grocery store on the way home to pick up something for dinner. Traffic was light as she drove over to the grocery store she realized she was back on track; this is the life she needed to be living. To feel complete, she felt whole and alive. Finding a spot with little effort, she grabbed her empty reusable grocery bags from the glove compartment and then headed inside. The cool air condition greeted her with fresh produce aromas. Grabbing a cart, she began down the fruit and veggie aisle. Picking through the many different kinds, she decided on some dragon fruit, kiwi, bokchoy and was moving over to the other veggies. She was looking forward to spending the night in, making a stir-fry of veggies and then watching some foreign movies on Netflix.

Her cell phone rang. Checking the caller ID it was Chris Douglas her ex-fiancé again. Curiosity caught the better of her as she answered. "Yes?"

"It's about time you picked up I've been trying to catch you all day."

"I do work."

"I know but I'm desperate I need your help tonight."

Groaning on the inside, she should have let his call go to voice mail. "I've got plans already."

"Dice eating a tub of ice cream and watching foreign movies isn't plans."

"Ha! A lot you know about me. Why are you calling me anyways?"

"Remember, I asked you last week if you would go to Jeff Biggins' birthday party with me and you did say yes. I remember you said yes."

Yes, she remembered saying yes. It was next month and she figured she had enough time to get out of it. Jeff was the creepy guy that just didn't understand the word no, he was supposed to be Chris's friend yet the moment he found out she knew about Chris sleeping around he was there trying to pick her up. "Yeah, that's next month what about it?"

"I got the dates mixed up its tonight."

"What?" she shook her head no, "No, I'm not going."

"Dice you promised me you would come."

"Alright, I guess we both made promises to each other that we aren't going to keep." She felt bad for saying that as soon as the words came out.

"You'll never know how much I regret doing that to us. I need you. You can network. There will be a ton of rich people at the party that you can pass your business cards out to them," he pleaded.

"Fine," she grumbled. "Fine, I'll just need time to have a shower and get ready. I'm not even at home right now."

"That's okay I'll be there in fifteen minutes to pick you up." He hung up before she could protest.

Making a face at her phone, she shoved it back into her purse and put her food back then headed out of the store empty-handed. She was home in five minutes and left the condo door unlocked. Chris was persuasive enough he could find his way in from downstairs.

She had to have her head examined, here she was rushing to have a quick shower to go out on a date with her ex, and to a birthday party for a guy she couldn't stand. All she wanted to do was sit on the sofa and watch some movies tonight eating some homemade Chinese food.

Dice showered in record time and when she came out she found a dress laid out for her on the bed with shoes. A small part of her was grateful that he was helping and another part was annoyed that he came into her closet and picked out something for her to wear. Slipping into the dress, she fixed her hair and makeup then gave herself the once over look in the mirror. She did manage to clean up very nice. Scooping up some of her business cards, she wasn't going to miss out on her network opportunity. The wealthy knew how to pay for services rendered.

Chris was in the living room waiting for her when she came out. "Wow you look beautiful."

"I always look beautiful," she laughed. "You don't look so bad yourself."

"I can't thank you enough for doing this for me."

"I'm not doing it just for you. I am going there to do some networking." She smirked at him. "Plus, you will owe me one."

"That's my girl," he grinned at her as he got the door.

She almost said something but refrained from it, no sense getting into a spat over choice of words, besides she had her own agenda tonight. Sure she was raking in the clients right now. It could be either two things she was just that good or it could be the fact that she was the new girl in town and people were just checking her out. She knew enough from working with her Uncle Eric who taught her, the tricks of the trade never give up the opportunity to make connections and pass out your business card. Meeting someone today could be a future client eight months from now or next year.

They took his car over to the party. She didn't mind and knew she could get home by herself whenever she wanted to. She wasn't reliant on her date to get home. Since they broke up, she had noticed he had changed a little. He was more … more accepting of her choices. He was also supportive and paid her compliments. It didn't matter because he had no say in what she did anymore. Her Aunt Sophie who had sided with Chris had accepted her choices and was being supportive heck she took over and decorated her office. They were both trying to stay in her good graces … and to be a part of her life.

Dice was very aware that they both looked for opportunities to show their support as much as possible. Her Aunt Sophie was a significant part of her life and that wasn't about to change. It was just that Dice was no longer allowing others to make decisions for her. Dice had taken the steps toward being an adult, taking charge and doing what she wanted to do. With that thought in mind, she also considered a partner for both work and home; but believed some people were just meant to be alone. It didn't mean they were lonesome or incomplete. Contrary to the general public's belief that you needed to be in a relationship to feel fulfilled and happy that was something she wasn't buying into. She felt more complete living alone, she didn't feel lonesome as she thought she would, in fact, she didn't have time since she closed her first case.

On the way over to the party, Chris was making idle chit-chat about the people at the office. She smiled and hoped he would find someone soon to replace her for these social engagements. This would be the third one since they broke up. She thought everyone at these gatherings knew the truth that they were no longer together but no one dared asked them about their wedding plans ... nor did anyone make any references to the blond girl he had been seeing. In fact people put on their smiling faces and made idle small talk, she was sure as soon as they were out of hearing they would chatter their rumors and speculations but that didn't bother her any. For the most part she was happy not having to deal with these people on a regular basis.

They made their initial rounds greeting the birthday boy and his date. Then going through and meeting the office gang, greeting them and their wives who flashed everyone their fake smiles with their fake faces ... most of them had plastic surgery done to look younger but in her opinion it didn't help, it just made them look sad as they tried to recapture their youth. There were about four women she learned to avoid because as soon as they caught a whiff of weakness they were all over it like a pack of wild dogs.

Chris found them a safe spot away from the action. He disappeared for a few minutes and she drank in the party. They were all dress up and looked amazing. She didn't stick out in a bad way. The dress he picked out allowed her to fit in. There was a couple standing across the way, they had looked her way a few times and were deep in conversation. Chris returned with their drinks and she was grateful for the distraction.

"Remind me why am I out on a date with my ex?" she looked up at him.

He grinned back, "Because I am irresistible and charming. Soon you are going to realize that I am perfect for you."

Drinking from her glass, she resisted the urge to counter that comment.

"I know I haven't given you much hope when we were together but when you left me I realized that you were the best time I had ever had. I'm not giving up on you Dice."

"I think that ship has sailed."

"I don't ... because if it did why would you be here with me now?" he flashed her a million-dollar smile.

She laughed and grinned back at him, "its' called an opportunity for networking, baby. Don't get it confused with anything else. This isn't a teen drama where I'm going to fall back into your arms and forgive you because you learned your lesson."

"Don't underestimate the power of a good teen drama," he chuckled.

His eyes sparkled at their playful banter and easy company. She remembered that was what attracted her to him in the first place. She reached out and grabbed his hand. Looking around, they had privacy where they were seated. Looking back at him, she didn't want him to get the wrong idea. "Chris, you are a great guy, you are. We all have our demons that we have to deal with but don't get the wrong idea please. There 'is' no us. If I am honest, I still care about you and I don't want to see you get hurt. With that being said, there is no us and there never will be. That ship has sailed. I love my life that I have now. I don't intend to compromise myself for anyone. You and me ... we are just friends and nothing more. We will never be anything more than that again. Do you understand?"

He leaned in and kissed her on the lips, pulling back he grinned. "I knew it you still cared for me. Mark, my word Dice we will be an item again."

"Oh my god, can you take off your man ears for a minute that's not ..."

"Chris! Dice!" one of Chris's partners came rushing over with his wife. "I am so happy you two could make it."

Dice bit back some angry words and forced a smile on her face.

Maybe coming to these parties with him was giving him the wrong impression. Smiling and nodding she acted like the good little date and joined in conversation as they discussed the war that might break out ... over in the Middle East. Then they moved on to vacation hotspots. Dice had some experience in a couple of places they were thinking of going for their twentieth anniversary and gave her two cents' worth of what not to miss as far as sightseeing went. Music started and the couple went off to dance but not before Dice offered them her business card. They were impressed that she was such a young professional, and asked for a couple more because the wife knew of a couple people who would be interested in her kind of work. Chris led her out on the dance floor. It was an outside patio area that had been set up for the party. He held her close she didn't dare bring up the subject again with so many ears listening in on their conversation. Instead they kept their conversation to work and what was playing at the local theaters. He got some tickets for a Mozart concert that was being given by the local orchestra, and knew she would want to go.

A part of her wanted to kick him in the shins and walk away ... maybe she should just run, chuckling to herself at the thought she shoved it out of her mind.

"What's so funny?"

Shaking her head, she looked away watching the partygoers. It never failed there was a lady fight breaking out over at the bar. Smirking she wondered how they lasted this long before it occurred.

"Oh just great," Chris grumbled as he noticed the commotion. "Hold on here honey I'll be right back." He went over and tried to help. Dice managed to find a nice spot and tried not to look too amused by the entertainment. Chris was a good guy when it came to these things he was in there doing his best to separate the ladies and to quiet them down. They both however had too much alcohol and refused to be stifled. Chris was just a nuisance and an obstacle that was in their way. Before he knew it, they both turned on him. The husbands of the ladies came to the rescue and grabbed their wives dragging them off to separate corners, giving them a stern talking to. They didn't seem to care. She watched as each of the ladies were still seething and glaring at each other. That fight wasn't over yet.

Chris got cornered by one of his co-workers. Dice looked around enjoying the cool breeze that crept in over the over humid evening night air. It was still very warm out.

"Hey pretty lady, how are you doing?" Jeff whispered in her ear.

Gritting her teeth, she forced a smile on her face as she stepped away from him and turned to face him. "Happy Birthday," she tried to be on her best behavior.

"Hey my offer still stands you can call me anytime," he grinned at her like she was a piece of meat.

"Thank you for being so generous. What about your girlfriend wouldn't she have a problem with you coming to my rescue?"

"Do you need rescuing?" he pinned her with his eyes.

"No, no I don't," she smiled at him. One of the ladies was back yelling at Chris.

"Are you and ...," he looked over at Chris who was now trying very much to fend off the angry wife who started hitting him. Her husband grabbed her around the waist and carried her away kicking and screaming profanities. Chris looked a little shaken as he readjusted himself. Looking over at her, he smiled and waved.

She smiled and waved back. "I'm sorry, what was your question?" Dice didn't bother looking back at Jeff. She could feel him watching her.

"You deserve better Dice."

His words were a slap in the face. Who was he to tell her what she did or didn't deserve? Turning she looked at him and tried to smile. "Don't presume to know me Jeff, nor what I deserve or don't deserve. You are in a relationship with a very pretty lady, you should be hanging on to her every word right now not over here disturbing me."

"You little ...," he grumbled.

"Hey, Jeff! Happy birthday," Chris interceded just in time.

"Hi Chris, I'm glad you two could make it."

"You know I wouldn't miss this buddy, where's Freya?"

"She is off chatting about lady things with a few of the other ladies."

"I heard you two took the next step." Chris shook his friend's hand and slapped him on the back. "Congratulations, did you set a date yet?"

Dice turned a smirk towards Jeff who looked a little sheepish. "Yes, we did, nothing set in gold yet. Anything can happen." He stared at Dice.

"That's a big step when a man makes that kind of commitment he takes himself off the singles market," she smiled and sipped her drink.

Both men looked sheepish and cleared their throats. Chris gave her a look to behave. She grinned back … she had them both and they knew it.

"I'll let you both know when we set a date so you can mark it on your calendars. We'll expect both of you there." Jeff recovered from feeling guilty pretty fast as far as she thought.

Men like him seldom felt guilty for long Dice reminded herself. "Did Dice tell you she opened up her own business?"

"Oh how nice, congratulations I'm sure you will be a success."

"Here's my card, I'm sure Freya may need my services in the future," Dice smiled at him.

He took it and his face fell as he read it. "Private Investigation … you?"

Dice nodded.

"She is good too," Chris put an arm around her. "Everyone is so proud of Dice."

"I'm sure they are. I mean, of course, we are." He forced a smile on his face. "You know I shouldn't ignore the rest of my guests here. I'm going to go mingle but be sure I'll catch up with you," he looked at her then continued. "… later. Enjoy yourselves."

"Thanks buddy," Chris patted him on the shoulder again. Turning to her, he smiled. "I do have the best friends ever don't I?"

"Friends like yours are hard to find," she smiled at him. Part of her wanted to tell him what a snake Jeff Biggins was but they weren't a couple any longer. As her friend what did the guy do to her? Come on to her a couple of times. She didn't owe Chris anything. Yet, with that being said she would keep an eye on Jeff if he stepped out of line again. His kind most often do.

The rest of the evening was nice. She found herself enjoying the dancing and the conversation with Chris. He was the supportive friend helping her network herself with everyone there. When people starting leaving they looked at each other and knew it was okay this was their chance. Thanking Jeff and his fiancée, they made their exit.

Once they were back at his car, he opened the door for her and paused. "Thank you for coming with me. I do appreciate it I enjoyed your company, and the way you smile."

"You're welcome."

"Did you want to stop and get something on the way home?" he offered.

"No thank you, I have an early day in the morning." She brushed pass him and got in the car. Dice did enjoy her evening out with Chris. It was unexpected and fun. A small part of her didn't want the evening to end. Then the smart responsible side reminded her that ending this evening now on a good note was the smartest thing she could do. If they lingered and prolonged their evening, it had a higher chance of not ending well.

He got in, started the car and looked over at her grinning. "I have to admit I don't want this evening to end. It feels like old times."

Smiling at him, she bit back the comments that would ruin this fun moment and just nodded. He wasn't a bad guy. It was just some decisions he made were not the wisest. Refocusing on the road in front of him, they crept down the street. It wasn't long before she was outside her apartment building. He stopped and got out of the car hurrying around to help her out on her side. By the time he reached her she was halfway out.

"Thank you Dice," he reached over and grabbed her around the waist then kissed her.

She didn't kiss him back but she didn't push him away either. He pulled back and looked at her hoping for a positive reaction.

"It was not horrible."

"The kiss or the evening or by chance did you mean both?"

"I was referring to the evening. As for the kiss, we've been down that road before. I'm sorry but that ship has sailed."

"Just give me a chance Dice, I won't screw up again. I promise."

"Thank you, for a lovely evening. Have a good night." She slipped pass him and headed for the front door.

"I'll call you!" he called after her.

She knew he would, not looking back she waved to him. "Good night!" Entering the front lobby she stopped, and checked her mailbox. Just a bill and advertising for herself. It was refreshing not having anyone else's mail in her mailbox. Heading over to the elevator, she pressed the call button and the doors slide open at a snail's pace. Stepping on, she pressed the number for her floor and the doors slide shut.

Smiling she laughed to herself how life had a funny way of

throwing you a curve ball from time to time. She had plans for the evening that got tossed and mixed like a salad. In the end, she had an interesting evening that wasn't so bad. When he had mentioned the party a couple of weeks ago she had to admit she was dreading it. She was thinking of excuses she could use to get out of it. In the end, it was something that she didn't end up hating. The partygoers were entertaining as usual. There were the same things that occurred at each of these parties but she had to admit she kind of look forward to watching the drama unfold. It was the party's entertainment. They never needed to hire any entertainment certain people that were invited each time were the free entertainment, it was simple just add alcohol and sit back and wait. It never failed.

Getting off on her floor, she was at her door within seconds unlocking it and heaving a sigh of relief. Home sweet home, her condo finally had that feeling and she wasn't going to let anyone mess it up.

CHAPTER TWO

SATURDAY 7:30 AM

The weather had improved a great deal in the last couple of weeks. She stepped outside and inhaled a deep breath then stretched her legs, back and shoulders. Taking another deep inhale, she grinned from ear to ear. Life was good ... life was so very good. Slipping her ear buds in, she set out for her morning run. She had gotten in late last night but once her head hit the pillow she was out. It was Saturday, she had no clients scheduled for today and her day was open, free and clear. Her Aunt Sophie had called earlier in the week inviting her over for dinner tonight, which she had accepted. It was hard to refuse her Aunt things since she was the one who had raised her after her parents had died when she was just a kid.

Crossing the street, she headed down to the lake and the running trail. Her morning and afternoon were clear just as clear as the big beautiful blue morning sky. Not a single cloud in sight, just clear blue skies everywhere she looked. It was one of the things she loved about living in Canada everywhere you look it was greens and blues. There were a few other runners out this morning, nodding and smiling at her as they passed. She just loved the solitude of running alone. It was her downtime, recharging her batteries and getting herself realigned. It was her form of meditation. Meditation in motion, she did a little ti chi when she felt stressed out, it was something else she just got back into.

Maybe she could go up to her Uncle's cabin? No ... wait ... she had dinner tonight. She could go tomorrow or after dinner depending on when she got done. She hadn't seen Ty in a while and wondered how he was doing. They were good friends he had helped her on her first case and introduced her to some very strange friends who seemed to have their own underground network of sorts going on. Then there was that secret room she had found ... her Uncle Eric had a secret office in his cabin. Ty seemed to be the only other person who knew about it. Perhaps she could investigate one of her Uncle's old cold case files? A grin spread across her face as she toyed with the thought. There were some things in life that might be better if left alone ... a little voice warned her in the back of her head. It was the nagging little voice. That little voice had a way of stifled her fun. Yet, it did keep her on track and out of trouble.

The thought of investigating one of those mysterious cases sent a little chill of excitement down her spine. There would be no harm in just peeking at one of those cases. Asking a few questions if the people involved were still around. That's assuming they were still alive. Finding out what caused the problem ... solving one of those mysterious cases. What did Ty call them? The Z files? No, that didn't sound quite right either. There were mysterious unsolved cases that came across her uncles' desk. She decided that was what she was going to do, unless something else better came along Plan A was to take a visit to check in on Ty and take another look at the cases in her Uncle's cabin. Why? Why go to the cabin when you already have a couple boxes of those cases from when you were up there last? The little voice scolded. Well, that was true too. Plan A go up to the cabin depending on the time, plan B pulls something from the box in her own home office.

She was almost back at her apartment when she finalized those decisions. Feeling good about her plans, she stopped on the way home at the bakery and picked up some fresh almond croissants. It was a naughty indulgent that she didn't do often but every once in a while she couldn't resist the urge. A few minutes later she was coming to the front of her building and slowed down.

Entering her condo, she stretched again on the elevator heading upstairs. Once back in her apartment she had a quick shower and slipped into her yoga pants and a tank top. Stopping by her home office she smirked, knowing all too well she couldn't let it wait until tomorrow. Picking up a box, she carried it out to her balcony and started a small pot of coffee. Getting her pastries out, she placed them on a plate, gathered some fresh berries from the fridge and washed them. The coffee was done. Placing her breakfast on a small tray, she carried it out to the balcony placed it on the table and opened the box.

Taking a moment, she inhaled the dusty contents ... old cases ... they were all at least four years old or older. These cases hadn't been touched since his death. A sad frown claimed her lips. She missed her uncle. When she had walked into his office as a teenager with her new private investigator's license in hand and looking for employment she had no idea he would have become a part of her family. After she had convinced him to give her a chance ... he was reluctant but she refused to take no for an answer. A few weeks later her Aunt had found out and stormed into his office to give him proper hell. After an hour they came out laughing and he had taken her out to dinner. Dice was still Eric Lawson's employee at the end of the evening and six months later he became her uncle and a year later he took her on as a partner teaching her everything he knew grooming her to take over his practice someday. It had turned out to be a win-win situation.

Here she sat staring at a box of old case files ... Eric Lawson's case files of mysteries. Unsolved cases that had an air of mystery to them either supernatural or alien origin or at least that's what Ty Morgan assumed. Ty was her Uncle's neighbor ... out at the cabin. He had taken over keeping the Lawson's cabin clean and up kept. Yet, he had done more than that when Uncle Eric was alive ... Ty worked with him on a couple of cases. Dice got the impression it was more than a couple and she wasn't sure who was helping whom. She hadn't been out to the cabin for a while.

Ty's place was still overwhelming just the thought of it. He had wall to wall to ceiling shelving in every room except upstairs in his bedroom. Books upon books, referencing the strangest things ... she shivered at the thought. How many of those things were real? He hunted supernatural beings. Things that she thought were just fantasy. It was hard to wrap her mind around. But when he was last here visiting her he kept getting a call from a colleague ... someone who needed his expertise in the supernatural.

Shaking the images of that memory off Dice pulled out the first file. Kallie Mitchell, a couple years younger than she was, she was the girl with the haunting eyes. Went camping one long weekend with her friends all five of them died without a valid reason except for Kallie. When they found her she was in shock and couldn't or wouldn't speak to anyone. Her five friends all died around the same time with what the coroner stated as a heart attack. What would cause five healthy teens to have a heart attack all at the same time? The young woman was hospitalized and cleared of charges. She had been checked over and there was no clear evidence that she was the cause of her friends' deaths. With her unable to speak they could not follow up and acquire any more information. The campsite did not look like it was ransacked or met with any ruckus. There was no evidence that these kids were murdered. In the margin of the case files, her uncle had scrawled the words 'murdered ... all of them'.

There were pictures of the campsite, police pictures. Dice wondered where her Uncle got these photos. There were also some police reports regarding the incident too. Some of the report was blacked out with a heavy marker it looked like a photocopy of the actual police report. Could someone on the force provide the info? Could someone on the force approached Eric Lawson with this case in hopes he could uncover something that they couldn't? Or were these files stolen? Examining the photos it looked like a regular campsite. There were three tents, a fire pit that had long burned out. The other campers were all lying around the pit. They look like they were hugging each other. It looked like three couples in total. There didn't seem to be anything that shouldn't be there. Holding up each photo, she examined them from side to side. Her eyes scanned for anything that didn't fit in for any little tell tale clue that might stick out.

Clicking her tongue against the roof of her mouth, she tilted her head to the side and absently took a drink of coffee. Sighing she put the photos back in the folder with care. There was nothing she could tell that stood out. Picking up the report that was on Kallie's mental state, Dice skimmed through. It looked like when they picked her up she was in shock, it was suggested that the shock was due to some great tragedy. Considering she was non-responsive, they could not gather any information from her.

Her Uncle Eric had taken notes too. He said he had visited the campsite and looked for anything that was out of the ordinary ... nothing stood out. He met with Kallie, while at the hospital where she was staying he was sitting in a chair beside her and notice a cold draft that came into the room. The air conditioner was broken some of the staff were complaining about that just a few minutes before and it was in the middle of a heat wave. At that moment Kallie turned to Eric and said, "Hi." A nurse was standing in the room with them and almost fell over. It was the first word that Kallie spoke since the accident. He tried to engage her in conversation but she never spoke another word. According to Eric's notes there was no other contact after that. He had gone back to see her, a couple of times since then but she just stared off into space.

Maybe she should go out and see if Kallie Mitchell was still staying at Shady Elm? She could also save herself a trip and call first.

Her phone rang. She felt reluctant but dragged herself up and went to answer it. "Hello?"

"Hi stranger, I was just talking to Tessa and we were thinking that we all should get together for lunch today. Do you have plans? If so can you clear them?" It was her friend Ronnie, who happened to be the lone computer whiz that she knew who didn't look anything like a computer geek.

"Well, I guess when you put it that way sure. When and where?"

"Let's go for noon at the Red Dragon I love their steak sandwiches," she replied.

"Alright, it's the Red Dragon at noon. I'll see you then."

"Great I'm just going to call Tessa back and let her know. Liam is coming too."

"Wouldn't have it any other way," Dice smiled.

"Aright dearest see you then." Ronnie hung up.

Returning to her patio, she sat down and checked the clock. She had an hour left. Sitting back in her chair, she looked out over her balcony to the lake. The sun glistening on the gentle waves, it looked like sparkling gems glittering. There were some children downstairs in the small playground laughing and running around. Looking across the way, she caught a familiar face staring at her. Sean Larke was sitting out on his patio with his new girlfriend. They were having brunch together. The woman was a petite, slender, redhead with a pretty face. The woman didn't notice her looking over at all. Looking away, she didn't want him to feel weird about anything. They gave it a go but he wanted something more ... he wanted a relationship and that wasn't something she could give him at the time.

Eating her croissant, she turned her attention back to the mysterious case files. So Kallie was one of the mysteries that were in the box. The phone rang again. Frowning Dice got up and went to get it. "Hello?"

"Hey, I heard you accepted lunch ... I want to tell you something. I don't think Sean is into the girl he's dating right now. I heard her whining that he didn't pay enough attention to her."

It was Tessa, sweet friendly Tessa who knew Dice since high school. Unfortunately, she was rooting for Team Dice-Sean ... which, wasn't about to happen. "Well, that is nice to know. I'm not interested."

"Oh come on ... didn't you notice how he lit up when you came by for lunch last week."

"No and it's none of my business."

"Dice, I'm telling you ... I think Sean and you would be perfect."

Sighing she blurted, "Okay he is sitting across on his balcony with the pretty redhead on his lap and she is wearing his bathrobe."

"Wha? What? No way!"

"Yup, sorry sister, but I think he's taken."

"I don't believe it. Take a picture with your cell phone."

"No! I will not do that."

"You must! I won't believe you."

"Okay, I am not spying on your boss. Nor am I taking pictures of him with my cell phone. I'll see you at lunch I'm in the middle of something right now."

"Fine party pooper, I'll talk to you in a bit." Tessa hung up.

Grabbing her cell phone, she went back outside and sat in her chair again. He didn't seem to notice she had come back out and was feeding his girlfriend breakfast or brunch. Holding up her phone, she discretely took a couple shots of the lovely couple. Tessa was going to be crushed. Dice was happy for him. He wanted a girlfriend, not a friend with benefits. She wasn't about to play the girlfriend roll for a while. Not after she got her condo back to herself. She loved having this privacy and sanctuary that she called home. She sent her friend the pictures through text. Tessa sent back a sad face.

Pulling out another file folder, she poured over another one of the mysterious files. This one was a boy who seemed possessed. He could move things with his mind. The file said he could make people do things they didn't want to. His name was Patrick Ford, twelve years old and an only child. The unusual thing about this boy was that he could speak in different languages fluently yet he never signed up for any other languages and he failed his French class two years ago. He became multi-lingo only after he was in a car accident.

Was it a possession? Couldn't be a brain tumor? Dice stuff that one back in the box. She would come back to it. So far she preferred Kallie Mitchell. Grabbing one more, she pulled out a file and was stunned to see the name on it. Joan and Tony Maddox ... they were her parents. Sitting up straighter, she swallowed hard and caressed the folder with unsteady fingers. Reading and re-reading the names on the folder it didn't change. How did her parents end up in the mystery slush pile? Did Aunt Sophie ask him to look into it? Licking her hot dry lips, her trembling fingers touched the edge of the folder.

Dice felt tears burning the back of her eyes. She wiped away the hot tears and realized she was breathing rather fast and shallow. Flipping open the folder, there were pictures of her parents on top. They looked so young and care free. Dice could hear her mother's laughter and hear her father singing off key not knowing the words for the song and making up his own which were not even close. They were such a happy couple. They had been such a happy family. Dice remembered them always laughing. Her father had that charming boyish grin that looked like he was always up to some kind of mischief. Tony had the darkest brown eyes, warm, friendly, and so kind. Tears slid down her cheeks as she stared at their pictures. She looked a lot like her mother.

Her mother had a light brown complexion and greenish-blue eyes ... her mother was such a looker. Her smile looked carefree and Dice remembered her. She had been five years old when they died. But she remembered them. Caressing the picture as if touching it, would bring her closer to them. The question that weighed in the back of her mind ...what was Uncle Eric doing with a file for them? It was a car accident. They had died coming home from a birthday party of a friend's and were hit by a drunk driver, killing them both on impact. She had checked the police report a few years back. Rick Li was a police officer at the time and pulled them for her, he was now a big shot detective for the department.

Sliding the pictures aside, she looked and found the familiar police report, she didn't need to read it again, she had read it so many times, she had it memorized. The offender had killed himself as well. Dice wondered what her parents were doing in the mysterious "Z" Files. It looked like … according to the notes attached, that Aunt Sophie was drinking one night and said their deaths were not an accident. Well, this was news to her. Her Aunt never once mentioned this in all these years that it was anything but an accident. Checking the date on the notes it was a year after Eric and Sophie had gotten married. He made a note if he found out anything he would tell Aunt Sophia. He wanted proof first. Looking through, he had tracked down the witnesses. The offender's family … everything checked out that it was just an accident. The offender Jordan Warless had just gotten laid off and he couldn't go home and tell his pregnant wife that he lost another job. Even though it wasn't his fault he ended up at the bar drinking all night … deciding he had enough he slipped out the back door telling the bartender he had called a cab. He found his car and drove across town he was three blocks from his home when he ran a red light and killing the Maddox couple instantly, he had hit them head on. They didn't stand a chance.

Uncle Eric spoke with Jordan's wife, Marcy who didn't know why anyone would want to ask her about her ex-husband. She had remarried and wasn't cooperative. Stating that she should never have stayed with him for as long as she did. He was always into 'get rich quick' schemes … shady dealings and he couldn't hold a job for more than a two-month basis. Her family and friends had warned her about him. Marcy had broken down and cried that she did love him it was just so hard being with a man who didn't want to grow up. She already had two children and another one on the way, she didn't need another child she needed a man.

Eric Lawson was very detailed with his notes. His conclusions were that there wasn't anything nefarious about Joan and Tony's deaths … so, why was it in the "Z" files slush pile? Perhaps it was just misfiled? Looking through it, she didn't see anything else that indicated otherwise. Maybe she would ask Ty about it when she saw him next time.

Folding everything back into the folder, she set it aside. Looking at the clock on her living room wall it was twenty to twelve. Boxing up her mystery files, she took them back to her home office keeping the Maddox file and the one of Kallie out. Then she went about to cleaning up after herself. She stopped in the bedroom and changed her clothes, put some make up on and ran a brush through her hair.

Staring at the woman in the mirror, she was proud to be that woman.

Chapter Three

S trolling into the Red Dragon, she waved to Gary who was not just the owner but the manager and bartender most days. He came over and hugged her.

"Hi Dice, are you meeting someone special here today?"

She laughed, "Come on now Gary I'm meeting someone special every time I come in here."

He grinned, "Right you are. See you tonight at dinner?"

"I wouldn't miss it."

He laughed again, "You're right ... she will hunt you down and I wouldn't want to be in your shoes after that."

Dice patted him on the shoulder as she looked over to the usual table, which Ronnie liked. Tessa and Liam were seated already but no signs of Ronnie. Strolling over, both Tessa and Liam got up and gave her hugs. Behind her Ronnie came rushing over, flinging her arms around her neck and almost strangling her in the process.

"You're so lucky you showed up," Ronnie grinned.

"I know, I know..." Dice grabbed a seat.

"What have you been up to?" Liam asked.

"Not much I have been pretty fortunate to be getting case after case lately. Just closed my last one yesterday, cheating spouse great photos for the lawyer."

"Good to hear, that means you are open to new endeavors," Tessa grinned. "I know you think he's moved on but he keeps asking about you at work. So if he has moved on why would he care?"

"He's a nice guy?" Liam offered.

"Oh shut it Liam. What would you know about men?" Tessa laughed.

"Apparently nothing at all," he busied himself with his drink. "You know you should ask my wife what my answer should be?" he chuckled.

They all laughed at that one.

"Stop! I am not a monster," Ronnie protested.

Her reply, elicited more laughter from everyone, she even joined in.

"No, she's not," Liam smiled at his beautiful wife as he put a protective arm around her.

"What else have you been up to?" Ronnie asked. "I have already caught up on Tessa's love life."

"Tessa has a love life?" Dice asked innocently.

Tessa stuck her tongue out at her and laughed.

"Well, nothing on the love front."

"I haven't seen any updates on your website. What's going on … are you giving up on the strange and mysterious?"

Dice wondered if she should tell them about the box. "Well," she began.

"Well, what?" Liam prodded.

The waiter came over and interrupted them. They all gave their drink orders first, than their meal orders. The waiter was a pretty young woman perhaps still in high school. She nodded, smiled and disappeared.

"Where were we?" Tessa asked. "Oh hello there Captain Obvious," she turned to the entrance as Sean Larke walked in with this pretty redhead girlfriend.

Everyone had turned to look he smiled and nodded in their direction. "Come join us!" Tessa shouted.

Dice kicked her under the table but kicked Liam instead who yelped. Liam looked at Ronnie thinking it was his wife. Dice stifled a chuckle, it would all have been quite funny except she was feeling a little embarrass.

Tessa still waving at them, with a big grin.

"What did you do that for?" Liam asked.

"Do what?" Ronnie looked at him as if he was asking her if it was still sunny outside.

"You kicked me," he looked a little hurt.

"No, I didn't."

"Shhh," Dice hissed. Sean came over with his lovely date.

"Hi," he smiled. "Alisha, please meet Tessa you've seen her at my office."

"Hi again," Alisha waved and grinned.

"Next to her, that's Dice, and Liam and next to him is Ronnie who is married to Liam."

"Nice to meet you," she smiled. "I love meeting Sean's friends he knows so many people."

Dice wondered when did her high school friends became Sean's friends. Then looking over at Tessa. Say what you want to say about Tessa, but when she got something stuck in her mind she was relentless. It was a plot and a plan. Dice was beginning to think this lunch was all pre-planned by dear sweet Tessa who looked over at Dice with the sweetest most innocent smiles she had. Dead give-away Tessa; Dice thought to herself with a knowing smile.

She missed what was being said but Tessa and Ronnie were making room for two more seats. Alisha smiled at all of them and fixed her gaze on Dice.

"Dice what an unusual name, is that a nickname?"

Liam laughed, "Nope, that's her name and she is an unusual lady. But we love her." He reached over and gave her a hug.

Dice forced a smile and snuck a glare over in Tessa's direction who smiled back at her this time with a grin that looked much like a cat who had just eaten a prize bird.

She was tempted to send a kick Tessa's way but she didn't want to get Liam again. Instead turning to Alisha, she said, "My dad was a professional poker player my mom a nurse they couldn't decide on a name and made a bet my dad won and I got the name Dice."

"Wow, you know I never heard your story about that. I've known you a long time." Liam looked at her and smiled. "What would your name be if your mom won?"

Dice grinned. "Lily."

"Lily?" Tessa shook her head. "Nope can't see it."

"I like Lily," Ronnie offered.

"It's nice but I don't see our Dice being called Lily," Liam offered.

"What are you saying? I'm not a pretty innocent flower?"

Everyone laughed. Dice stuck her tongue out at Liam.

"No, no I just meant. Oh forget it." Liam shook his head. Turning to Alisha, "How is the advertising business Alisha?"

"Oh it's been pretty busy this week. I have managed to acquire a couple new clients. A local musician who is looking at doing a road trip tour, she is so good."

"What kind of music?" Ronnie asked.

"Country music, she is this perky 20-year-old blonde who makes my job easy." Alisha grinned. The waiter came back with their drinks, took Sean and Alisha's orders then disappeared.

"Is that your first musician?" Tessa asked.

"Yes, so I am very much looking forward to getting her out there."

"You're using social media?" Ronnie asked. Alisha nodded then Ronnie started in on the pros and cons and the must-dos. She kept Sean and Alisha entertained with things.

"So what's with the website?" Liam asked Dice.

"Well, I've been a little busy."

"With work? Right, we know." Tessa rolled her eyes.

"Well, not just work," Dice began and noticed she had Liam, Tessa and Sean's attention. Sean was listening in and glancing over at her trying not to look obvious.

"Really? A new man?" Tessa said a little too loudly.

"What a new man?" Ronnie turned to Dice.

Dice laughed and shook her head no. Sean was looking right at her waiting for her to say it. "Not a new man." She didn't give him the satisfaction of looking his way. "I've found something at my Uncle's cabin when I was out there last."

"Yeah Ty, isn't he a bit old for you?" Liam gave her a stern look.

Licking her lips Dice stared down at the table. "What I do with my time and whom I spend it with is up to me. I like Ty he has no expectations. He's a grownup who knows how to treat a woman." She looked at them. Everyone was looking at her.

"Well, how much older is he?" Ronnie asked.

"Forget it. It has nothing to do with Ty. When I was up at my Uncle's cabin last time Ty told me about an office he had there."

"I went with you and Chris once how far from the cabin is the office?"

Dice looked at Tessa and grinned, "The office is inside the cabin."

"I didn't notice that."

"No, you wouldn't have because I didn't know it was there."

"You mean like a hidden room?" Liam asked.

"Really?" Ronnie stared at her. "And why wasn't I invited to this cabin?"

"We were honey," Liam consoled. "We were just too busy to get away at the time."

"Oh," Ronnie pouted for a few seconds. "Well, tells us about this mysterious room."

"It was just an office, a den of sorts."

"And you never noticed it before?" Sean asked.

Dice shook her head. "Nope, but get this. My Aunt doesn't know anything about it either. It's full of these old "Z" file cases."

"What's a 'Z' file?" Tessa asked.

"Some kind of science fiction show they had on a while ago," Dice replied.

"No, you have it wrong it's not 'Z' it's 'X' Files," Ronnie corrected.

"X?" Dice looked at her.

"Yes, it was about two FBI agents."

"Yeah that's what Ty said it was."

"So you found what that were alien related?" Tessa asked looking at her like someone had just farted.

"Well, kind of … that and supernatural."

"Supernatural you mean like ghosts, demons, werewolves?" Liam asked.

Dice nodded, "That's more it."

"No way," Ronnie gasped. "What are you going to do with it?"

"I don't know. I am thinking about checking some of them out."

"Stay away from that Dice," Tessa warned. "You don't need that kind of trouble."

"You know Dice I just met you but I think Tessa is right. My step dad once had dealings with a ghost when he was younger and his family had to move out of the house they were renting because things got very strange. Strange and dangerous, you don't want to mess with things like that." Alisha pursed her lips together and shook her head. The waiter came back with Sean and Alisha's drinks along with everyone's orders.

The food was delicious. Just because Tessa and Sean's new girlfriend Alisha agreed on it … made Dice all the more interested in checking it out. A small voice in the back of her head warned her not to be so childish. Perhaps Tessa and Alisha were right.

"Maybe Alisha is right," Liam smiled at Dice.

She wanted to kick him under the table again this time on purpose. Ronnie gave Liam a dirty look and shook her head. It felt kind of weird sitting at lunch with her friends who were being nice to Alisha when she knew what they were doing. They were trying to extract as much information from the woman to use against her. As far as Dice was concerned their efforts were fruitless. She liked Sean, but he was dating someone else. Someone who was sweet, smart, charming and was available for the relationship he wanted. Sitting back, she watched as her three friends work away. Knowing all the while it was shameful on their part. It was like Sean wasn't old enough to take care of himself or make his own decisions.

Sean barely looked at her for the rest of their luncheon. Tessa made a mention of how Dice showed up in the news two weeks ago for finding a killer that turned out to be innocent. That was by accident. She was hired by the guy's mother to find him. His mother was certain that he was innocent. When they found him it was his mother who knew after talking to him that he couldn't have done it, his mother was the one who in fact proved her son was innocent. All Dice did was find the guy.

Lunch was great. Dice loved hanging out with her friends and did it as often as she could. It was great to catch up on things going on in their lives. She smiled at her friends around the table.

"You were great." Tessa smiled.

"The camera really likes you I saw that clip," Liam patted her on the shoulder. "Look I'm famous by association."

Everyone laughed. "You guys are too much." Dice shook her head.

Gary came over and tapped Sean on the shoulder. Sean got up and they stepped away from everyone else. Chatting among themselves, Dice tried not to notice. She still kind of liked him more than she should. It was nice to see that he had moved on. A small part of her wish he hadn't and wished he had waited for her. Yet she couldn't offer him the girlfriend he wanted.

Sean came back and sat down as the waiter was clearing the table. "Well, we should get going."

"Wait," Liam smiled at everyone. "Ronnie and I have an

announcement."

"Now?" Ronnie asked with a grin.

"Why not?" Liam smiled back. "Do you want the honors?"

"No go ahead," Ronnie smiled and blushed.

Dice was curious as to what the announcement was. It was not like her friend to blush for anything.

"Alright, Ronnie and I are going to have a baby."

"What?" Dice squealed. "Oh my god, that is awesome!" She jumped up and hugged her friend.

"Wow, it's about time!" Tessa hugged Liam.

"Yeah, that's what our moms said," he laughed.

"Congratulations." Everyone was hugging each other. Somehow Sean was standing next to her.

"How are you really doing?" he asked softly next to her.

She looked over at him and smiled, "I couldn't be better. I'm glad to see you so happy with your new girlfriend. She seems good for you."

His smile faltered, looking over at Alisha he looked back at her. "A man can't wait forever Dice."

"I never asked you to."

"Yes, you did."

"There is nothing between us, why are you bringing this up."

He looked a little hurt. "Nothing? Yeah right, I'm sure Ty is keeping you busy."

"What Ty and I do is of no concern for you." She felt a little annoyed that he would be bringing her fling with Ty up. Sure Ty and she had sex but it wasn't a lasting relationship. They just wanted different things in life. Plus she kind of felt, he was holding out for someone else."

"Really?" he growled. Clearing his throat, he looked back at their friends. "You're right. We didn't mean anything to each other."

"I didn't say that."

"You didn't have to."

"Sean ...," she stopped as she saw Alisha coming over and was in earshot.

"A baby how exciting," Alisha grinned.

"Are you interested in having children?"

"Yes, I can't wait ... I know I'll be an awesome mother," Alisha smiled glancing nervously over at Sean.

"Well, you and I are like polar opposites," Dice looked sadly at Alisha's face. "Lucky for you I heard Sean wants a big family. Well, I should be going," Dice flashed them all a smile turned. Her smile faded within seconds as she headed for the door.

Gary stopped her at the door, "Are you okay honey?"

"I'm fine, just have to get going I'll see you tonight," she brushed pass him and out the door.

She heard him saying, "well, you don't look fine."

Down the street she was back at her car within minutes and safely seat belted inside hidden from the rest of the world. Looking around, she pulled out and went for a drive. Finding herself downtown in the shopping district, she tried for a little distraction of what every other woman loved to do... everyone except her. If she was feeling a little sour she might as well complete her afternoon with a little must do shopping. She needed to buy herself some more socks ... no matter how many she had ... they seemed to disappear every time she did laundry.

Chapter Four

Returning home, she managed to accomplish something this afternoon, she bought herself some new underwear, socks and another pair of dress slacks. It was a shopping success. The normal outcome for her shopping expeditions would be with Dice returning empty-handed and annoyed. She removed all the tags. Looking at the clock it was going on 4 pm, which meant she had enough time to throw a load of laundry in before she left. Each condo came with the hook-ups and a small closet that could be an extra storage space or a small laundry room. She stuffed her clothes in the washer and she poured laundry soap and fabric softener in the correct compartments. She turned it on. The machine barely made any noise just the swoosh swooshing of the water moving around. Closing the door, she changed her clothes and went downstairs to the gym to sneak in a quick workout.

Dice reminded herself that she didn't need any male distraction and Sean being with another woman was just what she needed. It was better for them both. Especially, when Alisha with the perfect hair and waist wanted to have children … having children was a sore spot for Dice. She didn't think it was something she would want or be very good at. Chris would have liked someone like that. Her line of work didn't make for the safest of environments for children. No, she just didn't have that motherly instinct in her and she couldn't risk faking it until she acquired it. What if that never happened? It would be so unfair for the child and her would-be spouse. No, some women

29

were just not meant to be parents. Maybe in her next life she would want to try her hand at that.

The gym was empty and she had the place to herself. First, she went over to the stair climber and then finished off with a swim. The water was cool and refreshing. There was just one other couple in the pool and they were off in a corner by themselves looking a little romantic. After a couple laps she went back upstairs and had a shower. She took her laundry out and threw it in the dryer. While she waited for that to dry she went about getting dressed, fixing her hair and putting a little makeup on. If she showed up without makeup at her Aunt's house her Aunt Sophie would think she was coming down with something and mother hen her to death. No, that was the last thing she needed.

Giving her apartment the once over everything looked neat and tidy as usual. Taking her clothes out of the dryer, she folded and put them away. Grabbing up her keys and purse, she headed out. It was a short drive and she knew if she didn't get over there soon her Aunt would be calling her. She didn't want to wait for it to get to that. Aunt Sophie could be a bear about those things.

Pulling up outside her Aunt's house, she spotted a couple cars there already. Groaning on the inside, she recognized Sean Larke's car. Not again. Why couldn't she escape that man?

Taking her time, she trudged up the walkway. She was going to be on her best behavior. She wasn't going to do anything to come between Sean and his new lady. He really deserved to be happy, she reminded herself. It would be wrong. Yet, why was she still feeling a little hurt by his choice? Why couldn't he find some unpleasant dwarf of a woman ... or some tall yet hideously deformed super model? This woman he was with ... looked perfect, she was sweet, smart and wanted to be someone's girlfriend. Alisha was probably one of those women who thought he completed her. Frowning, she reminded herself not to be so judgmental. The woman did nothing to her ... plus, she made him happy. For that, if she liked him she would be happy for him.

Walking in the front door Dice called, "Aunt Sophie? Aunt Sophie, I'm here."

The living room was deserted. Walking through she found herself alone in the kitchen. Then she saw a balloon floating in front of the kitchen window. Groaning on the inside, she just hoped it wasn't a birthday party that woman threw. That would explain Sean's car out front. Swallowing hard, she headed over to the back door and pushed it open stepping out into the back yard where she was greeted with a big crowd of "Surprise!" from all her friends. Looking around, she saw Liam and Ronnie, Tessa with her arm hooked around a happy fella, Chris, Ty! Sean and his girlfriend … Gary, a few of her clients and then a bunch of people she didn't know. Almost twenty people she surveyed that she didn't know. They had to be Aunt Sophie's friends.

Fixing an, 'I'm so happy to be here,' smile on her face, she crossed the patio and stepped out in the back yard. Her Aunt had a couple tents and tables set up. Looked like a barbeque, a table with fresh salads, fruits, and other tasty side dishes out and a bar was set up at the back. That could be her first step.

Chris was at her side before she knew it. Kissing her on the lips and giving her a hug. "Happy belated birthday Dice, you look amazing." She wanted to run away but didn't dare.

Chris wrapped an arm around her waist and whispered in her ear, "I tried to tell your Aunt this wasn't a good idea. That you wouldn't like it but you know what Sophie is like."

"Really? No, no really I should have this every day," she smiled with gritted teeth trying to look appreciative when she just wanted this evening to be over with as fast as possible.

He gave her a little squeeze, and whispered in her ear. "Well, you look great and stop gritting your teeth. Try to look natural. Oh, oh incoming, incoming." He chuckled.

Aunt Sophie came over and hugged her to death. "Dice I know you undoubtedly are thinking of a way out of here … if you leave before I say you can you'll be in big trouble young lady." Aunt Sophie kissed her. "Happy Birthday baby."

"Thanks Aunt Sophie," Dice smiled.

Sophie took her around to the mystery guests and introduced her to everyone. When she looked Chris had disappeared over to the bar. She wanted to join him over there. Sean and Alisha were standing around talking with Liam and Ronnie. Comparing couples notes, she gave herself heck for thinking that way.

They reached the end of people she didn't know which felt like it took forever. Greeting her clients and then her friends everyone spread out and mingled. Grabbing Tessa by the arm she growled,

"You could have warned me earlier."

"What fun would that be? You should have seen the look on your face, it was priceless," Tessa laughed.

"You're a riot," Dice sneered.

Tessa laughed harder. "Oh Dice we do this because we love you."

"Love me less," she grumbled.

Music began and dancing ensued. Dice looked over and saw her Aunt dancing with Gary. How could she stay mad at that woman when she looked so cute with her boyfriend? Dice knew her Aunt meant well.

"Hey gorgeous birthday girl, can I have this dance?" a warm inviting voice asked from behind.

Turning she saw Ty looking ravishing as usual. Dice couldn't help but smile back at him. "Sure," she said.

He took her by the hand and over to the dance area. Wrapping his arms around her, he pulled her really close.

"I was surprised to see you here."

"I was surprised to get an invite, but your Aunt called me and insisted that I come telling me you would appreciate my presence here. How could I refuse?"

She grinned, "Really that's all it took?"

"That and any excuse not to have to cook."

"I thought you liked cooking?" she countered.

"Awe it depends," he shrugged. "Depends on who I'm cooking for, if it's just me I know all my tricks. If it's for someone else then there is a reason. I get to show off my skills. So which guy are you with?"

"I'm sorry what?"

"I noticed there is the old flame kicking around here, Chris he came alone and is keeping a very close eye on you. But there's that guy that I saw at the hospital Shane? Sean? He looks like he brought a date but he seems still interested in you. So which one are you trying to make jealous by dancing with me?" he bent close to her and nuzzled her cheek.

She laughed. "Neither. Chris and I are just friends and nothing more is going to be happening on that front."

"Are you sure about that? The look he's giving me isn't one that suggests just friendship intentions."

"Too bad for him," she smiled up at Ty. "As for the other one, his name is Sean. He's dating someone else. That ship has sailed as well."

"Well, sugar, I'm glad you think those ships have sailed but I think you should have informed the captains of those ships."

Shaking her head, she cringed at his analogy. "You know that is seriously not my problem."

He grinned at her. "I'll bet you any amount of money those two guys are going to make it your problem."

Rolling her eyes, she shook her head again. "Why are you talking about them? What have you been up to lately?"

"Work as usual"

"Do you recall a case with Joan and Tony Maddox?"

"Your parents?" he looked at her a little surprise.

"Yes, I found their file mixed up with some that I grabbed from Uncle Eric's office. I was surprised to even see their names on anything that would be there."

"No, I don't recall anything about them. I can check my records all the cases I've worked on with your Uncle I kept track of but that is back at my place."

"Well, when you get a chance that would be really lovely. I would love to know if there is any connection to an 'X' file."

Ty laughed, "I heard you were calling them 'Z' files earlier."

"From someone who has a big mouth that is who." She laughed.

"Well, it was funny. When you get a chance you should stream some of those old TV shows and see what they are about."

"Yes, maybe I will do that."

"I think you might like some of them." They were still dancing and the song was done. "Do you want to get a drink the music has stopped?"

He leaned into her ear and began humming, "not when I'm with you."

She laughed. "You're too much."

He gave her a little dip and then hugged her in a big bear hug. Some of the new people clapped and thought they were a cute couple. Ty kissed her cheek and walked her over to the bar.

"That was fun," she smiled up at him.

"Oh you are fun to hang out with."

"Thanks so are you. How long are you in town for?"

"Well, that all depends on who can put me up for the night," he gave her a wolfish grin.

"Well, we will have to see about that then," she smiled at him.

"See about what?" Sean came up behind her and ordered a drink for his lady and himself.

"Where I'm sleeping tonight," Ty smiled at him. Grabbing Dice around the waist pulling her closer he gave her a hug. "Dice was contemplating how generous she was feeling."

"You can always stay at my place. I have a guest room made up." Sean offered.

"Well, that is very generous of you. If my other plans fall through, you can guarantee I'll be knocking on your door tonight," Ty grinned.

Dice laughed, "He might have to take you up on that offer Sean."

"Oh how you tease me sweet Dice."

"Oh keep it up dear Ty," she teased back.

"What's keeping you so long honey?" Alisha was by Sean's side.

"I was just inviting Ty to stay over with us tonight," he handed her a glass.

"That was some fancy footwork out there," Alisha nodded at Ty.

The music had started again. "Do you want to dance?" Ty offered.

Alisha looked at Sean who just looked at her. She looked back at Ty, and nodded. They went over to the dancing area and he sauntered her around. Alisha looked like she was having the time of her life.

"Don't you dance?" Dice asked Sean.

"Yeah," he snorted. "But not like that."

"That's too bad," Dice sipped her drink. Watching Ty dance Alisha around, she didn't feel jealous at all.

"Come on," he grabbed her hand and pulled her out on the dance floor.

She hadn't expected that. Before she knew it, his hand was on her back and the other one was holding her right hand. Her throat felt dry, his eyes were burrowing into her soul as he stared at her.

"You look great," he cleared his throat and tried to smile.

"Thank you ... so do you," she managed to get those words out but it felt like they were the only two people in the backyard dancing. He kept staring at her and she didn't want him to stop.

"I miss you."

She cleared her throat. "I noticed that ... Alisha suits you better."

"Dice," he began. He looked hurt. "We both know I can't give you what you want. Don't say anything. It feels so good to hold you."

"Please don't do this."

Before she knew it the song was done and Alisha was at his side, cutting in.

Aunt Sophie came over smiling at her. "Dice I have someone I want to introduce you to."

"Sure," she excused herself from Sean and followed her Aunt across the lawn and into the house. It gave her a few minutes to gather her composure. In the living room there was a middle-aged man who looked a little nervous as he smiled at her when she entered the room.

Dice said nothing but crossed over to him and waited for her aunt to make the introductions.

"Kyle Barnett this is my niece Dice Maddox, Dice this is my dear friend Kyle. Kyle and I were talking a few days ago and discovered that his situation needed someone who would be sensitive to his current situation."

Dice felt a little intrigue; she reached out and shook his hand. Aunt Sophie pulled a chair over for her to sit on. Dice accepted it with a "thank you."

Turning to Kyle Barnett, she looked him over. He was a little salt and pepper on top, his eyes had dark circles and bags making him look like he had been under some kind of stress. His skin looked tired and lifeless, his shoulders slumped … he looked like a man who was defeated.

Clearing her throat, she smiled and nodded at him, "how can I help you?"

"I'm glad you asked young lady. I'm sure you must have heard about the situation with my wife."

She began to rack her brain trying to remember what she had heard regarding Kyle Barnett and his wife. Nothing came to the forefront on the subject. Pursing her lips together with a fixed frown, she shook her head. "I'm sorry I'm drawing a blank … could you refresh my memory."

He looked genuinely surprised. "Wow, you must be the single person on the planet that didn't hear."

"Dice last year, I told you about him and his wife she went missing. Linda Barnett, she was the physics teacher at the university."

"Oh yes you're right I remember. Is there any more news about your wife?"

"They tried to send me to prison for her death but there was no body so without a body how can you prove she is dead? It was a good thing I have money and a good lawyer or I'd be talking to you from behind bars right now."

"I take it you are innocence?" Dice asked. They all say they are but she always watched them when they claimed to be innocent ... sometimes there were telltale signs of a lie.

He looked directly at her didn't blink ... didn't twitch ... point blankly replied, "Young lady, I love my wife. It is true we were going through a divorce but I still love her. I wouldn't want anything bad to happen to her. I did not kill my wife. I don't think she is dead. She can't be. I have paid a couple of private investigators to find her and everything they found is in this file here." He held out a thick manila envelope for her. It was thick and looked like it had seen better days. He had large elastic bands around the middle for extra support, which it seemed to need.

Taking the envelope, she watched him as he passed it to her. He was very careful and gentle with it.

"I don't know what happened to her. We were having dinner and gotten into an argument. She left in her car. Twenty minutes later I followed her to apologize for being an ass. When I finally caught up to her I found her car on the side of the road with the gas tank nearly empty, the lights still on, the keys in the ignition and the driver's door hanging open on the side of the road. Linda wasn't there. I looked everywhere. I was frantic I called the police to help me. I told them I had just found her car by the side of the road and felt she met some kind of danger. They sent a patrol car out to me an hour later. Do you know when a person goes missing every minute counts? The longer you wait the higher chance of them not coming back to you."

"What happens next?"

"Well, when the guy ... the single police officer came out to investigate ... I had already scoured the area. At this point I was afraid someone took her away. I was frantic and in tears. I was so scared for her. Then the next thing I knew I was in the backseat of the police cruiser and brought into the police station where they questioned me for hours. All that time they wasted on me ... meanwhile ... whoever had Linda was getting further away." He swallowed hard.

Dice noticed his eyes looked a little watery. She wondered how she would have handled that if she were in his position. "How long have you two been married?"

"It will be twenty years next month. I was beside myself when I realize they thought I was a suspect. They talked to people who witnessed our argument at the restaurant and thought I was a raging lunatic. Before I knew it, after being grilled ... they booked me for her murder. I thought they found her and she was dead. I was a complete mess. I had called my lawyer when I realized what was happening. He came down and I was out in a few hours but it didn't change the fact at this point I thought they found her dead. My lawyer was the one who found out that they didn't find her and they were still looking for her. It was all over the news that she was missing and I was the prime suspect. It just hurts to think that anyone would think I am capable of hurting her. Yet, at the same time I was so grateful for the news coverage because every chance I got I was begging people to find her ... to look for her and to keep an eye open for her. My only thought was to find her. If people thought I was guilty so be it. But if there was a chance that I could use the media and have them find her for me I was up for anything."

"No one came forward with any news?" she watched him as a tear slide down his cheek. He tried to ignore it.

Sniffling a bit, he cleared his throat and managed to recover. Shaking his head no, "I thought someone would have come forward. It's like she dropped off the face of this world. I put up posters and ads ... I hired private detectives like yourself and no one could find a thread of ... or a clue ... nothing. Which meant the suspect ... the number one suspect was still me. They figured I killed her and buried her somewhere. I lost my friends ... family ... her side of the family thinks I'm guilty. They even hired people to prove that I did kill her. It was all circumstantial evidence the whole case. There just was no proof. Some of my family won't speak to me because they think I did it."

"Who in your family thinks you did it?" Dice asked with a raised eyebrow.

"My younger sister adored Linda. I can't believe she would think I did it, but she told me to confess and tell them where the body was. I was crushed even more." Tears came more freely. Aunt Sophie sat beside him and comforted him.

"You couldn't have done it Kyle, I won't believe it for anything. Even if you told me you did it, I still wouldn't believe it." She hugged him.

He leaned towards her and appreciated her faith in him; Dice watched the emotions play across his face. She didn't think he killed his wife. Which left her wondering who did? And where was Linda Barnett's body? Dice knew she was going to take his case in that moment.

"Young lady I couldn't have hurt Linda, she was the one who wanted the divorce I would have given her anything she wanted. I just love her so much, I wanted … want her to be happy, even if it means she isn't with me. Linda is a free spirit she can light up the room. Everyone wants to talk to her when we go to parties."

"Did she have any enemies?" Dice asked.

He shook his head. "There is no one that I can think of that would want to hurt her. If you knew her, you would know what I mean. No one could hate her."

"Okay, what about at work? Did she have anyone who might be in competition with her for anything?"

"Competition?"

"You know for a promotion or the limelight?"

"No … no I don't think so."

"Alright the week before she disappeared, did you notice anything different about her?"

"She asked me for a divorce."

"Was she seeing anyone?"

"You mean another man?"

"Yes or woman?"

"No, not that I know of. That wouldn't be Linda's style."

"I see … what kind of activities was she into?"

"She is a very active lady. She was a member of the Tennis and Boating Club downtown, she volunteered, she also participated in many marathons, and she biked most places unless it was after six in the evening. She did yoga, ti chi and she ran her own book club."

"She sounds like she was a busy lady."

"She was … is … no one has heard from her. It's not like her."

"I see …," Dice grabbed a pen and was jotting down some notes on the outside of the envelope. "Who was her best friend?"

"Jasmine Foster they were like sisters and inseparable."

"Does Jasmine think you killed her?"

Kyle looked at her and shook his head no, "no, she was one of the people who believed in my innocence right from Linda's disappearance."

"What about her parents?"

"They are both dead, they were both older."

"What about your parents?"

"It's just my mother and no she doesn't think I did it."

"Good." Dice stood up "Alright, I'll take a look at this tomorrow and I'll need you to stop by my office to sign a standard contract and drop off a retainer fee."

"Actually …," he looked over at her aunt.

"I already took the liberty of printing the contract and the retainer fee is included in the envelope," Aunt Sophie smiled at her. "I hope you're not mad."

Dice laughed. "How could I be mad?" Sitting back down, she opened the envelope and found two copies of the contract with his signature and her Aunt's signature as a witness besides his name. Dice signed both pieces one for her files back at the office and passed the other one over to him. Looking at the contract it was dated for today's date as well. Her aunt had planned this meeting in advance for her. Aunt Sophie continued to look out for her, even now as she was working a job that her aunt thought was too dangerous for a woman, she was still helping her. Sending her clients that she thought might be less dangerous. Her aunt seemed to believe in this man's innocence.

"Alright, then I'll look over these files tomorrow. Check out all the leads and see where it goes from here." She pulled out a business card and scrawled her cell number on the back. "Here is my cell-phone number, if you think of anything else please call me. Don't give this out though because not a lot of people have it."

"Thank you." Then he closed the gap between them and hugged her. "I knew I could count on you. Your aunt is the best. She told me you could find anyone. Even when no one else can … you have a nose of a bloodhound."

"I will do my best." She wanted to give her aunt a dirty look for setting this man up with such high expectations, but when she looked at her aunt who was beaming and grinning from ear to ear she couldn't. Her aunt believed in her … her aunt thought she could do anything. That filled her up with such pride. She waited for him to let her go and then smiled and nodded at them both. "Okay I'm going to go put this in the car and I'll start first thing in the morning."

"Thank you Dice," Aunt Sophie came and hugged her.

"No problem," Dice hugged her back. For her Aunt Sophie she would have taken this case as pro-bono.

Dice headed out the front door and across the lawn to her car. Unlocking it, she stuffed the envelope in the glove compartment and locked it back up. When she got home tonight she might take a look at it. Turning she walked smack into Chris.

"Are you ignoring me?" he grinned steadying her so she wouldn't fall over.

She laughed, "like the plague."

"What?" he looked hurt.

"No, no I'm not." She patted him on the shoulder. "Why didn't you bring a date?"

"I'm not seeing anyone. There is someone very special I would like to ask out."

She patted him on the shoulder again and started to move around him. "You should do that."

"What if she says no?"

"You will never know unless you ask."

"Wait," he grabbed her arm and spun her around. Then he leaned in and kissed her. It was a soft needy kiss. This wasn't like him. She tried to back away but he held her close. Deciding to wait until he was finished she didn't enjoy it. Chris had always been a good kisser there wasn't any question about that. She was grateful no one was around. He pulled back and she wiped her hand across her mouth.

"Umm, ah thank you," she looked at him a little confused. "I thought we had this conversation before? There is no chance of us ever being a couple. We can be friends but that's it."

"Dice you are the only one for me."

"Why? Because I kicked you out and called you on being an ass."

"No, because, when I hurt you I never saw anyone who had cared about me like that before in my life."

"That's why you were still dating that girl. Listen this is not a conversation I want to have with you. I am not interested in starting anything up with you. We are friends and that's it. If you want more than that we shouldn't be friends."

"I can wait for a lifetime for you Dice. But I will take friends only for now."

"That's all I can give you."

"Alright," he smiled. "Sorry about the kiss."

She laughed, "well, it could have been much worse."

"What you don't like how I kiss?"

"I never said that."

"What are you saying?"

"I just meant it's better than a kick in the ass. You know you are a good kisser. So stop fishing for compliments," she slapped him in the arm.

He wrapped an arm around her waist as they walked back into the party. Once back inside she checked on the new people and had small conversations with them. She worked the room then made her way back to her own group of friends.

"So what's going on with you and Chris?" Tessa pulled her aside.

"Nothing," she looked at Tessa feeling a little confused.

"That's not what I heard. Apparently, Sean's date went out to the car to get her shawl and saw you two kissing."

"What? That little spy ..." Dice swallowed some of the choice words she had for Alisha.

"She couldn't wait to tell Sean. He said she was lying and not to talk like that. Then the next thing I know they are fighting sounds like he's more interested in who you are kissing than kissing his new girlfriend, according to Alisha."

"What?" Dice felt a little giddy and reminded herself that she didn't need any more complications going on in her life right now. There was a small part of her that was dancing with joy on the inside.

"Yes," Tessa hissed as she grinned from ear to ear smiling and nodding. Looking around at the others, she continued, "The next thing I see he's trying to deny it and she is storming off out the other side of the house."

"I was going to say I didn't see anyone pass me on the way back in here."

"Well, why were you out front in the first place with him?"

"I wasn't out there with him ... well, yes I was out there with him but I wasn't WITH him. I had a meeting with my new client in the house. A friend of Aunt Sophie's, I had gone outside to put the file in my glove compartment and when I turned around he was there."

"Next time kick him in the shins and shove him down then run away screaming," Tessa hissed.

Dice laughed, "you're crazy. I wasn't doing anything wrong. Sean is with someone else. It's none of his business who I kiss or not kiss for that matter."

"He looks like he's alone right now." Tessa nodded to Sean who looked like he was leaving the party by himself. "You should go and stop him."

"What? He's a big boy if he wants to leave," she watched as he was heading around the side of the house … walking away.

"What kind of host are you if you don't say goodnight to your guests?" Tessa shoved her.

"Okay I'm going," Dice gritted her teeth as she hurried across to around the side of the house he was leaving on.

He was in the front yard and moving a little slower now.

"Hey," she called to him.

He paused.

"Hey, are you leaving without saying goodbye?"

He turned around and looked at her. He looked so serious she froze in her step. She was half way around the side of the house.

"Who says I was leaving?"

"Sorry," she smiled and started to turn back.

"Wait," he called to her.

She turned around to face him. He slowly walked over to her; she watched his face as she saw him struggling with something. Sean Larke had something on his mind but what? She knew she was about to find out.

"Where's Alisha?"

"She had to go home."

"Oh," Dice nodded stupidly.

Within a few seconds, he had closed the gap between them. Looking at her, he searched her face for something.

"Did you want something?" she choked out the words.

"Do I want something," he snorted. "Really Dice?"

"You asked me to wait just now … and I waited."

"Yes, you did," he frowned. "Yes, you did."

"How much did you have to drink?"

"Not enough."

"Okay," she stepped back one pace. "Did you want to talk about something?"

"Talk?" he looked a little irritated. "Talk?"

"Or not, that's okay too."

"Am I scaring you Dice?"

"No," she didn't know why he would want to scare her. His behavior wasn't like the Sean she was used to but then again she hadn't seen him lately.

He reached out and caressed her cheek sending shivers down her spine. What was it about this guy? He wasn't that tall, however, he was slightly taller than her. His dark eyes looked stormy and she wondered what he was up to. He stepped forward and she stepped back. A couple more and she had run out of space to back up to. She found herself pressed up against the side of the house and he was brushing her hair aside. Leaning in, he kissed her hard on the lips, then it softened and she found herself wrapped around him not wanting this kiss to end. He tasted so sweet, wet and warm. Dice wasn't happy when he pulled back she was gasping for air. Looking at her sheepishly, he was gasping for air too. Maybe she imagined that?

"I'm sorry," he whispered then turned and walked away.

Leaning up against the house, she used it for support. Her legs felt weak as she sank down to the grass. He didn't look back he just strolled away. A small part of her wanted to chase him down and kick him for not wanting to stay. Then sense of reasoning gnawed at her and reminded her he had kissed her out of spite. He just had a fight with his girlfriend. She was not his girlfriend. She was no better than Chris … Sean was no longer on the market and here she was lip wrestling with him or was it called tongue wrestling? Heaving a sigh, she admired the well-manicured lawn for a few minutes. Regained her composure and went back to her party.

Tessa came over to her and wanted to know what had happened. She lied and said she caught up with him but he wanted to go home or catch up to Alisha. Her friend seemed disappointed with the response and dropped the subject.

Ty seemed to have found a lady friend who was not just attractive but a couple years older than Dice. She was one of the invited guests that Dice just met tonight. Checking with Aunt Sophie, she confirmed the lady was single, levelheaded, and quite brilliant. Ty took her out dancing on the dance patio. Dice joined him with Chris. It was a gorgeous evening. The food the drinks, she had limited herself to two for the whole evening because she wanted to get up in the morning, have a run and get started with her new case.

She waited with her Aunt until it was going on two am when the last guest left. Dice began cleaning up.

"No, no honey, leave it tonight. Gary and I will take care of it in the morning."

"Absolutely, don't worry birthday girl I'll help your charming auntie," he said then nuzzled her aunt's neck. That was her cue to leave. Laughing she nodded.

"Okay night you two. See you later."

"Don't be a stranger," Gary called out to her.

Heading around the front, she found Chris waiting for her.

"Hey," he smiled.

"What are you doing still here? I thought you left a while ago."

"I just wanted to make sure you got home safe."

"What are you going to do … follow me?" she laughed.

"I was thinking about it."

"Don't!" she laughed. "Did you enjoy yourself?"

"Absolutely, I saw you talking to Carol Keyes, she's nice."

"The blonde?"

"Yes, she is sweet and single."

"Are you trying to set me up with someone else?"

"Would that be so wrong?" she teased.

"Dice there is just one person for me … that's you."

"Didn't we have this conversation already? If I recall it didn't end well for you. It's insanity to keep doing the same thing over and over again and expect a different result."

Pressing his lips together tightly, he nodded. "I hear you," he said.

"Do you really?"

"Dice I hear you."

"Good, then what are you still doing here?"

"Just making sure a friend gets home in one piece."

As she stepped closer, she noticed he had one too many to drink. He was in no condition to drive.

"Come on let me take you home," she held out her hand for his keys. "Fork over your keys buddy."

"Sure," he grinned from ear to ear. "You do care about me."

She led him over to her car and opened the passenger's door for him. He got in without complaint. Dice went around and got in on her side. Starting the car up, she looked over at him as she pulled out. "So where do you live now?"

"Over on Browns Line," he grinned as he looked out the window. "Tonight was fun."

"Yup," she nodded as she drove across town. Coming up to Browns Line she asked, "What is the street number?"

"For?"

"Your home, what number do you live at?"

"I don't live over here."

"I'm sorry what?" Biting back the bubbling anger, "Where do you live now?"

"I don't remember," he started to drift off.

Pulling over, she shook his arm. "Chris, Chris!"

Searching for his wallet, she pulled it out of his back pocket and turned the inside lights on … rifling through she searched for some tale-tell sign or indication of his current address. Nothing … it was too late to call anyone. He snored softly in the passenger's seat. Heaving a sigh, she was just too tired to care at this point. Turning the car around, she headed home. If she could get him upstairs, she would let him sleep on the sofa, otherwise, he would have a very sore neck in the morning and it would serve him right.

Traffic was light and she took the expressway and was home before she knew it. It was a struggle to get her ex on the elevator when he decided he wanted to break out in slurred songs and press every button. It took forever to get him inside her condo, and once inside it wasn't too much trouble to get him over to the sofa. His feet hung off the sofa but that was something she could live with. Getting a blanket, she came back downstairs and covered him up. He was snoring again. He must have known he had too much … at least he was smart enough to wait for her to come out. Tucking the blanket around him, she knew it was what he liked and he got the best sleep that way. Then she went and had a quick shower, changed and as soon as her head hit the pillow she was out like a light.

CHAPTER FIVE

SUNDAY 9:34 AM

She had slept in but then again it was the weekend and she was out pretty late. Getting up, she got her running outfit on and headed out. Glancing at Chris still snoring, she would leave him sleeping until she got back. He would need a ride back over to her aunt's home to pick up his car.

Downstairs the fresh cool morning air greeted her like an old friend. Stretching she loosened up her muscles and started out slow. Last night was fun she got to meet some new people. Sean Larke kissed her and she liked it too much, but that was just out of frustration she reminded herself. He did leave and he still has a girlfriend.

The morning began warming up as she ran along the trail. There was a cool morning breeze that felt great. Last night as it got later … Ty had come by and gave her a hug, telling her he had found a place to stay and thanked her for her generous offer. She had laughed and told him anytime. The woman he left with had looked eager to get him alone.

The new case that rested in her car's glove compartment was waiting for her at home. Kyle Barnett had intrigued her. Thinking back, she remembered him on the news a few times last year and once when over at her aunt's house someone had brought it up and thought he was guilty. Aunt Sophie had stuck up for him and said there was no way he could have done it. Aunt Sophie reserved her tenacious unwavering solidarity for those she cared about. If she didn't know you then you got her scrutiny.

Dice stopped at the bakery and picked up a few pastries. Her new case had her interest. It tickled the back of her mind all the way home. Stepping in the underground garage, she picked up Kyle's file and headed back upstairs. Dumping the keys in the bowl, she left the pastries on the counter along with the envelope. Dice made a pot of coffee and saw Chris still snoring on her sofa. Men they were like big kids.

She headed upstairs to her bedroom, retrieved fresh clothes and then found sanctuary in her bathroom. The warm water felt like heaven as it drizzled over her skin. Wanting to get a look at the case notes, she made it a quick one. Dressing in the bathroom since she had a houseguest over and she didn't want him walking in on her by accident. Tidied up after herself she went back downstairs to the living room and found the blanket folded and resting on the end of the sofa. Two steaming mugs of coffee and breakfast sitting out on the patio table waiting for her along with Chris who was sitting in her favorite chair grinning at her.

"Hey I hope you didn't mind."

"Not at all, I am starving." She motioned for him to move over. He got up and she sat down.

"I've got to use the bathroom but I'll be right back. I brought your envelope out as well not sure if it was something you were working on or not." He went inside.

Dice caressed the envelope and pushed it aside, she started in on breakfast first just nibbling a bit. Within minutes Chris was sitting down beside her. He had positioned himself so he could sit closer to her. Dice said nothing.

"After we eat I can take you over to Aunt Sophie's to get your car," she said in between bites.

"That would be great, thanks. There is no rush I have nowhere to go today."

She smiled and nodded.

"Did you want to go get a movie?"

"A movie?" where was this coming from she wondered.

"Yes, it's no fun to go alone," he said in between bites.

"What did you want to go see?"

"There is a new one out with Tom Cruise. I've wanted to go see it."

"Is there an early manatee?"

"I can check," he pulled out his phone and was pressing on the screen, searching for movie times. "Yes there is one," he paused looking up at the clock. "It starts in two hours ... how about it?"

"I guess we could stop there on the way to get your car," she nodded. "I'll just need to change my clothes."

"Why? There is nothing wrong with what you have on."

"Just like a man. You guys just don't care." She shook her head. "It will take a couple minutes."

"So what's in the envelope?"

"Case notes for a case I'm working on."

"Oh I see. Can I help?"

"No," she smiled.

"I'm going to go watch some sports if you want to work on that now."

"Sounds good," she smiled at the thought.

He got up and kissed her on the cheek, then cleared the table. She casually glanced over in Sean Larke's direction and saw him sitting out on his patio too. His girlfriend was hovering around him. Dice tried not to notice or let on it bothered her. Besides she had her ex here ... if Sean saw, he may not be too happy either. Then again he may not care at all ... what was worse? Chris had cleared the table she had the patio to herself. Taking the contents out of the envelope, she saw the retainer fee, which was more than she normally asked for. The contract they both had signed yesterday and the stack of notes. She got up and went inside grabbing up a notepad and pen. Coming back outside, she couldn't help but glance over at Sean again. Mentally giving herself a slap she sat down and forced her mind back on the task at hand. She was hired to do a job. Looking through the case notes it looked like he had been to a few people looking for help.

The first one was a man from out of town. He had interviewed everyone that knew the couple ... there was a list of interviewers. The detective seemed very thorough. The notes were all neatly typed and consisted of twenty sheets. There was forensic analysis that determined if Linda was dead she didn't die in her car. In fact, according to the report "Unofficial" report, there were no signs of a struggle either in the car or around the car. Which meant she got out of the car on her own accorded and simply walked away. There were no tire marks near the vehicle other than Kyle's. So it made sense that the police thought he was a suspect. He lured her out of the car and then knocked her out or did something to take her to another location. Yet ... could he have had the time? She thought she read something about twenty minutes ... was twenty minutes enough time to catch up with her, disable her and hide or murder her and cover his tracks? The hypothesis is that he killed her somewhere else. It would make him one diabolical killer. After all, he played the grieving husband perfectly. Was he acting? She didn't see any hints he was lying or acting.

She made a list of all the names to check and their contact numbers she would double check with her system.

Chris peeked around the corner and was smiling at her. "Hey we should leave now if we are going to make it."

Smiling up at him, she nodded. Packing away her case notes, she scooped them up.

Chris tilted his head to the side looking out pass her. "Hey is that Sean Larke?"

She tried to scoot him inside. It was too late. He came out and was waving at them. "Sean! Alisha!"

Dice slipped inside, "We're going to be late if we don't go now."

"Yeah I'm coming honey," he was too busy having a conversation with her neighbors. Honey? She wondered if she should slug him? If she could just hide, instead she took off to the bedroom and changed. When she came back out he was standing at the door ready to go. Sighing with relief, she was grateful.

"Hey great news, Sean and Alisha are going to join us."

"Great," she looked at him feeling like she just got hit in the face with a ball.

"Hey, I thought you guys were good friends. Did I do something wrong? You don't look happy."

"No," she sighed. "The more the merrier, come on." Maybe he could invite all her ex-lovers to join them!

He followed her out and was concerned she was upset with him. When they reach downstairs she had reassured him it was a fantastic idea and she couldn't be happier having Sean and his beautiful girlfriend tag along on their non-date for a double date.

They met Sean and Alisha at the movie theatre. Alisha looked less than thrilled by the company she would be keeping this afternoon.

Sean and Chris started talking sports and they were like buddies all of a sudden. Dice wondered if anyone would notice if she casually slipped away. Maybe and it wouldn't bode well for her in the long run.

"Hi Dice thanks for the invitation," Alisha glared at her.

No, this was not going to be an uncomfortable afternoon at all … she forced a smile on her face. "I need popcorn." She let Chris get their tickets she went and bought them some snacks.

Alisha followed her, of course. "Don't think I don't know what you are up to. He's mine and I intend on keeping him."

"I'm not sure where you are going with this, but I am not interested in your boyfriend if that is a concern of yours." Even saying the words out loud she wasn't sure if she believed it herself.

"Really?" she snarled. For a small thin pretty lady when she was angry she wasn't so pretty anymore. In fact, Dice had seen pit bulls that looked friendlier. "Don't play coy with me, I see the way you look at him. Chris is a great guy you should stick with him."

"Thank you for your great advice." Turning to the Cashier, she made her purchases and was looking for Chris, not wanting to be near Alisha any longer than she had to be. Chris and Sean were chatting up a storm by the entry gate.

"Hey thanks for inviting us, Chris said it was your idea." Sean looked at her watching her face, she felt like he was drinking her appearance in with his eyes.

"He did, well, I don't like to take all the credit."

"I had wanted to see this movie too."

"Perfect," she was counting the minutes on the inside of when this torture was going to be over with.

"Dice stopped at this bakery down the street this morning and picked us up breakfast on her way home from her run. Do you still run?" Chris asked him.

"I do, I just try to get up as early as possible and do my running."

Dice felt a little hurt that he hadn't joined her for a run lately. Since she closed her first case, he seemed to have been avoiding her. Alisha came up behind her and accidentally bumped into her spilling some pop on her back. "Oh Dice I'm so sorry," she apologized.

Gritting her teeth, she wanted to snap what are you five? I get it … he's yours! Keep him! In fact, you can have this one too! Instead, she smiled.

"It's okay. It was an accident," she heard herself saying as she took her sweater off revealing the tight tank top she had on. Both Sean and Chris looked at her chest and smiled. Feeling a little subconscious about it, she shook out her sweater and draped it over her arm grabbing back the popcorn bag to block the view.

If looks could kill, Dice knew she would be dead. Frowning a little, she didn't much care for the attention herself. In fact, if the truth was put out there, she hadn't planned on going to the movies this afternoon. It was a spur of the moment kind of thing and she knew Chris didn't do these things by himself. If she had known Sean and his crazy girlfriend was coming, she would have been more than happy to let them babysit his ass. Yet, here she was trying to stay out of Alisha's way and keep her distance from both men. Sighing she chuckled at the situation, she needed to learn to say no. Even a HELL NO, when she didn't want to do something. Then she wouldn't be in this situation.

"What's so funny?" Chris asked with an eager smile.

Sean reached over and helped himself to her bag of popcorn waiting to hear the joke. She shook her head. "It's nothing."

"Oh come on you laughed," Chris smiled at her. "Didn't she laugh Alisha?"

"I heard a laugh," Sean replied for him and his date.

Alisha just glared at her. It was funny how the guys didn't see the dirty looks. She hovered behind Sean off to the side. He reached over and wrapped an arm around his date. This seemed to please her.

"Let's go get our seats before the best ones are taken."

Inside they decided on the middle. They ended up sitting Alisha, Sean, Dice and Chris. Much to her dismay, she was sitting between both men, to watch a movie she knew she wouldn't have come to see by herself. It was science fiction and it had Tom Cruise in it. She didn't expect it to be good.

Ten minutes later the lights dimmed and she couldn't see in front of her face. Sean reached over and grabbed her leg, giving it a gentle squeeze, then his hand disappeared as the screen lit up. Dice wondered if she imagined it. No, ... this was not weird at all she thought darkly to herself. Keeping her arms tucked in, she ate her popcorn. Chris put an arm around her shoulder and helped himself to her popcorn. She wondered when did he like popcorn all of a sudden. The movie turned out to be very good. Dice was surprised she enjoyed the movie. A part of her was glad she came to see it. Next time, she would come alone. She didn't need the weirdness that her friends were sporting for her.

As they were filing out, Sean had turned and was talking to Alisha but grabbed her butt. Dice bit her tongue and vowed this was the last movie she was ever coming to with these guys. Back out in the front lobby. It was accidental she told herself. Sean and Chris started talking about what parts they liked and didn't like.

"Hey want to go grab a late lunch?"

"Sure that's a great idea," Sean agreed.

"Great," Alisha flashed them all a fake smile.

Let the joys of this double date that I don't want to be on continue, she kept the sarcastic thoughts to herself. The guys debated on the restaurant options but then they decided on the Red Dragon.

"That was so much fun," Chris gushed as he got into her car. "I like hanging out with them. I think Alisha likes you."

"I'm sorry what?" Dice laughed.

"She is always being so nice to you."

Dice wondered where he was the entire time. "You think?"

"Oh yeah, you should invite them over for dinner sometime."

Dice bit back a comment. Instead she changed the topic of conversation to the movie Chris had picked out a good one, … which brought them to the topic of how he often did pick out the good movies. Dice wondered how much longer would this get together last for. All she wanted to do was dump his ass off at his car and get back to work. He was having a good time. Her aunt had told her last night that she heard he didn't take their break up so well and that she should be nicer to him. Dice also reminded herself that she didn't own him anything.

They arrived after Sean and Alisha got there and had found a table. Chris held out the chair for her and she sat in it. He sat down beside her and the waiter came over. Recognizing Dice right away, she smiled from ear to ear.

"Miss Maddox can I get you your usual?"

Dice nodded, she wanted to add make it a double but refrained.

"You come here too much," Chris teased. "I'll have what Miss Maddox is having."

"Hi again Mr. Larke, will it be the usual for you as well?"

He looked across the table and smiled at Dice, "yes, that will be wonderful Lily thanks."

"And for you miss?"

Alisha smiled sweetly at them all, "I'll have a rum and coke."

"Super, I'll get your drinks and come back for your orders." She was gone.

Dice avoided looking at Alisha and studied the room.

"That was a great movie, Dice admit it," Chris reached out and grabbed her hand.

"I thought it was better than it was going to be." Sean nodded.

"I could watch Tom Cruise in anything," Alisha gushed. "He's so scrumptious."

"He's not one of my favorites," Dice pulled her hand away and picked up the menu. "But he did a great job in this movie."

"I think he's getting better," Sean added.

"For sure," Chris checked the menu out as well.

Lily came back with their drinks swiftly and took their orders. Within minutes they were being served their lunch choices. Dice couldn't get this lunch date over fast enough. When the guys weren't looking Alisha was flashing her dagger eyes.

It was an excruciating thirty minutes. "Well, we should get going I gotta drive you back to pick up your car."

"We should do this again," Sean smiled at them.

"Yes, I think that would be a fantastic idea," Chris agreed.

Dice was heading for the door.

"What do you think Dice?" Sean asked he was right behind her. Turning around she almost bumped into him.

Swallowing hard, she lost her voice. She overheard Alisha telling Chris what a great couple they were. She felt like she was dropped into the middle of the sea and was drowning. "Yes," she whispered. "Sure."

He grabbed her arm and she felt tingly with his warm fingers on her cool skin. Looking into his eyes … those eyes that she wanted to avoid since they started this date, she wanted to kiss him but took a couple steps backwards.

"What about tomorrow night let's do dinner?" Sean suggested.

All she wanted to do was to get away from him, drop Chris off at his car and get on with her life.

"That works for us," Chris answered for them both.

"Sure," she heard herself saying. "Sure." Turning she escaped the bar into the fresh afternoon air. Getting away from them was her sole goal today.

Fumbling with her keys, she opened her door, got in and reached across unlocking the passenger's side. Sean and Chris were shaking hands like they were old friends. Alisha hugged Chris and gave him a kiss on the cheek. "See you tomorrow night. Bye Dice," she waved at Dice.

Chris took his time getting in the car. As they were driving away she reminded herself, in a few hours this would mean nothing. It was a short drive over to her aunt's house and she dropped Chris off.

"I'll call you later," he promised.

"Sure, have a great night." She didn't wait. She just drove off and headed straight for her home.

Locking her door behind her she was so grateful to be home again. Making a pot of coffee she went to change into her shorts and tee again. Emerging from the bedroom, she stopped at the kitchen to pour herself a cup of coffee and then scooped up her case and notes. Heading back out to her patio, she sat down sinking into the chair and feeling finally at ease. What an awkward afternoon. She should have left him at her aunt's house ... let him sleep on the front lawn. That's what she got for being a Good Samaritan. Inhaling deeply then letting it out, she took a gulp of coffee and then re-read the case notes from her predecessors. Sitting back, she decided to read them first then re-read them and then take notes after. Kicking her feet up on another chair, she felt relaxed and comfortable for the first time today.

Shoving the weird events out of her mind, she cleared her mind and zeroed in on her case. Kyle seemed like he was innocence, it was split, half the people he hired came to the conclusion that he had taken her ... his wife and killed her somewhere else.

The other half felt like there wasn't enough information to base his innocence or his guilt on. In their professional opinion, they didn't get the impression he had killed his wife. Then again, most serial killers look like your neighbors. They were the friendliest people and you would never suspect them to be raving lunatics.

Dice went back over the files six times and made her own notes, a list of people who had been called upon, checked out and interviewed. A list of theories it was short. A list of suspects ... was even shorter. Dice knew there was something that was missing. She had no idea what it was yet, but she knew it was something. She decided she wanted to check with her friend at the police department to see if they had any other mysterious disappearances or was there some killer on the loose. She also decided she was going to give each one of these people on the list she made a thorough background check. There had to be something missing. There were little loose threads hanging out all over all she had to do was pull … tug on the right one and that would give her some idea who was behind this. She could not have just disappeared without a trace. There was always a trace. The trace in this case must have been overlooked or thought to be of an insignificant importance at the time. Digging into things was what she was good at. Dice felt this was the challenge she needed.

First, she called her friend Detective Rick Li, "Hello?" he answered sounding a little grumpy.

"Rick, hey it's Dice."

"Dice now is not a good time."

"Are you at work?"

"Not at the moment."

"This will just take a couple minutes."

"Alright, girl you better make it fast. What's on your mind?"

"Do you remember the missing lady Linda Barnett?"

"Wait …," she could hear him moving something around and then he came back to the phone. "Yeah, I remember that everyone thought the husband did it."

"What do you think?"

"I was one of the few who thought he didn't do it. There was just something about him that made me feel he was innocent."

"Do you remember if there were any other missing ladies around that time? Matching her description?"

"You don't think we would have thought of that?"

"Can you check?"

"Dice if you are going to play detective you need to do some of this yourself."

"I just want to know what you guys know about it."

He laughed, "I'm sure you have our notes that are on file somewhere. I know how you work. Fine I will check around. Quit calling me. The next time you call me it better be for lunch, dinner or something fun like sex and Netflix."

"Come on Rick solving cases is our idea of foreplay," she laughed.

"Oh so are you saying that I'll be getting something else later on?"

"Just my undying gratitude," she replied.

He snorted a laugh, "yeah, like I need that. I mean it quit calling me." He hung up.

Smiling to herself, she got her laptop out and began a basic search on people who were on her list. Dice checked the 411-information directory to see if their addresses and phone numbers were the same. It had been just a year but a lot could happen in a year's time. There were a couple people out of the dozen names she had that didn't come up. Not bad. Dice noted the updated information for each.

Dice had checked, over the last year, with the other investigators they all tried to track her whereabouts by checking the usual; Social Insurance Number, bank accounts, credit cards, cell phone, email and social network that she had all her personal accounts that if she was still alive she would have accessed at least one of them in one way or another. Her driver's license expired and she never renewed it. Chances of finding Linda Barnett alive were next to nil she was a goner. But who? Who had the opportunity and motive to kidnap her and kill her? It had to be someone she knew because there was no evidence of a struggle at the location of her disappearance.

The single tire tracks were her husband's. Could someone have walked up to her and have her walk away with them? She either walked away with someone or they carried her. According to Kyle she had a twenty-minute head start on him. If it was someone coming from his direction, he would have noticed the perpetrator. Could there have been more than one? Yes, but then it gets a little messy. There should be tracks or something along the side of the road. It had rained a little that night. Looking at some of the photos, she was right about the rain. The side of the road was a little muddy. There were footsteps all around her car. But were they Kyle's or someone else's?

That was the problem with people rushing into or onto the crime scene. They mean well, but they have a habit of messing up the crime scene. Dice picked up the phone it was still early evening so she decided she would call a few people and see if she could set up some appointments to meet with Linda's friends tomorrow.

Dialing the first number on her list, a man answered the phone. "Hello?"

"Hello, may I speak with Mae Johnson please?"

"MAE! The phone is for you." He yelled into the receiver.

Dice gritted her teeth. Then a young woman picked up the phone with a cheery, "hello?"

"Hi Mae Johnson, this is Dice Maddox I was hired by Kyle Barnett who is looking for his wife. I was wondering if I could meet with you?"

"I don't know anything about it like I told the other detectives."

"May I come by tomorrow?"

"Yes, you can come over any time in the morning but I have a couple classes that I'm teaching in the afternoon so, if you could get here before ten I would appreciate it."

"Sure I can be there at 8:30 unless that is too early for you?"

"No, that would be great. I just don't know how I can help you. Linda was a dear friend of mine I would love for you to find her."

"Thank you for your time, I'll see you in the morning."

"Thanks." She hung up.

Dice marked the time for her Monday 8:30 – 9 am. Then moved down the list to the next person, dialing the number she waited for it to ring. Voice mail … she left a message, her name, and why she was calling and that she would like a few minutes of Danielle's time. Ending the call with the number where Dice could be reached.

She met with three more answering machines but pressed on. Dice managed to book five more people for Monday and had Tuesday and Wednesday half-full when she was finished, with the rest on her list she left messages and decided to wait a day and see if they got back to her otherwise she would follow up either by another phone call or a stopping by their home addresses.

Looking up at the clock, she noticed it was going on nine. Deciding to take a break from this, she bound everything up together with the elastic bands then took it inside and left it on the kitchen counter. Picking up the phone, she decided to order a pizza, placing her order she poured herself a glass of wine and went back outside on the patio with a throw blanket. Sitting in the lounge chair, she sat down and watched the night sky … which was fading into twilight, goodbye weekend she said to herself. What a weird day. She had plans and they got rearranged. Yet, in the end, she got to sit alone in the comfort of her own home. It felt like bliss.

There was a buzz of noise down below with traffic and some

teens in the park area. Her eyes traveled over to her friend's condo and all the lights were off. A part of her was relieved it meant that crazy girlfriend of his wouldn't be eyeballing her from there. Nor did she have to worry about them seeing her and wanting to come visit her. It was just some quiet time. She got up and went back inside grabbing a couple of candles and turning on the stereo low … but loud enough for her to hear it out on the patio. Getting a book, she turned on a couple lamps and then went back outside. Curling up on the lounge, she lit the candles and a nice aroma of jasmine and vanilla filled the air. Opening her book the lamp in her living room gave off enough light for her to read her book. She felt her body and mind unwinding … this weekend was weird and she wasn't looking forward to tomorrow night. Having dinner with her ex and the guy she was crushing on with his crazy girlfriend wasn't her ideal way of spending Monday night on the town. Maybe she could make herself busy with the case she was working on. Chris and Sean seemed to have hit it off they may not even notice that she wasn't there. Alisha would be grateful not to have to lay eyes on her.

Sighing Dice tried to shove the thought out of her mind, she would worry about that tomorrow. Now was a nice quiet evening alone … with a pizza on the way over, she had a book to read and a glass of wine to keep her company.

She was just getting to a good part in her book when the buzzer for her home rang. Getting up, she went inside and checked the little view screen it was the pizza guy. She buzzed him in. Then went to get her wallet, she found it just as there was a knocking at the door.

The pizza guy knocked on the door and she answered it, she paid for her pizza, closed and locked the door behind him. Cleaning up after herself on the patio, she came back inside and turned the television on. Flipping through the channels until she found some kind of detective mystery solving show on, she got her food, a drink and snuggled into her sofa. It was great. Smiling and nodding this was the life. No one to tell her what to do, or how to do it, sole control over the remote … it was freedom! She ate some pizza and fell asleep watching television.

CHAPTER SIX

MONDAY 6:05 AM

Waking up too soon was never fun. She had been dreaming about Sean Larke. He had come over and she held him captive. This had to stop she scolded herself. It wasn't healthy. He had a girlfriend she had ... well she had complications all over the place. Her neck felt a little sore and she realized why ... she had fallen asleep on her sofa. Frowning she cleaned up her pizza mess, wrapped up her leftovers and put them in the fridge. Stretching she checked the clock and decided it was a good time to start her day. Tonight she made a vow to go to bed early with a good book and fall asleep there. Stretching she got up and then slipping into her running gear. Stepping outside, she had the morning air greet her like an old friend. This was good she was up early enough for a run. After this she would shower, have a leisure breakfast and still had time to get to her first appointment.

Stretching she took a few deep breaths. Then set out with her ear buds in. She didn't notice someone had been following her for a block. Pausing at the Lake, she sat down on the bench and drank in the beauty around her. She had a full schedule today and knew she wasn't going to be up for a replay of yesterday afternoon. That she could do without. She needed to call Chris later and make an excuse maybe she has a late meeting? Yeah that would work. Then she could just take a drive somewhere and have dinner out away from all her normal hangouts. Or she could tell the truth. That she didn't want to hang out with them. That would hurt their feelings. How could they not see that she was uncomfortable yesterday? No one seemed to notice. She reluctantly got up and stretched a bit and continued with her run.

Getting back, she had plenty of time to shower and dress for her meetings. Leaving the underground driveway, she pointed her vehicle in the direction of her first meeting. Today was going to be a busy day. It was a ten-minute drive she arrived a little early but gathered her belongs up. She had a small recording device that would record up to 20 hours of feed. Checking to see if it was on she dropped it into her pocket. The little device was something her Uncle Eric gave her. It helped out with recalling information later, which no one had to know. She had asked once wasn't it illegal to record someone without their knowledge. He said if she planned to use it against them there could be complications. They used the devices to help write up their reports and chase leads. Recording devices were inadmissible in court anyways. So it was kind of a moot point.

Collecting her briefcase and purse, she headed up the steps and knocked on the door. A young woman answered looking frazzled. Her hair was a mess and in knots, she still wore her pajamas that also wore her breakfast on them. No makeup, dark circles under her eyes … she croaked, "Good morning, you must be the lady I spoke to last night."

"I am Mae Johnson," she smiled.

"My name is Dice Maddox. I am a private investigator working for Kyle Barnett. I understand you were friends of Linda. May I come in?"

"Yes, yes, of course," Mae stepped backwards. "I don't make it a habit to have people over in the mornings but when I heard it was someone looking into Linda's disappearance I made an exception. To your left come sit in my sitting room."

Dice stepped inside and slipped her shoes off by the front door, then went to the sitting room. The room was a mess. It looked like a frat party occurred in there last night. Half-empty glasses of water everywhere. Clothes stuck in the sofa and littered the floor. Dirty plates that looked like they have been there a couple of days piled high on the coffee table.

"Sorry about the mess I haven't been picking up after myself … what I say, it's my mess and if you don't like it don't look."

"Right you are," Dice put a smile on her face and tried to ignore the room around her. Clearing a corner, she sat down inspecting the spot first just to make sure nothing was going to bite her. "Can you tell me what Linda was like?" she pulled out her notepad and got ready to take notes.

"She was a great girl I mean she was old enough to be my mum but she was fun to hang out with. She didn't judge me like other people tend to do. I miss her ... I miss her a lot. We would always get together for tennis on the weekends unless she had something going on with Kyle. Then every Wednesday night we met at her house for our book club."

"What kind of books was she into?"

"Linda was into reality things ... non-fiction that sort of thing. She was a physicist you know. Very brainy, but not like a snobby brainiac ... Linda was super smart but she was down-to-earth. You could have a conversation with her and she never made you feel stupid. In fact, on the contrary, she made sure everyone felt good about themselves."

"Was she like that with everyone?"

"Yes, you should have met her she was great."

"Did anyone not like her?"

"There was one lady in our book club that was a little jealous of Linda. She thought Linda got things handed to her all the time because she was also very pretty. I knew Linda and I can tell you, she worked very hard to get everything. Nothing was handed to her."

"Who was jealous of her?"

"Her apparent best friend Jasmine Foster, I don't like her much."

"Jasmine Foster was her best friend did everyone know this?"

"Oh yes," Mae nodded.

"What about at the tennis club? Was anyone there that didn't like her?"

"Everyone liked her, some people were just jealous."

"Were you ever jealous?"

"A little bit at first but then when you get to know her ... I mean once you get to know her you can't be jealous of her. She is just so genuinely kind."

"Did she talk about work?"

"Sometimes but it was for the most part, boring."

"Did she get along with everyone there or did you ever hear of an argument, someone who might have been jealous or someone who didn't get along with her?"

"Well, there was one guy that worked in her department Ishia Wren, he was also a physics professor and in a way her competitor for the dean position. From what I heard though there was no competition ... she was the sure win. She had it all brains, beauty and she could speak in public as well as in three different languages."

"I didn't know that. What languages did she speak?"

"She spoke English, French and Mandarin fluently."

"Interesting," she thought about the notes but no one had mentioned that or her work rival.

"Did she mention anyone at work that she liked?"

"She had a friend that she consulted with a lot Dale Stein. He worked in the English department though."

"Were they more than friends?"

"Oh I wouldn't know that. She was married after all."

"That doesn't mean anything. Since you brought him up how was her relationship with her husband?"

"They got along very well. He was her best friend at least that is what she said a few times."

"No mention of any friction that might lead to a divorce?"

"Oh god no, I wouldn't think so. I don't remember that at all."

"Do you think her husband could have killed her?"

"Who Kyle?" her jaw dropped. "No way," she shook her head no. "Not in a million years. Kyle treated her like a princess. He was always calling and checking up on her. He loved and supported her, you know. A good husband, he was always sending her flowers too with little love notes."

"Do you know what her favorite flower is?"

"Lilies, she loved lilies."

"Did she have any odd hobbies that you knew of?"

"No, well she likes tennis, she could drive a boat. She wasn't a swimmer though. She liked cross-country skiing in the winter but as far as I know I don't think she ice skating or did downhill skiing."

"Tell me what do you think happened to her?"

"Someone had to have taken her. I watch TV and know that the chances of her being alive after all this time is unlikely but she was the most helpful person. If someone approached her on the side of the road they could have taken off with her. She was so trusting."

"Do you have any pictures with you guys together?"

"Yes, hold on." She popped up and disappeared. Five minutes later she came back with an armful of scrapbook albums. "Here I found a couple." Mae gently placed them on the table.

Dice watched as she pulled one out of the stack and plunked herself down beside her. Flipping open the book, they leafed through the sheets. Every so often she would ask for a picture and reassured Mae that she would return it.

"I have a ton of these. Don't worry you can have the pictures I gave you."

After looking through six albums Dice was ready to leave. Before she got up to leave she asked, "Is there anything you want to tell me about her that I didn't ask?"

Mae stared quietly at the mess on the coffee table ... she nodded slowly, "she wanted kids but Kyle couldn't give her any. She had once said that she loved him very much but at the same time she couldn't imagine her life without having any children."

"She was getting a little up there in the age department wasn't she?"

"Yes, I think it was passing the point of having children. She was in her forties but I she knew wanted a baby of her own."

"Do you think it would have been enough for her to want to leave him?"

"It could be. I know he was satisfied with how their life was set, but if it was me ... I would have just artificially inseminated forget him. But that wasn't Linda's style. If Kyle said no, she would have let it go."

"Was Kyle the boss in their relationship?"

"Yes in a way."

"Did she mind that?"

"No, I don't think so."

"Alright if you can think of anything else that might help me out with this case please give me a call day or night." Dice wrote her cell phone number on the back of one of her business cards and handed it over to Mae Johnson. "Thank you so much for your time."

"You're welcome."

Dice packed up her bag, grabbed her purse and left. Driving down the street and around the corner, she pulled out her recording device and turned it off. Then she made her own notes more or less about Mae Johnson and her impressions upon the young woman and the information she received from her.

Checking her car clock, she had twenty minutes until her next appointment. It was going to be a long day. Driving over to her second stop she got out and turned on the device again and slipped it into her pocket, grabbing her bag and purse. Walking up the steps to the second home, she rang the doorbell.

A few minutes later the door opened and a middle-aged woman answered looking tired and frazzled. "Hello?"

"Hello Mrs. Shirley Lamont?"

"Yes."

"My name is Dice Maddox. I'm a private investigator working for Kyle Barnett. We spoke on the phone last night and you suggested that I come by."

"Yes, I remember. You want to know about Linda."

"Yes, I would like to ask you a few questions. Can I come in?"

"I guess," she stepped back making Dice squeezed in passing her and through the doorway. She closed the door and Dice took off her shoes. "This way," the woman was short and not at all sociable.

Dice followed her down the hallway until they came to the kitchen. It was quite different from the last home she was in everything was in its place and it looked super neat and tidied. Dice loved to clean up after herself but this kitchen made her feel like a slob.

"It's a mess, sit anywhere," Shirley Lamont waved a hand as she went over and got a cup of coffee. "I just made coffee would you like a cup?"

"Sure thank you, a little milk and sugar in mine please."

Shirley nodded. She brought over a small tray with fresh mugs of coffee and sliced cake on a plate. Then she pulled out a cloth and wiped the sterile clean table down. Placing her mug on a coaster and she nodded to the cake. "Try the coffee I'm sure you will love it. You're not allergic to cinnamon are you?"

Dice shook her head no and sipped the hot brew. It was delicious she could taste the hint of cinnamon in the coffee. "I love that, is it just the cinnamon you added?"

"Yes, it's a secret of mine, but yes. I like you. Please try some of my coffee cake. It's homemade." She grinned.

Dice couldn't refuse taking a bite-size piece off the plate she popped it into her mouth careful not to drop a crumb. It was like tasting heaven. She moved it around in her mouth savoring the yummy sweetness. Swallowing she moaned. "Wow, that was incredible."

"I know. I am very good at these things. Just for the record, you mix the cinnamon in with the coffee ground beans before you brew. It tastes better that way. So how can I help you?"

"I was hired by Kyle Barnett to find his wife. What do you remember about her?"

"Linda was ... I say was because her disappearance was sudden and chances of her being found alive is slim. I'm a realist and understand those aspects of that. She didn't have any real enemies not Linda. It was so hard not to like her. When I first met her ... I was like great, another blond bimbo then she started talking and I was like hey this one has a brain. She was gorgeous, fun, adventurous, and very witty. The only person I could imagine who would find that offensive was an insecure man or woman. Once you got to know her there was no way you could hate this woman. I mean even Kyle ... I know their relationship was a little shaky, which was due to her wanting a baby and he couldn't give her one."

"Was that why they were getting a divorce?"

"I think there may have been other things too. He was jealous. Linda was a free spirit and everyone liked her. Yet, she would never have crossed the line and she gave him no reason to be jealous. If you saw pictures of her you would understand. She looked like she could be a swimsuit model." Shirley got up and left the room for a minute and came back with a photo album. Sitting down in the chair beside her, she flipped it open.

"The woman was in her forties but looked like she was twenty-two."

"She was gorgeous," Dice agreed.

"Yes, and she wanted a baby she was going on forty-six I think. There was one other guy I know who had an issue with her and it was her co-worker he was a real douche bag. I told Linda she should have reported him, but she wouldn't. He went online and took her pictures she had and then placed them on other women's body. Then posted them around the university where they worked. He was such a pig. They were nude photos. He tried to discredit her and get her fired because they were both up for the same promotion. No matter what he did she would have still beat him. He even went so far as to pay a student to go forth and claim Linda tried to make sexual advances at him. The kid admitted that he was lying and mysteriously dropped out of school. I think he was just too embarrassed to show his face."

"Do you remember what his name was?"

"Yes Milton Hunter."

"Did he say it was her rival what was his name again?"

"Ishia Wren? No Milton Hunter did not come out and say it was Ishia Wren but he did say someone had paid him to say that."

"Is there anything else that Ishia Wren had done that you can think of?"

"There were other petty things but those were the major things that caused her trouble until it was discovered she was the victim of some small man ego. Ishia Wren was never really brought up on any charges or let go from the university. He did end up getting the job of Dean for their department. There's justice for you. She had disappeared before the decision was finalized. I'm sure if she was still here she would have gotten it."

"Wow that is something. I didn't know. Did you mention this to any of my other colleagues who interviewed you before?"

"They never asked. They assumed Kyle was the main suspect. No one ever asked if there was anyone she worked with that could have been causing her trouble."

"I see … is there anything else that you think might be relevant to the investigation?" She found it hard to believe no one asked this woman but she wasn't going to press it.

"I think she might have been interested in another man. She was a woman after all and if her husband isn't supportive or doesn't provide for her in all areas that make a woman feel like a woman then yes they tend to look for those emotional needs to get met elsewhere."

"Makes sense who was the lucky guy?"

"Well, I think he was a fellow teacher … in the English department I don't remember his name. But he was a good friend and supportive when Ishia Wren was stirring up shit for her."

"I see isn't that guy married?"

"I'm not sure. So was she. Does that make a difference Dice?"

"I guess not." She snuck another piece of cake. Dice couldn't help it Shirley Lamont knew how to bake.

Shirley continued to flip through the photo album.

"What kind of activities was she in?"

"Tennis, cross-country skiing, boating, she had a book club that was fun. She had a science club started at the university where her students got to go and test ideas ... she was very passionate about her work. She did have an assistant who was like family to her. What was that young woman's name?" Shirley pursed her lips and tapped her finger on the table. "It was an odd name."

Dice took the opportunity to sneak another piece of the coffee cake. It was the best thing she ever tasted she was making a mental note to keep Shirley's number for future reference. Maybe she could get some to take with her.

"I'm sorry Dice I can't think of her name. It was unusual though."

"That's alright."

"She also volunteered every second weekend down at the soup kitchen she believed that it was more important to give back. I had gone with her a few times."

"Was there anyone who took an interest in her ... perhaps an unnatural interest in her?"

"No, they were a very nice people ... just down on their luck kind of people she treated them all with kindness. That was another thing about her it didn't matter if you were homeless or the president of a big corporation she treated everyone the same. With kindness ... I think that had been both endearing and at the same time it caused some people to find her a threat."

"A threat? Are you thinking of anyone in particular?"

"No again, in general it was men who found her a little intimidating when they realized she was more than just a pretty face. Humble was a good way of describing her. She never bragged about anything. At least not that I have ever heard of."

"Wow you have been a great help."

"Thank you, would you like it if I wrapped up the rest of the coffee cake for you to take with you?"

"Normally I would be gracious and say no but your cake is too good to be gracious I would love it all," Dice laughed.

Shirley laughed, "I know."

"Why are you not opening your own bakery?"

"Oh no dear, that is not my thing ... I bake when I get stuck on a problem ... I am a psychologist and I have been mulling over a patience's issues since last night. I think I have figured out an approach but I just bake when I am stumped."

"Wow, if you get stumped again," she hauled out her business card and wrote her cell number on it. "Or if you can think of her assistant's name and contact number I would appreciate it."

"Most definitely ... I honestly can say I don't think I have forgotten anything this time. You were a wonderful treat to chat with today Dice I appreciate you stopping by."

Shirley handed her a little bakery box with the coffee cake in it. Walking Dice to the door, she shook her hand and they bid farewell. Dice got out to the car and peeked inside the box. It was a fresh whole cake and a couple small slices. Dice took the recording device out and turned it off.

Ishia Wren was someone she had already booked for on Wednesday afternoon. That was going to be an interesting meeting; she added Milton Hunter to her list of people she wanted to interview and the mysterious assistant. Dialing Kyle Barnett's private number she let it ring.

He picked up on the third ring, "hello?"

"Hi Mr. Barnett this is Dice Maddox. I was just wondering did your wife have an assistant that worked with her?"

"Yes, she did."

"What was her name?"

"Oh what was that girl's name ...," he pondered. "It was a strange one I think the last name was Grey something."

"No worries sir I'll find it. I'm off for another meeting but I hope to have some more information for you soon."

"Thank you Miss Maddox."

"You're welcome bye for now." She wrote down on her notebook Grey something...

Putting her car in gear, she drove off to her next appointment. This was another friend from her book club. Annie Wells. She asked if Dice could meet her at work. Popping by the Greek restaurant Phoenix's Spoon and Fork, she parked and went inside. It was a little more posh than she thought it would be by the title of the establishment. Dice looked around for someone. A host approached her right away. "Your name madam?" he asked.

"Madam? I like that, it's Dice Maddox."

"Yes, you are a little early but your table is ready. Right this way."

He led her to a table that was close to the window.

"Thank you, I'm supposed to be meeting someone."

"Yes, your guests will be with you shortly. Would you like a drink?"

"I'll take a hot tea please."

"Very well, here is your menu. Today's special is lamb with our house rice special, soup and salad. I'll give you a few minutes to make your decision and to wait for your guest to arrive." He bowed and disappeared.

Dice looked through the menu. The food was expensive but it wasn't a regular restaurant. She couldn't wait to try the food. She wondered if they did delivery.

A woman with dark black hair that had a tinge of blue sheen shining through came over and sat down. She smiled and shook her hand. "Hi Dice Maddox, I'm Annie Wells nice to meet you. I hope you don't mind but I start my shift here in an hour and the food is to die for. Try today's special I took a peek it's one of the better dishes if you like lamb."

"I will," Dice smiled.

Annie waved to the host and held up her fingers for two. He nodded. "Are you working for Kyle?"

"Yes, I am," she nodded.

"He's so nice. I never once thought he could do it. It's just not his style."

"Do you know him well?"

"No, I've met him a few times, but the way Linda talked about him I couldn't imagine."

"I see you were part of her book group right?"

"Yes, we met every Wednesday night at her place. We were supposed to rotate and take turns hosting but everyone liked it at Linda's. In fact everyone preferred her place she would always have snacks and drinks for everyone. She was a great hostess."

"Did she ever talk about work?"

"No, I have never heard her say anything. I know a couple times she was upset but she wouldn't talk about it."

"Had you heard of anyone having a problem with her?"

"A problem with Linda? Are you mad? She was a darling. I think Linda was one of the most genuine people you could meet. She wasn't fake Linda was always genuine. You know some people just want to be liked but others don't care and Linda was one of those people who didn't care ... everyone just liked her."

Their lunch came and they began to eat.

In between bites Dice nodded, "this is very good."

"I know right. I work here and another job. However, this place I come to eat lunch every time before my shift starts. It's the best food in town."

"Do they deliver?"

"We do, remind me to get you a take home menu on the way out."

"What kind of activities was she into?"

"Linda?" Annie chewed then swallowed. "Sorry," she laughed. "Well, from what I know of she was into tennis, boating, skiing I think it was downhill don't quote me on that. She volunteered I know that because she took me a couple of times to the soup kitchen. She had a group at the University for her students and it was open to the public if you were interested in physics. It drove this guy she worked with crazy that she would just let anyone walk in off the street. That was Linda she didn't care about those things like status ... like most people do." She took a bite.

Dice grabbed a drink, "do you remember if she had an assistant?"

"Yes," she nodded and chewed. "Di she was awesome."

"Di?"

"Yup short for something else but can't remember. Don't ask me her last name couldn't tell you what that was."

"Okay thanks, more than I had before. When you were interviewed before was there anything that you remember that you didn't think was important that might be?"

She laughed. "That a tough question, the other detectives were more interested in if she had any enemies. I couldn't think of any. If you knew Linda, you would understand."

"What about her husband?"

"Nah, they asked me that too and I said I couldn't imagine him doing it. I know spouses are the main suspects but I saw him a few times ... the way he looked at her ... there's no way."

"Is that what you told the other guys?"

"Yup."

"Was she talking about getting a divorce?"

"One of the lady detectives told me she was getting a divorce, I told her that she was mad. There was no way she was. Linda was happy. They said something about her wanting a baby and he couldn't give her one. I know she was looking into adoption. She would have been happy with an adopted baby. That was Linda. She would rescue the world if she could."

"That's what I heard from a couple of her other friends too. I'm sorry I didn't get a chance to meet her."

"How did you get into police work?"

"I'm not a police officer I'm a private investigator."

"Sorry I have a tendency to get them mixed up. You remind me of Linda you could have been a model."

Dice choked on her food. Drinking down some water, she recovered.

"I'm sorry are you okay?"

"Yes, I'm fine."

"I just meant you're very pretty like Linda."

"Far from a model but thank you," Dice laughed. "I was made to be a private investigator it's what I am good at. Tracking people down is what I do."

"No, that is cool too. Did you want to join our book group?"

"I will think about it. So you girls are still meeting?"

"Yup, Wednesday nights we tend to meet at Jazz's place."

"Jazz?"

"Yes, Jasmine Foster she is a great girl."

Dice looked down at her plate and was surprised that she had eaten everything. It was just so good. "Well, thank you for the invitation."

"Let me get you that take out menu unless you want to try some desert?"

"Oh no, I don't have any more room left," Dice got up and headed over to the checkout. She paid for lunch and got a receipt to put in her file.

"You have my number if you want to join us this is Jazz's address we often meet there on Wednesday nights," she wrote the address down on the back of the receipt.

"Thank you," Dice nodded.

"You can't leave without taking home some of our famous Balaclava. It is delicious."

"Thank you again, here's my card if you think of anything else please let me know." She passed her business card over to Annie who took it and stuffed it in her pocket.

"Thanks for stopping by."

Dice left the restaurant and when she got outside reached into her pocket and turned off mini recording device. She got into her car and made a couple notes so, it seems that not everyone knew about the divorce and when they heard about it, they didn't believe it. No one thought Kyle was a suspect except for her predecessors. They thought Kyle was guilty but why? Di the assistant no one could remember her name. Dice turned on her car and headed to her next appointment it was a manager of an insurance company. Parking she went inside and asked to speak with Sandra Miller.

The receptionist dialed a number on her phone and relayed the information that her 12:30 appointment was there.

Within minutes a large woman came ambling out to greet her. "Dice Maddox?" she held out a meaty hand.

Dice grabbed her hand and shook it. The woman had a strong grip.

"Come this way back to my office." She turned around with great care and Dice followed as she led them down the hall turned right and ducked into a little office.

"Please sit down." Sandra waved at a seat.

Dice took the seat and pulled out her notepad. "You know I am working for Kyle Barnett, Linda's husband."

"Yes, so were the others."

"How did you know Linda?"

"We belong to the same boat club, and were in the same book club we met every Wednesday night it was fantastic."

"How did you meet her?"

"School I was taking a refresher course about two years ago and met her in the cafeteria."

"I heard she was kind and nice to talk to," Dice prodded.

"Yes, I was looking for a seat in the cafeteria and the people that were in my class were being a little rude because of my size. These are adults we are talking about too which just added salt to injury. Linda told them all off and she took me aside and sat with me. She introduced herself and we just hit it off. We kind of had the same problem people would just look at us and make judgments and assumptions based on how we looked. We were more than our outer shells. She referred to our bodies as our space suits. I liked her a lot. She was one of the few people that saw me for who I was when they looked at me. I have this condition and I've tried to lose weight. Doctors suggested surgery but you know … I can still get around and I am okay with the way I look."

Dice nodded, "did Linda have any enemies?"

"No one … no … wait there was this one guy who was a bit of a jerk that worked in the same department as she did. What was his name … his last name was a bird's name … Seagull? No, that's not it … Eagle? No, that's not it either … Robin … no … Wren … Wren that is it."

"Did you ever witness anything?"

"While I was there … a student came forward saying Linda had made sexual advances at him. It was all lies. She made the news for it. It was to tarnish her good name. The kid couldn't even look her in the eye. I knew he was lying. It was a couple months later the kid confessed he was paid by someone to say that. He wouldn't say who … then the next thing everyone knew he dropped out or transferred not sure what happened to him. The whole time, Wren was there taunting her every chance he got. It never came to light as to who put the kid up to it but my money is on Wren. Even six months before she disappeared, there were naked pictures of her up all over the university. Even in her lectures someone would pin them up on the blackboard. She would take them down but it didn't matter they kept showing up everywhere. Someone cropped her head and put it on someone else's body. Then it went viral. It was all over the internet. The sexy physicist's but the thing was it wasn't her body. She was suspicious it was Wren. I have to say a couple times he made snide remarks about her and the pictures. It was later realized that the pictures were fake and it started to die down."

"Do you have any idea why someone would want to do that to her?"

"You must have seen what she looked like … she was a looker. Hell if she wanted she could have been a model. She had the right look and bone structure for that thing. She was up for a promotion but with the bad publicity, I think that weighed on her chances. If they were grading her on her merit alone, hands down she was brilliant she would have won. She wrote and published papers of her research. She was a force to be reckoned with. But Wren was such an asshole."

"Was there anyone else?"

"No, not that I could think of ... there was one lady whom I didn't trust ... what was her name she had one of those princess names. She had the hots for Kyle. I warned Linda to watch out for her but nope she wouldn't hear me. I think she wanted to have Linda's life. What was her name ... Ariel? Belle? Jane ... Jazz ... Jasmine Fox or something."

"Was it Jasmine Foster?" Dice offered.

"Yes, that is the wench. She was the one ... I told Linda to be careful. She told me that they knew each other for a long time. Linda wouldn't believe me. But if you saw the way she looked at Kyle you would know I wasn't making it up."

"Thank you," Dice nodded. "Do you still go to the book club meetings?"

"No, I thought they stopped happening after Linda disappeared."

Dice changed the subject, "had you ever seen Kyle fighting with Linda?"

"No, he popped by the meetings a couple of times. They were picture perfect in my mind they were the perfect couple. I don't think he saw anyone else he had eyes just for Linda. Jasmine didn't stand a chance."

"You didn't hear any rumors of divorce?"

"Linda?" Sandra laughed like it was the funniest joke in the world. "I couldn't imagine it."

"Okay what about kids?"

"No, they didn't have any."

"Did she ever mention she wanted kids?"

"I think she may have when she was younger but she chose her career. She was like me in that respect. We love doing what we do. Being the best we can be in our field is important. Some women are just not meant to be parents."

"I can respect that."

"Well, look at you, do you see yourself having children?"

"No," Dice shook her head.

"You're a private investigator ... would you want to bring kids into this world in your line of work?"

"Agreed, what kind of activities did she do in her down time?"

"As I mentioned, I know she was a member of the Tennis and

Boating Club, she loved both. She also had this group for scientists at the university. It was open to the public."

"Is there anything else that I might not have asked that you think might be important?"

She paused and thought about it. "No, no I can't."

"Okay here's my business card if you can think of anything please give me a call." Dice wrote her cell phone number on the back.

"Will do," Sandra took the card and placed it in the top drawer. Dice figured it was her catchall drawer.

Standing up, she held out her hand. "Thank you very much for your valuable time."

"Oh anytime young lady, anytime. Do you need me to walk you out or are you okay to get out yourself?"

"I should be good." Dice nodded. With that, she headed back out the door and down the hall nodding to the receptionist as she left.

Dice knew she had to hurry to get to her next one. She shouldn't have booked them so close. Skirting across the street it was in the office building that Chris worked at. Finding her next appointment she checked her voice mail one of her appointments canceled for this afternoon, which meant she had just three people Jasmine Foster, Mike Sundar both in the same building, and Jon Cousins.

CHAPTER SEVEN

Jasmine and Mike worked in the same office. Finding the Whitman and Schultz Attorney's office was easy they operated the whole fifth floor. Taking the elevator up Dice stopped at the receptionist desk and asked for Jasmine Foster. She was told to have a seat and Ms. Foster would be right with her.

Sitting down in the waiting room there were a couple of others with grim faces waiting for their attorneys as well. Picking up a magazine, she flipped through noticing the date it was this month's. Putting it back in the pile, she shuffled through the rest and all of them were recent magazines. Nice to see in an office, the lawyers wanted their customers to feel they were current and up to date right down to the finest details.

"Miss Maddox ... Miss Foster will see you now. This way to the board room," the middle-aged woman pointed and she got up and followed her down a short hallway to a room that had frosted glass walls. Soft clean carpets in a dark slate gray, mahogany table, black leather chairs with wheels and swivel attraction. Dice took a seat facing the door. She pulled out her notepad, the little recorder was already on.

"Can I get you some kind of refreshment?"

"I'll have a coffee with one milk and two sugars," Dice nodded.

"Right away miss." She took off and returned a few moments with a hot cup. "If you need anything else, just pick up the phone and press 1, you will be directed to me. She'll be in soon."

"Thank you." Dice waited.

A few minutes later Jasmine Foster walked in. If this woman felt insecure around other women Dice couldn't tell. She wore a sexy yet conservative blouse that matched her pinstriped double pleated skirt that showed off all her curves. She must have been Linda's age but she took care of herself.

Dice stood up and smiled. "Hi I'm Dice Maddox, a private investigator working for Kyle Barnett. I spoke with you on the phone last night."

"Right," she didn't look impressed. "I'm sorry I thought you were the secretary setting up the meeting. Anyways let's get this over with shall we?" She closed the door behind her and sat down.

"What is it that you want to know? I'm an open book and I have nothing to hide." She grinned at Dice.

Dice knew from experience anyone saying that really meant they had something they didn't want revealed and they intended to keep it that way.

"Sure, well the first question I had was when did you meet Linda for the first time?"

"Oh god, that was so long ago, grade school I think. Maybe grade seven. Yes, I think it was grade seven."

"Oh so you were long-time friends then?"

"Well, not at first in truth we couldn't stand each other. It wasn't until we were in high school that we started to hang out. From then on we were inseparable."

"You two must have had some fights then?"

She laughed, "Are you kidding me? You have never met her because you couldn't be mad at Linda no matter what she did. She stole a few of my boyfriends in fact quite a few of my boyfriends in high school and in university. But it was Linda she never did it on purpose and she wouldn't date anyone I was interested in. Men just liked her. Until they got to know her ... she was more than just a pretty face. If you weren't smart, you didn't stand a chance. Most of my boyfriends she had stolen were dumb as dirt but they were lookers. When they met her they dumped me like a sack of potatoes and they would chase after her constantly."

Dice nodded and made a couple notes. "Did she date anyone you were interested before she knew you were interested?"

"My ... my, aren't you a clever girl? Yes there were a couple of them. I never complained much because when they found out she was brilliant most of the time they couldn't keep her interest. So I got all her leftovers."

"Did that ever make you mad?"

"Are you kidding me? You should have seen her leftovers. I married two of them and still collect the alimony. I don't ever need to work, but a girl needs to keep busy. I remember in university she wouldn't wash her hair and pulled it back in a ponytail wear frumpy gym wear, no makeup and glasses and the guys would still follow her home. No matter how unattractive she tried to make herself it never worked. She was cursed."

"Did anyone take a dislike to her?"

"Not that I can think of, there was her co-worker at the university that was an ass. He was a real loser I think he's the Dean of her department right now. I forget his name."

"Did she confide in you that she was having family issues?"

"Linda Barnett having family issues, not in this lifetime? Dear girl, are you serious? You mean with Kyle?" her eyes lit up. "No, did you hear something?"

"No, nothing at all I was just wondering what was their relationship like?"

"In truth, she was the one that chased him. At first, he thought she was just a bimbo when he realized she was more than just a pretty face he dumped the girl he was dating and went out with her."

"Do you remember who he was dating at the time?"

"Yes, I do."

"Can I have her name please?"

"You are looking at her."

"I thought you said she didn't date the men you were interested in."

"No, it wasn't something she would do but Kyle was different she fell for him hard. They had a romantic courtship. When he took the time to get to know her he fell hard. He never looked at me the way he looked at her. I was happy for them," she scratched her nose and wiped the corners of her mouth, looking at the table.

Dice didn't think she was as happy as she wanted people to believe maybe Sandra Miller was right about Jasmine.

"What else can you tell me about her?"

"What do you want to know?"

"Is there anything you thought about that you forgot to mention to the other detectives?"

She paused staring at the table again and shook her head. She looked like she was lost in thought. "No ... not a single thing."

"What kind of things was she into? Did she like shopping?"

"Linda? Shopping," Jasmine laughed. "No, she didn't but I use to drag her out with me all the time. Her husband hired a personal shopper for her too. She looked great in anything it was like having a grown-up Barbie doll to take along with you. A wet paper bag would have looked awesome on her."

No ... not jealous at all, Dice just smiled and nodded. "What kind of activities was she into?"

"Well, you must already know she was an excellent tennis player, she loved boating, feeding the poor, we had a book club that she started, I continued it after her death. She couldn't swim, ski, roller-skate, we tried those things but she couldn't do anything like that. We tried rock climbing and she sucked. We signed up for ballroom dancing, salsa, jazz and skydiving. She wasn't very good at any of those things." She chuckled at the thought.

"Oh that's interesting, no one mentioned that."

"They probably wouldn't, everyone remembers just the good things. She was afraid of dogs. I remember poor Kyle bought her this little toy Chihuahua for her birthday and she broke down in tears he had to give it away to a friend."

"Do you remember who they gave it to?"

"I should it was me I still have the dog called snowball."

"I see was there a reason why she was so scared of dogs?"

"From what I heard when she was four years old she was bitten pretty bad by the neighbor's dog. From then on she didn't like dogs."

"Who could blame her?"

"Are you kidding me? It was a freaking baby Toy Chihuahua. Snowball wouldn't harm a fly. If you ask me, I think she was being ridiculous about the whole thing. She really needed to get over it. God it happened to her when she was four. I mean she broke down sobbing at her own party for Christ sakes." Jasmine pursed her lips and shook her head. "What an embarrassment."

"So everyone knew she was scared of dogs?"

"Pretty much it was the talk of the night. Everyone was trying to console her."

"Did she ever want to have kids?"

"Kids?" she made a face as if Dice had asked her if she ever wanted to start a spider farm. "Oh no, they weren't a couple that would ever want kids. That was something I couldn't see happening in this lifetime," she chuckled. "God ... kids ... you're a real comedian."

"Hey I try." She pulled out her business card and passed it to Jasmine, "Here's my card thank you for your time if you can think of anything else that might help please give my office a call."

She took the card and looked at with a little disgust. "Sure." She slowly got up and strolled out. Dice made a few notes. Holy crap this woman was too much. Picking up the phone, she dialed 1.

"Hello Miss Maddox, how can I help you?"

"I have an appointment with Mike Sundar could you let him know I'm ready for him and that I'm in the boardroom?"

"Right away Miss Maddox," the line went dead and she put the phone back on the receiver.

Dice continued to make some more notes until she heard a man clearing his throat standing in the doorway. Looking up, she found Mr. Mike Sundar staring at her with a dazzling white smile. He looked East Indian but more like a movie star. With his good looks she was sure he had women swooning for him. For a brief moment she thought she had a small orgasm just looking at the man. She stood up and held out her hand to him trying to shove the amusing thought out of her warped mind.

"Hello, Mr. Mike Sundar my name is Dice Maddox. I am a private investigator who was hired by Kyle Barnett. Please sit down so I can ask you a few questions."

"Oh baby you're cute," he drawled. "You can ask me anything." He had a hint of a British accent.

"Are you from here?"

"No darling I'm from England but I have migrated to Canada when I was in college. I've been trying to get rid of the accent for a very long time. Are you married?"

Dice laughed, "No Mr. Sundar that's not how this works I ask you the questions." She went over and closed the door shut then returned to her seat.

"How did you know Linda Barnett?"

"I met her through my wife."

"Linda was friends with your wife?"

He nodded.

"Who's your wife?"

"You've met her already pretty lady. Jasmine Foster, she kept her name."

"You and Jasmine Foster ... the woman who works here?"

"Yes, I know I could have done better but I fell in love with her pretty face ... when I got to know her ... it was too late. I was married to the bitch. We divorced a year and half ago. Since then I met and married my fourth wife. She is a bitch too, but at least she loves me." He laughed at his own joke.

"Did you know Linda and Kyle well?"

"Well, enough I had been to their house on occasion. I like Linda because she was funny and she understood my sense of humor. You could just be yourself around Linda."

"Did anyone not like Linda?"

"My wife not my current one I mean Jasmine," he laughed. Then he leaned closer and lowered his voice. "You won't tell her I said this right?"

"This whole conversation is confidential it's between just you and I."

"Good. Yes, she hated Linda. I found out she had a thing for Kyle. That's been part of our marital problems that and she is a crazy bitch. She always pretended to be what do you ladies call it besties with Linda but every chance Jasmine got she tried to make Linda look bad. Linda didn't notice. For someone who was so brilliant, she was dumb when it came to her friends. She didn't know. Sandra Miller I liked her. She was a little bit puffy but that was a medical problem ... she is funny and smart too. If I didn't meet my current angel ... Sandra, I would date her if she was interested."

Dice was getting a bunch of imagines in her mind she cleared her throat and took a sip of her coffee. "What kind of things was Linda into?"

"Oh I'm sure you heard the usual. Tennis, boating, God this woman was too nice ... she even went down and fed the poor people, I caught her volunteering at the hospital once too. I don't think she had a bad bone in her body. Vices ... I would have to say Linda's consisted of picking out the wrong friends. So trusting she trusted everyone around her. That would be her vice. From what I understand, she didn't like heights either."

"What do you think happened to her?"

"With Linda … you never know. If Jasmine isn't a suspect then I would say she picked the wrong random crazy person to trust and she is buried in the woods somewhere. Like I said she was too trusting. You must have heard about her co-worker. He was an asshole too. What he did was uncalled for. You don't treat women like that."

"The previous detectives that came and asked you questions was there anything you thought about after you talked to them that you wished you were asked or wish you told them?"

"I told you more than anyone else. I never told them about Jasmine. They interviewed us together since we work at the same office. You were the first one that didn't."

"I see …," she nodded and made a note of that. "Did you ever hear of Linda and Kyle fighting?"

"No, they were like my parents. They never fought and if they did they did it when no one was around, which was nice for everyone else. I'm sure they must have. Hey I have been married five times and I fought with every one of them. Makeup sex is the best. I'm sure you know this too."

"May I call you again if I think of anything else?"

"You can call me anytime."

She passed him her business card. "If you think of anything please call me, this is my office number. Call anytime and I'll get back to you as soon as possible if I'm not in the office."

He took her card and slipped it into his jacket pocket. "Any time pretty lady, anytime," he grabbed her hand and kissed it. He turned and left.

She sat down wrote a couple more notes, packed up her belongs and took her mug with her out to the front reception. Dice left her mug on the counter and thanked the receptionist for her assistance. Then she left. On the way down she reached in and turned her recorder off.

Since one of her meetings canceled she had just one more left. Hurrying across town to her next appointment, she found her next appointment at the university's library. Students were littered everywhere. She went over to the counter and the librarian behind she smiled at the young lady and asked, "I'm here to see Jon

Cousins." She slipped her hand into her pocket and turned on her mini mic.

"Yes, he is in his office. Hold on I'll ring him for you." She picked up and phone and in such a soft tone told Mr. Cousins there was someone here to see him. He must have told her that he was expecting someone and to show them in because she smiled sweetly up at Dice and nodded in reply into the phone with a quick soft and sultry, "sure no problem."

The pretty receptionist hung up and pointed to the door across the way. It was unmarked. "He's right in there."

"Thank you." Dice turned and walked over knocking on the door.

"Come in," a male voice called.

Opening the door a man that was on the short side, a little muscular wearing a short sleeve dress shirt and slacks stood up. He looked like he was in his thirties. He held his hand out to her.

She closed the door behind her and shook his hand. It was a firm strong shake. "Hi there, my name is Dice Maddox. I am a private investigator working for Kyle Barnett, investigating Linda Barnett's disappearance."

"Nice to meet you young lady, please have a seat."

She sat down across from him. "What do you think happened to Linda?"

"Well, I guess that's what you're here to find out. I wouldn't presume to know."

"Fair enough, how did you meet Linda?"

"Through working here, I helped her on a couple projects."

"Can you elaborate on that?"

"She was framed by some kid who claimed she came on to him. I found an email from the kid to another email address that turned up dead. We had our IT guys look at it but they couldn't find whom it belonged to. But it did prove that the kid was paid for his lying when we confronted him, he cracked."

"Didn't he tell you who hired him?"

"He said, he didn't know. He only got the emails and money slipped under the door."

"Who did Linda believe it was?"

"Well, she couldn't believe anyone would do that but we had our suspicions we just didn't have anything to back it up with."

"You mentioned you worked on a couple projects with her. Did one happen to be some scandalous photos?"

"Yes, you heard about those too."

Dice nodded.

"Yes, I was able to prove that the person's body that her face was cropped onto wasn't hers. The model had this really tiny tattoo on her ankle which Linda didn't have."

"Clever boy," Dice jotted that down in her notepad.

"I would like to think so," he chuckled. "Rookie mistake."

"Was there anyone else that didn't like Linda?"

"No ... everyone loved Linda."

"Did you hear of any marital problems?"

"Linda and Kyle? I couldn't imagine that, they were great together."

"Did you hang out with Linda after hours?"

"I went to her book club every Wednesday night and we played tennis now and again."

"Do you remember who Linda's assistant was?"

"Linda's assistant? No ... I remember she had one but I can't remember her name it was unusual though. Not like Lisa or Lori or whatever."

"You were on the interview list, was there anything you want to tell me that you may have forgotten to tell someone that interviewed you before?"

"No, they were pretty thorough."

"I see. Well, if you can think of anything else please let me know. Here's my business card." She handed him her card. "Thank you for your valuable time."

She got up and left. Turning her mini recorder off Dice headed back out to her car. It was a day. Dice didn't want to go home because Chris and Sean would find her there. If she went to her office, they probably would find her there too. Unless ... unless she parked in the back of the Red Dragon? At least she would have access to her computer and she could make up some notes for this.

With that decided she drove over to her office and parked in the back behind the Red Dragon, no one would even think of looking for her in the back. She slipped into her office and locked the door behind her. Slipping into the back office she closed the door behind her and turned the lamp on. Starting up her computer she decided she had better call Chris and let him know, she couldn't make it for dinner. She felt a little bad about lying to him but then remembered yesterday's double date. What ill feelings she had about lying soon melted away.

Deciding to text him it would be easier, he wouldn't be able to hear her voice and know she was lying. She decided to tell him she was stuck out in the field on assignment couldn't make dinner, sorry. She pressed send. Then set her phone aside. Sighing in relief, she started a file for Kyle and Linda Barnett.

Deciding to double-check it, she ran a check, on Linda's driver's license and her social. Checking her email, social media nothing looked like it was accessed except for the last time she was being traced. Credit cards … bankcards nothing had been touched.

She started with the interviews she had today. Then short listing some of the more interesting things she found out. Noting the fear of dogs and that she was attacked by a dog when she was four? Was she afraid of heights? Was Jasmine dating Kyle before he dated Linda? She wondered what Ishia Wren was like? Was he behind the photos and the student accusing Linda of sexual advances? Who was Di? Why couldn't people remember her?"

Pulling out the photos that she received today, she laid them out on her table. Grabbing printer paper, she began by putting everyone name on the top of the page then she put down what they thought of Linda, how they knew her and anything else she felt was relevant.

Then she got her white board out and taped all the sheets with potential suspects listed up on the wall. The photos she had gathered gotten taped to the white board. Under the photos she put 'where is Linda?' She grabbed another piece of paper and wrote suspects on the top, then listed 'Ishia Wren motive Dean's position,' beneath him she wrote, 'Jasmine Foster motive Kyle' … she sat down in her chair and hauled out the pastry box of coffee cake. Putting her feet up on the table, she stared at the wall and the board. She needed to find Linda's assistant. Maybe she could tell her something more? The kids in the after-school science group she created. Someone had to know what happened to her.

Dice grabbed her phone and called her friend, Detective Rick Li who worked for the police department.

"Detective Li," he answered.

"Rick hi, how are you?" she said cheerfully.

"Dice Maddox if you are hovering over another body hang up and call 911," he growled.

"Rick is that any way to talk to an old friend?"

"If there is no dead body then you must be calling to invite me out to dinner?"

"Did you look into that matter I had asked you to?"

He sighed, "I did, in truth I was about to call you anyways."

"What did you find out?"

"There was nobody, no other people matching her description went missing. In fact we couldn't find any other mysteries of missing people at all for that time period. I don't know what to tell you Dice. The lone suspect is your client. I wish I could tell you something else there just isn't anything to offer."

"Thanks for trying."

"I'm not joking the next time you call me it better be for food or sex or both I don't care what order either," he laughed.

"Right because that's what I do just randomly call people for food and sex."

He laughed again, "Well if you ever get those urges put me at the top of your list. How do you find it going solo?"

"I like it," she smiled and looked around her office.

"I heard just good things about your recent work Dice."

"Thanks for saying so."

"I gotta run but the next time it'd better be more than having me run a check for you."

"Thanks, Rick I appreciate it."

He hung up. She returned her attention back to her wall again. There didn't seem to be any paper trail suggesting she was living her life somewhere else. She was all over the news a year ago. If she had hit her head and had amnesia someone would have recognized her she was a looker so that helped in that department.

She checked her list of meetings for tomorrow she was meeting the guy who was in charge of the soup kitchen Rob Martin, then Linda's sister Lori Bowen, Derek Holbrooke who was a manager for the Tennis and Boating club, and finally Tracey O'Connor another friend from the book club. Then on Wednesday, she was meeting Danielle Poulin in the Human Relations department at the university, as well as Sammy Whyte who was a colleague of hers, Dale Stein and Ishia Wren. She needed to meet with Milton Hunter and Di the assistant. None of the other investigators ever interviewed the assistant.

The assistant was something that she could ask Danielle Poulin on Wednesday about unless it came up before then. As her luck was persisting, she didn't hold much hope for that. Reviewing the old case notes from the previous investigators, she poured over them. Reading and re-reading them nothing came to light. Nothing new surfaced. There was no mention as to the animosity that Jasmine Foster felt towards her friend. Mike Sundar knew but he was married to her for a short spell. Sandra Miller knew but she was also excluded from the book club. Was that the reason that Jasmine Foster didn't invite Sandra because she knew how she really felt towards Linda? Jasmine Foster knew Linda Barnett the longest. It was funny why people still hung out with others especially if they couldn't stand them. Revenge? ... Wanting to watch someone fail especially? Jasmine was upset with Linda for always stealing her boyfriends even when she wasn't trying to. That was the salt in the open wound. Maybe she cracked and couldn't take it anymore? Everyone thought Kyle was the main suspect even the people whom he hired to prove otherwise. Dice was piling up more questions, rather than answers. If there was some way that Linda could speak to them and tell them the truth. "Linda Barnett what had happened to you?" Dice asked the photos that were on the white board. Just Linda's smiling face staring back at her. She was quite the striking beauty even as she got older she had a certain beauty to her that didn't go away. She just got better, that's what Uncle Eric would tell Aunt Sophie when she worried about her looks. He told her she was crazy and that she was aging like fine wine ... gracefully.

Dice decided she needed a break from this and her stomach was growling. Looking up, she noticed it was going on eight o'clock. Packing up her notes, she left the wallpaper and photos up. Grabbing her briefcase and purse, she turned off her lamp and then headed out. Locking up after herself, she figured it was safe and stopped in at the Red Dragon.

Stepping inside the place looked full. Dice went over to the bar and found a seat.

"Hey Dice, you're running late tonight," Gary smiled at her.

"I was working in the office. How are things?"

"Not bad. Your table is waiting for you."

"My table?" she looked at him surprised and confused. "What

table?"

He pointed behind her to the dates she was trying to avoid. Chris, Sean and Alisha were all sitting at a table. She instinctively reached for her briefcase and purse. If she snuck out they wouldn't see her then, she could escape without having to endure that too.

"Dice!" Chris looked up and waved at her as she had dismounted from the stool.

"Crap," she grunted under her breath. Sighing she plastered a fake smile on her face and waved to him. What the hell were they still hanging out together for? Trudging over to their table, he had a chair pulled out for her. "Hi guys," she said cheerfully.

"Hi, we knew you would show up eventually," Sean smiled at her as he gave his date a little shoulder squeeze.

"You guys know me so well," she sat down putting her bags on the empty seat between her and Alisha. "You guys were here the whole time?"

"No, we went miniature golfing earlier than decided to come back here figuring you would make a stop by if you were working," Chris grinned at her.

"I'm so predictable," she frowned. "Who knew?"

Sean and Chris raised their hands and said, "Me!"

Narrowing her eyes at them, she stuck her tongue out.

"So how was your day?" Chris asked.

"Interesting ... and so long, I was just planning on grabbing a bite then heading home to soak in the tub. How about you guys?"

"I saw you in my office building earlier."

"Yeah, I had a couple interviews."

"What are you working on?" Alisha asked.

"It's confidential," Dice smiled at her.

"I just thought maybe we could help you."

"My client wants his privacy," she didn't want to share anything with Alisha.

"That's understandable. If you need our help you know you can count on us," Sean smiled.

She nodded. Then Alisha started talking about their miniature golfing experience. Gary brought her hot tea and rubbed her shoulders.

"You need to loosen up, girl. Best thing for that is sex," he laughed and walked away.

Not uncomfortable at all. Could she just melt into a puddle of embarrassment now?

"Well, if you need some assistance, I can offer my services," Chris reached out and grabbed her leg giving it a squeeze.

Sean stared at her waiting for her to say something. She just took a sip of her drink and grabbed the menu ignoring them all. Alisha flashed Dice a glare and then kissed Sean on the cheek regaining his attention. Not awkward at all? She shook her head.

Resting the menu down, Alisha hauled out her phone and popped up some photos of Chris, Sean and herself. There were several photos of Sean hugging her and Chris showing her how to hold a golf stick. She smiled and nodded at each picture counting the minutes of how much longer this evening had to endure. Chris and Sean were talking about some game that was on the big screen. They were discussing how some hockey player was injured. How long he would be out. They rehashed the guy's injury and how it could have been prevented. Then she just blocked the rest out it was just a bunch of blah blah blahing as far as she was concerned. It wasn't anything that held any interested for her. Much like these photos that Alisha had with her and the guys, Alisha was making a statement to Dice. Dice got it. Alisha thought Dice was trying to move in on her territory. It didn't matter what Dice did or said there was nothing she could do to get this crazy woman to see that she wasn't trying to steal anyone away from anyone. In fact, you couldn't steal somebody from someone else. Sighing Dice was grateful the noise drowns the sound out. Plastering a smile on her face, she waited until the picture show was over with and was grateful that Gary sent over some food. Everyone else had already eaten.

Twenty minutes later she had eaten and drank her tea. Chris tried to order her a drink. "No thanks, this has been fun but I have another early morning. So I'm going to duck out. You guys have a great night, Alisha it's always a treat," she grinned as she grabbed her briefcase and purse. She stopped at the counter to pay for her meal but Gary said next time. She was too tired to argue and decided to just forget it. Outside the night air greeted her. A shiver crept over her. Momentarily she forgot where she parked her car ... and then remembered it was in the back. Hiding ... incognito ... so much for that! She shook her head and grinned. Heading around the building it was just a couple minutes and she found her car. Unlocking it, she was grateful to get that evening over with. How funny she tried to avoid them and then ran smack into them when she didn't want to. Karma the little voice in her head whispered, that's what you get for trying to ignore them in the first place.

"Dice!" she looked up to see Sean crossing the parking lot.

Tossing her briefcase and purse over on the passenger's side, she half turned towards him. He came up to her breathing a little hard and standing a little too close. Swallowing hard, she could feel his breath on her skin.

"Yes?" she asked.

"Yes?" he grabbed her face and kissed her. Wide eyes she stared at him. Grabbing her car for support, she found herself pressed up against the car sandwiched between her car and Sean Larke. Why was he doing this to her? Pulling back, he stared at her.

"What? Why?" she stammered. Flustered and turning red she felt her cheeks flaming.

"Why do you always make me crazy?" he gasped.

She noticed he was very short of breath as well. "What are you doing? Alisha?"

"She's a little crazy if you haven't noticed. I'm breaking up with her tonight."

"So you thought coming out here to molest me was … what a good idea?"

He grinned, "it depends do you want me to molest you?" he ran a hand down her shoulder and then to her waist.

Inhaling deeply, she shook her head, "I'm sorry. If I gave you any indication that I was interested in starting a relationship … I'm not. I love being single. I miss hanging out with you but I really love having my own space."

"I know … I get it," one hand was resting on her waist the other caressed her cheek.

"I am not looking for a boyfriend."

"Dice I know I hear you. I just want you to know I am available for whatever you have in mind. Friends … friends with benefits … just friends … whatever … I really miss hanging out with you. I just want to be able to hug you and hold you, to kiss you and not have to hide how I feel about you."

"Umm, I have to think about this." She swallowed hard. Dice wasn't sure what she wanted. But she didn't want to be the reason

Alisha was single either. It wasn't her decision, she reminded herself.

"That's fine," he leaned close and gentling caressed his lips against hers. It sent shivers from her lips to her toes. Perhaps Sean Larke was very dangerous? Dice was having trouble breathing and was grateful she had her car to hold her up.

"I think your date is waiting for you," she rasped.

"All I want is to hang out with you."

Swallowing hard, she forced a small smile. "You said that already. I'm going home. Good night Sean," she managed to get out.

"I don't see you leaving."

"I am."

"You're still here."

"I'm going now."

"Are you?" he grinned.

She hated it when he grinned at her like that it was very distracting. Those very talented lips shouldn't be allowed to do that. Licking her lips, she shoved his hands back. Then slide into her seat. He closed the door once she was inside. Grabbing her seat belt, she clicked it into place. Not daring to roll down the window she just waved and started the car. Checking her mirrors briefly, she backed up. He stood there watching her leave.

What a weird night. It was such a long day she was grateful for finally getting home and being able to lock the door behind her. Dropping her keys in the dish, she kicked off her shoes by the door and left them on the shoe rack, taking her briefcase and purse she left them on the counter. Dragging her butt upstairs, she went directly into the bathroom where she stripped off her clothes. Looked at herself in the mirror and wondered who that woman was staring back at her. Shaking her head, she got into the tub, pulled the curtain and started up the shower. The hot water felt like heaven. She could no longer think. Her brain was in overload and today was just long and tiring. Not to even think about this evening ... so strange. Did Sean actually kiss her again? Did it mean he would go running with her again? More kissing? She smiled at that thought. Well ... whatever it was ... she pushed it out of her mind and just focused on the hot water washing away the day's stress, dirt and grime. Staying in the shower a little longer because it was just so comforting. Finally, giving in to it she turned the water off and got out grabbing the towel from behind the door and wrapping it around her. She gathered up her clothes and dumped them in the laundry basket. Padded across the soft carpet in her bedroom she pulled open her drawer and pulled out some clean clothes, she dressed within seconds returned the towel to the rack in the bathroom and then headed back to her bed. Crawling into her bed pulling the blankets up over her body. As soon as her head hit the pillow she was out.

CHAPTER EIGHT

TUESDAY 6:02 AM

She couldn't believe how tired she was last night. Getting up, she stretched and yawned. Within minutes she was dressed for her morning run and was standing in the kitchen peeking out her window across the balcony to Sean Larke's place. Looking for any signs of life … that he might be up and preparing to run with her this morning.

The door opened from his place and Alisha stepped outside wearing a big smile and very messy hair. Sighing sadly, she frowned. "I guess he changed his mind," she whispered just to hear the words how they sound out loud. Bittersweet.

Nope. That was it … she had to cut her ties with that man. She could see him coming out after her trying to scoot her back inside. Instead, they look like they ended up hugging and kissing. It was her fault the little voice whispered if she hadn't been so stubborn about it. She wanted to be single well now she was very much single. What was she complaining about? It was what she wanted right? She nodded, it still hurt seeing him with someone else. If they were right for each other they would be together … obviously, they weren't. Pushing her sad little love life out of thought, she had another day of interviews she wanted to get through today. First, she needed to get out there and get her run in.

Holding her head up high, she got her iPod and ear buds, grabbing her keys and headed for the door. Within minutes she was downstairs standing outside, giving a little stretch here and there.

Inhaling deeply, she shook off her disappointment and started

93

out. Focusing more on her case at hand, she reminded herself she didn't have time for anything else. She had four people she was going to meet today Rob Martin told her to come by in the morning he was down at the Soup Kitchen. After which she was meeting with Linda's sister Lori Bowen. Then across town, she had an appointment with Derek Holbrooke who was the manager of the Tennis and Boating club as well as Linda's friend. Finally, her last meeting scheduled for today was Tracey O'Connor who worked at Tea, Books and Candles. She decided she would pick up some more candles if they had some that she liked. She was supposed to have met Tracey O'Connor yesterday but something had come up and she needed to reschedule. Dice still needed to find Linda's assistant, who was the mystery girl?

Dice looked up and realized she was standing back outside her building. She had ran her usual trail on auto pilot the whole time. Her mind took leave and was engrossed in her case. Heaving a sigh, she stretched a bit and went inside.

Twenty minutes later she was showered and dressed. Ready for her day ... the only problem was ... she didn't have an appointment for another two hours. Grabbing her phone, she dialed Kyle Barnett, he answered on the second ring.

"Hello?"

"Hi Mr. Barnett, I was just calling to check in with you. I met with a few people yesterday and I was wondering if this morning you might remember Linda's assistant's name?"

"No sorry, just Di comes to mind. Did you find out anything new that the others didn't?"

"Do you have a couple of minutes?"

"Yes," he hesitated.

"I'm on my way over."

"Right now?"

"Yes," she hung up so he wouldn't be able to say no. Grabbing her briefcase, purse and keys she headed out the door.

It was a short ten-minute drive. As she was pulling up in the driveway, she noticed he was peeking out the front window. Stepping up the walkway the front door opened as she neared it. Kyle Barnett greeted her with a big smile.

"What a lovely surprise. You're so much like your Aunt Sophie," he held the door open for her. "No, no keep your shoes on."

Dice followed him through his home and outside to the backyard.

Sitting on the patio, he had a small kitchen cart with breakfast items and fruit on it.

"Please, Miss Maddox help yourself to breakfast unless you have already eaten."

"Thank you," she helped herself to some strawberries. Flicking the switch on to her mini recording device in her pocket, she took a seat and smiled at him. Rearranging herself in her seat, she pulled out her notepad and grabbed a pen. Then took a bite of strawberry, chewing ... she smiled at him. Swallowing she cleared her throat and smiled again. "I hope I am not being too intrusive by popping by this morning."

"Not at all Miss Maddox, it's a pleasure to see you as always."

"I hope you still feel that way after I have asked you a couple questions I have on my mind."

"I'm sorry?" he looked at her as he leaned back in his chair. "What is on your mind Miss Maddox?"

"Jasmine Foster," Dice said her name and paused watching his face for a reaction. There was none. Dice eyed him suspiciously but he just watched her. "She was or is Linda's friend. Are they close?"

"It would seem so," he said carefully.

"Were you dating Jasmine before you started dating Linda?"

"I was ... what does that have to do with anything? We were casually dating nothing serious. We were so young at the time."

"Do you recall how Jasmine took it?"

"We were young. She wasn't that into me as you young people say. She was looking to party and have fun. When I met Linda everything changed for me. I wanted to settle down and be with just her."

"What you are saying, is that you and Jasmine were casually dating it wasn't anything serious and you both went your separate ways without giving each other a second thought?"

"Why would we? It wasn't serious."

"What if I told you ... Jasmine was crazy about you?"

He laughed, "yeah right."

Dice could not believe he didn't know this or notice at the time. Jasmine Foster believed her friend stole her man from her. She could very well be a suspect. "Not only was she very much in love with you. Jasmine was very upset that Linda stole you away from her."

"What?" his smiling face faded, "You're serious about this aren't you?"

"I am very serious."

"Who said this to you? They were lying. That's not how it was at all."

"Really?" she just watched him. "Think back about that time in your life. Did Jasmine give you any indication that she was interested in anyone else but you? Did she seem hurt or angry when you went your separate ways? Did she blame you? Or did she blame Linda?"

That caught his attention. He gasped and held his chest, with his mouth gaping open as the words sunk in. Tears welled up in his eyes. Shaking his head no, "I won't believe it until I hear it from her first. Are you trying to tell me young lady that Jasmine ... she ... no, there is no way, she could have hurt Linda. There is just no way."

"I'm not saying she did anything to Linda but how could you not have noticed?"

He didn't reply. He just shook his head.

"I've talked to Jasmine yesterday and she seemed pretty upset about Linda being gone but at the same time she did mention that she had a thing for you."

"I didn't know," he whispered.

"My other question was about her co-worker Ishia Wren, have you met him?"

"Yes on many occasions. He has even been here and sat in that seat that you're sitting in," he nodded at her.

"When the pictures of Linda went up all over the place, the nude pictures that were not really her body, do you think he could have been behind it?"

"I know at first everyone was shocked and he was the only one that seemed to take pleasure in the subject whenever it came up. Linda believed he was behind it. Not at first ... at first, we had no idea who would do such a thing. It wasn't until a month into it that she became suspicious that it was him behind it. I, on the other hand, didn't see why someone of his stature would stoop to such a level."

"Alright, what about Milton Hunter?"

"What about that little lair?"

"Do you think Ishia Wren was the one who put Milton Hunter up to that?"

"I don't know him that well. I remember when it had happened Linda was devastated at first. She couldn't believe someone would be so cruel to make such accusations against her. She had gone over to Mr. Hunter's home and when Mr. Hunter's mother yelled at her then punched my wife in the face. Linda was crushed. It later came out that Milton Hunter made it all up. Some people thought I paid him off, which I had nothing to with him coming forward and retracting his accusations. He admitted that someone hired him to do it. Claiming he had no idea who was behind it because they contacted him through notes shoved under his door or some fake email address. Linda believed Ishia Wren was behind it."

"He got recently promoted didn't he?"

"Yes."

"If Linda was still here do you think he would have been promoted?"

"No if Linda was still here, she would have gotten that position."

Dice watched him again, made a couple notes. "So my question to you is do you think Jasmine or Ishia are capable of murder?"

"No," Kyle shook his head. "I can't believe Jasmine would be capable of anything like that. Nor Ishia, I don't know him that well but to gain a promotion. It seems absurd."

"Is it?"

"Do you have proof?" he narrowed his eyes at her.

"Not yet," she smiled.

"You shouldn't go making accusations without proof young lady."

"I came here to ask you a few questions about people you think you know. Do you still feel confident that you know these people so well?"

"Young lady I don't like that tone you are using with me. What do you want from me?"

"Well, I got what I came here for. I have an early appointment today. I should be heading out. I just wanted your impression of these individuals that have caught my attention. I have not accused them of anything for the record. I am curious though if their motives for having Linda out of the way ... how far would these individuals go to do that."

"I am running late for work too."

"Well, thank you for your time," she got up and showed herself out.

She headed over to the Soup Kitchen and parked outside in the back. Leaving her briefcase behind, she grabbed her notebook and pen stuffing them in her purse. Rolling up the windows, she locked up. Heading to the front door, she noticed the door was locked. No one was around. She walked back around to the back of the building looking for another entrance.

At the back she saw a big burly guy hunched over a box. His clothes looked like they had seen better days she wasn't sure if he was the guy that ran the place of if he was a customer of theirs.

"Excuse me," she interrupted him. "I'm looking for a man by the name of Rob Martin. Is he here?"

"Yes, he is."

"Mr. Martin?"

"Yes, I am."

"I'm Dice Maddox, I'm a private investigator working for Kyle Barnett. I was just wondering if I could ask you a few questions."

"What kind of questions? Did I kill her? The answer is no. Do I think she is still alive? I don't know. Do we miss her here? Yes, we do." He straightens up, turned and looked at her. Checking her over from head to toe, frowning slightly like she didn't quite measure up to his idea of something. "You're a detective?"

"I am a private investigator, looking into Linda's disappearance."

"Alright come with me I don't normally take a break but I could sure use an excuse to sit down right now." He held the door open for her and gestured for her to go inside. She stepped inside, the kitchen was hot, it was like stepping into an oven. Hot just didn't quite cover it. Dice felt beads of sweat formulating on her forehead. Inside there were seven people working frantically at making food. A couple of the ladies were singing bible songs. The others just smiled and chatted eagerly among themselves as they worked. No one looked like a slacker from what she could tell. Everyone was moving quickly in the small kitchen going about their tasks. Rob Martin came in and nudged her.

"This way young lady," he nodded to a small hallway.

Everything about this place smelled delicious. Everyone seemed happy to be there. The place looked old and a bit weathered. The hallway wasn't much different the tiles were lifting and there were a few that were missing. Yet the place felt warm and inviting.

He opened a door and they went inside. Closing it behind him, he ambled over to the chair behind the desk. The room was compact and really organized.

He sucked in air like it was his last breath and heaved it out in a big sigh. She could feel his warm onion breath as he sighed. Even his table was on the small side, which made him appear larger.

"Let's make this quick. I don't have all day," he grumbled.

"I understand Linda Barnett worked here on every other weekend. Is that right?"

"Yes," he nodded.

"How did she get involved, do you know?"

"Linda was an upstanding citizen just like over three-quarters of my volunteer staff. The other quarter is usually made up of community service individuals who are generally wonderful people either who made a mistake or were misunderstood. I met Linda once in the supermarket and she struck up a conversation with me. I explained what I did. She seemed interested, told me she would be out the next weekend to help. True to her word she showed up. We are open in the afternoon every day of the week and rely on funding from donors. At the time I didn't really know who Linda was. She not only came to roll up her sleeves but she donated money on a regular bases which makes a huge difference. Since she has disappeared, her husband has taken up the donation portion of helping out which we are really grateful for."

"Does he come down and roll up his sleeves?"

"No."

"I see," Dice nodded. "Did she bring anyone with her on a regular basis?"

"Yes, Dale Stein he is a close friend of hers and he still volunteers every weekend on Saturday and Sunday. I can always count on him."

"While she was here did you notice anyone she didn't get along with? Did she fight with anyone?"

"No, I have never seen her raise her voice not even once. Everyone loved Linda she has been missed terribly since she disappeared."

"What about any of the customers that come in? Did any of them take an extra interest in her?"

He laughed, "Are you asking if one my friends that come in here could have killed her? Is that what you are asking young lady?"

"I am just wondering if someone took a liking to her and she didn't reciprocate the feelings?"

He narrowed his eyes at her, pursed his lips and shook his head.

"No, I think you are barking up the wrong tree here young lady."

"Had you overheard of her talking about any problems with anyone? Not necessarily here but maybe at work when she was here with Dale Stein?"

"No … nothing had been said from what I can recall. Who could hate Linda? She was the closest thing you could get to an angel. We all miss her."

"And you don't recall anyone here that might like Linda too much? Having a crush on her … following her around … that sort of thing?"

He pressed his lips together, "no nothing that I would say was verging on the sick side of things or stalker like. You must have seen pictures of her. She was a looker. Of course, men admired her, but they all knew she was married. I never saw anyone here that would harm her in any way. In fact quite the opposite … one weekend she was coming here and someone tried to rob her, one of our regulars stopped the guy and the robber was arrested. These guys that come in here are more honest than regular citizens. They just have stuff they are having trouble dealing with on a personal level."

She nodded. "I see. I appreciate your time. If you can think of anything else, please give me a call." Dice hauled out her business card and scrawled her cell number on the back, then passed it to him.

"Will do, I hope you find out what happened to her. Like I said we miss her terribly here."

Dice shook his hand and showed herself out. Getting back to her car, she unlocked it and hopped in. Rolling down the window, she was just about to start it up when one of the ladies from the kitchen approached her.

"Excuse me miss, are you looking into Linda Barnett's disappearance?"

"I am … do you have something to tell me?"

The woman peered around her craning her neck to see if anyone was coming out. Taking another shaky puff on her cigarette … inhaling deeply it was like watching a prostitute going down on a john and taking it all in. The old woman smiled broadly and exhaled circles of billowy white rings.

"I saw her bring a man here a few times and they looked a little more than just friends. I hear she was a married woman too but it wasn't her husband. Back in my day things like that were unheard of."

Dice just nodded. Figuring the woman was referring to Dale Stein. The investigator in her wanted confirmation. "Are you referring to Dale Stein?"

"Yes, of course, that is the English teacher right?"

"Yes, it is."

"Yes, that is the man she paraded around with. We had a name for girls like that. It isn't very nice either."

Dice nodded. "Did you see them kissing or anything?"

"Good lord girl! Did you not hear me? She was a married woman? She had the decency not to do that in public but it certainly looked like they were more than just friends."

"Your name is?"

"Mrs. Caroline Riker, I am a widow, my dear. I know what it is like to be married. That woman … she was one of those floozies."

"Mrs. Barnett was a professor of physics at the university."

"That's the problem with you young folks today. Back in my day, the ladies stayed at home and watched the babies, took care of the house and volunteered in the community."

"Carol?" Rob Martin called to her. "Suzie is looking for you."

"I'm coming!" she shouted back and her whole body shook a little. "It was nice talking to you young lady, but mark my word women need to be at home."

"Thank you, Mrs. Riker you have a good day." Dice stabbed her car key in the ignition; bit back a few thoughts of her own on that subject. Waited for the old woman to get out of the way and backed up. She was heading over to Lori Bowen's home next. Lori was Linda's younger sister. It would be nice to see what she thought of her sister's disappearance.

Dice found the woman's home it was in one of the less nicer neighborhoods. Driving down the street, she noticed that there weren't a lot of people out in the yards. In fact, the street seemed unusually bare. It didn't feel right and it didn't sit well with her. The front gate opened automatically when she approached it. Pulling into Lori Bowen's driveway, Dice noticed the high wrought iron fence that encompassed the whole property. The front gate opened automatically when she pulled up to it. It reminded her of horror movies just before one of the main people disappear.

As she approached the front steps, the front door opened and no human seemed present. Creepy Dice thought, very creepy.

Stepping up to the door she called, "Hello? Hello, Lori Bowen? Hello?"

No one seemed to be in the hallway. Stepping inside, she held the door open. As her eyes adjusted to the room, she called again, "Hello? Mrs. Lori Bowen we have an appointment this morning. Hello?"

"I'm in here dear!" a voice called out sweetly.

Closing the door behind her, she tried to locate the person with the voice.

"Hello?" she called again.

"Keep coming dearie down the hall to the kitchen!" the voice directed.

Dice continued and found the woman who looked just like Linda except a little younger, smiling back at her.

"Sorry about that but I'm right in the middle of catering this big party tonight. If I stop now, I'll be screwed."

"If it is a bad time I can come back," Dice offered.

"Nonsense, grab yourself a cup of coffee and there are snacks on the tray by the coffee pot. I understand Kyle hired you to find my sister?"

"Yes, my name is Dice Maddox, I am working for your brother-in-law. How is your relationship with him?"

She laughed, "well we still see each other on special occasions. I don't wish anything bad to happen to him. He's a nice enough guy, yet I've been related to him for gawd … I think it's like twenty years. Look at me, I'm a wreck," she laughed. "Well, my sister never did pick the right kind of guy for her … she stole him from her friend Jasmine you know. I don't think it settled well with her. However, Jasmine would never admit it. The last party I was at I saw Jasmine there making googly eyes at him. He was clueless. Typical man … they never catch on to anything you want them to and the things you don't want them to … they are all over it. I'm sure you know what I'm talking about. Wow, you are so young looking. Are you fresh out of high school right?"

Trying not to show her any disparagement she grinned, "I'm not telling. Was Linda seeing anyone else?"

"You mean having an affair?" Lori laughed at the thought. "You would have to know Linda, that would be scandalous and she wouldn't want that. My older sister could have had any man she wanted. Everywhere she went men would fall all over her. I lived in her shadow for many years because I was a late bloomer. There were some things that Linda would be adventurous and do, but that my dear isn't one of them. Her pride couldn't take it. There was this one guy that came to a couple of her parties that she worked with I thought he was dangerous. He watched her every move ... it wasn't that he was interested in her in that way. He was looking for any weaknesses. When I say dangerous I mean it. I think he was the one behind those nasty pictures thank God our mom wasn't around to see that. I don't think her heart could have taken it. Even though Linda got cleared of it. It wasn't her body. The idiot didn't even have the smarts to edit out the tattoo. It was almost like he wanted to get caught. Then, there was that nasty young man who claimed my sister the prude would make passes and advances at him ... HA! In his dreams! These people just didn't know Linda Barnett at all. If they did they would know that wouldn't shake her. Yes, she was upset but it was only because it started affecting what her peers thought of her."

"Was she ever upset that she didn't have children?"

Lori laughed again, Dice was thinking wow I am so grateful I can keep you amused lady.

"Linda ... well there was a time when Linda would have wanted children but those days long left her. When she started her career that was her baby ... those after-school clubs she created to connect the students with the community by offering it open to the public was her baby. Taking care of Kyle ... that was her baby. Her husband was such a suck. I thought he would have crawled under the bed without her and died when she disappeared. I'm surprised he is able to still dress himself. My sister did a lot for that man. He was the one who was impotent. They talked about adopting but he wasn't keen on it. It would mean less time Linda would have for him. Considering all her extracurricular activities he complained about. Could you imagine if they had a child?"

"I'm sure they would have managed. People do it all the time," Dice helped herself to a cookie. Biting into it, she could taste the oatmeal and raisins in it. It was delicious. Say what you want about this woman she could certainly bake.

"You like that?" she nodded to the cookie.

Dice nodded.

"Yes, I know everyone loves those cookies. But as I was saying Linda couldn't have children if she stayed with Kyle."

"What about Dale Stein?"

"Dale?" Lori made a face. "No, he was cute and all but no. That would be weird. I don't see them as a couple."

Deciding to try a different tactic, she changed the line of conversation, "What was it like growing up with Linda?"

"It was great I suppose at times, she was a great sister. She was fun and always included me in everything. I was an ugly duckling until I blossomed. Linda always looked out for me. I always heard from my mom especially why can't you be more like Linda? Gawd even the year before she died she was still saying that to me. Like get over it, I'm not Linda alright?" she waved a spoon around. "My mom thought Linda was perfect. My dad was a little different he liked my sister and I for the people who we are."

"Is your dad still around?"

"Oh yes, he's visiting my aunt in Chili."

"You have an Aunt in Chili?"

"Yup she was the adventurous one, found a hubby who was an exchange student. They fell madly in love and then she moved back home with him. They have six kids and are very happy. My sister was a lot like my aunt. They both were free spirits that weren't afraid of taking chances."

"What do you think happened to your sister?"

"Well, if you are asking if I think my brother-in-law could have done it? No chance. That Dale guy I doubt it. I don't know anyone who would want to hurt her on purpose."

"What about Jasmine Foster?"

"I wouldn't put it pass her. If she thought she could get away with it. She pretended to be friends with my sister but that old saying of keep your friends close and your enemies even closer comes to my mind when I think of that woman."

"I see, and her co-worker that may have been behind the nude pictures and the kid who claimed she was making the moves on him? Ishia Wren?"

"I'm not sure about him. He was an odd one, very observant." Lori nodded.

"By any chance do you happen to remember Linda's assistant?"

"You mean Divya Grayson?"

"Is that who was Linda's assistant?"

"Yes, she was a great girl. Smart girl, she was Linda's shadow."

"How do you spell her first name?"

"Sure it is a little unusual. D-I-v-y-a the young woman was very unusual as well. I think it was one of those relationships of Divya being the daughter that Linda had always wanted. She was into everything Linda was. I thought even for a short span that Divya had a crush on Kyle. Nothing would have ever happened there … if you recall, I had already said he only had eyes for Linda."

"Do you know where she is now?"

"Not a clue I assume she is still at the university maybe she is working for that Professor Wren?"

"I see. Did you ever meet Milton Hunter after his accusations?"

"No but if I did I would have torn another hole in his ass. People like that don't deserve to live. What was he thinking? He almost ruined her career. It was a good thing he stepped up and confessed it was all a lie."

"Would she have lost her job?"

"She took a leave of absent for a short period while they investigated. I thought she was going to lose her mind. Kyle and her career were everything to her. Even Divya couldn't help calm her down. Sense of reason went out the window in her home."

"How did you finally get through to her? Reacting to something like that could have dangerous consequences. Did she ever face her accuser?"

"It wasn't me, our dad sat her down and talked to her. They were alone for an hour. Kyle and I stood outside and tried to listen at the door. But my dad kept her in the den and when they finally emerge she was calmer … not only was she calmer but she said she wasn't fighting it. If people wanted to believe that about her it was too bad for them."

"That must have been a tough decision."

"All I know is one minute she wanted to rip Professor's Wren and Milton Hunter to pieces the next thing it was water under the bridge. Well, not so easily I did see her wince a few times every time that came up but she held her head high and refused to play into it. That's one of the things I admired about her … Linda was always so strong. That and everybody loved Linda."

"Can you think of anyone who would want to harm her?"

"Wow, umm," Lori shook her head. "No, no matter how mad she would make you … you wouldn't want to hurt her. I can't see it. I know Jasmine was a little crazy. She blamed Linda for losing Kyle. She moved on and had two or three more husbands in the span of Linda's marriage. She is single again … I think she may still be interested in Kyle as a friend but more than friends. Nah I think the woman moved on from that. Professor Wren," she paused and shook her head. "Well, if he was behind those things like Linda thought then he would certainly want her out of the way but playing some cruel pranks on Linda is a far cry from killing her. He's smart … and I would like to think smart enough to know that he would eventually get caught."

Dice knew from experience that it didn't take much to push someone to that next level of violence. She still felt both Jasmine Foster and Professor Ishia Wren were on her short list of suspects.

"Did you hear the rumor that Linda and Kyle were breaking up?"

"What?" Lori paused and looked at her. "Who said that? I'll bet it was that bitch Jasmine. You can't trust a thing that comes out of her mouth. Kyle and Linda would never break up. Never."

"What about the baby issue?"

"No, that wouldn't do it, I'm telling you there is no way they would break up. Even if they talked about it, I know they would never go through with it. They depend on each other too much for little things. Not to mention the big things in life. No whoever said that they were lying."

"Well, I won't take up any more of your time. Here is my business card, on the back is my cell number if you can think of anything else please let me know." Dice left the card on the counter.

"Thank you dearie, good luck with the investigation. I hope you find her. Not knowing where she is …," Lori tears up. "It's so hard on all of us that love her."

"I will do my best."

"What is your track record at resolving cases?" Lori asked.

"I just started back into this business last month but even before that I have solved every case."

She smiled at Dice, "I'm so glad Kyle hired you then."

"Me too," Dice nodded. "Have a good day and good luck with your event tonight."

"Thank you."

Dice showed herself out and was back in her car before she knew it. Pulling back out the gate that mysteriously opened again for her and she exited into the street. She had an hour to kill before her next appointment heading back to the office she decided she would try to get a lead on Divya Grayson. As she was pulling into her parking spot, her phone rang.

"Hello?"

"Hi Miss Maddox this is Shirley Lamont, I remember Linda assistant's name, it was Divya Grayson, spelled D-I-v-y-a and last name G-r-a-y-s-o-n. I hope this helps."

"Well, thank you so much it does. I appreciate you calling me."

"No problem dear, I have to go, my client is coming in. Do let me know if you find out anything about Linda please."

"I will."

"Good luck," she hung up.

Dice smiled and remember she had left the coffee cake in her office. Crossing over to her inner office, she put some coffee on and found the cake. She had about fifty minutes until her appointment with Derek Holbrooke the manager for the Tennis and Boating Club. Turning on her computer and pulling up her software, she made a few inquiries as she sipped her coffee and ate some of Shirley Lamont's delicious coffee cake.

Finding the last known address for Miss Divya Grayson, she jotted it down. She tried the phone number listed but got 'this number is no longer in use,' message. She would pop by there after her meeting with Holbrooke.

Feeling a little satisfaction as things were moving forward, she saved everything and shut down her computer. Grabbing her purse and brief case, she carried her coffee cake that Shirley Lamont made in her arms and searched her pocket for her car keys.

Coming out of her office, she was surprised to see Alisha standing in the waiting room. Slipping her hand into her pocket looking for her keys something told her to turn on her mini recording devices. She did.

"Alisha? What are you doing here? How can I help you? Is Sean okay?"

"Dice," she sneered. "I'm here to tell you to back off and stay away from my boyfriend. He's mine. I don't need you sniffing around and trying to snatch him away from me."

"Okay, I think you are barking up the wrong tree lady."

"Am I?" she shouted. "I saw you last night kissing him in the parking lot! I am warning you … you little bitch to stay away! Stay far away from Sean! Do you hear me?"

"I think everyone down the block heard you." Dice narrowed her eyes towards the angry little red headed woman.

"If you don't," she growled. "I will make your life miserable."

"Right, by coming to my office and threatening me? You are aware what you are doing right now is illegal, right?"

Alisha came storming at her. Dice didn't move she didn't need to. She was more than capable of taking care of herself.

Waving a finger in her face, "I will make you pay. I am so warning you lady, back off or you will seriously regret it. What do you guys call it … the big sleep. I will end you."

"The big sleep? You will end me?" Dice raised an eyebrow thinking 'this woman is crazy'! Dice wondered what Sean saw in her. "Are you threatening me Alisha?"

"Oh Dice Maddox, I will do so much more to you than just threaten you. I will kill you if you come near him again." She turned and stormed off.

"Wow okay crazy," she reached into her pocket and turned off the mini recorder. Should she report her? Alisha was a little crazy but she was probably just angry. If something else happened then she would make a stop by Rick Li and say hi.

Giving her office the once over nothing seemed out of place. She headed out to her next appointment. Driving down to the waterfront was a nice drive. It was short and as she approached she could start to smell the fishy smell that was synonymous with the area. Finding the visitors parking was easy she had been there a few times with Chris, one of his friends had a boat and they used it a few times. Parking her car, she got out and paused. Inhaling deeply, she loved the fresh air with the hint of fish. It was bright and sunny. The sun danced across the ripples in the water, glittering like shining gold chipped blanket. The blues were deep and refreshing. She felt instantly recharged by her surroundings.

Heading over to the main office, she marveled at how brightly painted everything was. The building was bright white and trimmed with navy blue. Very nautical and yet it wasn't obnoxious or overly done. It suited the place. Going inside she found a small store of sorts. There were newspapers, snacks, a few staple goods and candy.

The young woman behind the counter smiled sweetly at her and nodded. "Good afternoon, is there anything I can help you with?"

"Yes, I'm looking for Derek Holbrooke, we have a meeting scheduled."

"Sure, just give me a minute I'll find him for you."

She picked up the phone and dialed for him. "Your appointment is here. Yes ... yes ... okay." The young woman hung up. Looking back at Dice, she smiled. "He'll just be a couple minutes. Come I'll show you to his office. Would you like a cup of coffee? Snacks?"

"I'm good," she smiled and followed the young woman.

"By the way, my name is Katie, if you need anything just call." Katie opened the door to the room that had a gangster feel to it.

"Ah looks like someone is a big fan of ...," Dice's voice trailed off.

Katie laughed, "yeah I know he's a big fan of the gangster movies. He was in a couple movies that came through town ... he was only an extra but he's got pictures of every one of them." She pointed to the wall with pictures scattered all over in frames, Derek Holbrook dressed up and in costume with other cast members and he looked like a director.

"Nice," Dice smiled and nodded. "Very impressive."

"Isn't it though, I keep telling my wife how people really like these things and she won't allow me to bring them into the house," Derek Holbrooke stood in the doorway. Smiling at his picture collection, he shook his head. "I just don't know what that woman is thinking sometimes. Ah well," he looked over at Dice. His admirable smile turned to a wolfish grin as he sized her up.

Dice nodded.

"Well, Miss Maddox had I known how beautiful you were I wouldn't have kept you waiting."

She groaned on the inside. Katie rolled her eyes and ducked out. Derek Holbrooke came over and shook her hand, hanging on to it a little too long. Dice pulled it back and forced a smile on her face. "Yes, I'm a private investigator working for Kyle Barnett, I'm here to talk about Linda Barnett's disappearance."

"Please sit down. That was a tragedy. They never did find her."

Dice took a seat. Pulling out her notebook, pausing she smiled at him. "Mr. Holbrooke …"

"No, no," he interrupted. "Please call me Derek."

"Alright, Derek how would you describe your relationship with Linda?"

"My relationship with Linda … hmm, well I would say we were erroneous lovers," he laughed. "No no we were great friends I knew her back in high school. We never dated. It wasn't that I didn't want to but we didn't have much in common until later in life. Then we discovered that we both loved tennis and boating. I had taken over my father's business and she came into my little shop here. We were both married and were only open to friendship. If I were to cross the line and my wife found out I'd be singing soprano for the rest of my life and sleeping on the couch both of which do not appeal to me. My wife is just under five feet and the cutest thing you would ever lay eyes on but when she gets mad … god look out. She would make Al Capone look like a nurse maid."

Dice smiled and nodded. "Do you think Linda was fooling around on Kyle?"

"Linda? No, I don't see that."

"Do you think they were tight or maybe on the rocks?"

He inhaled deeply and thought about the question hard. Shaking his head he replied, "no I think they were pretty tight … I mean they were married people have you ever met a married couple that hasn't had a fight? Really, if you are married you are going to fight or have a disagreement at some point they had been together forever. I know she wanted kids but it was a no show happening there. I just don't see them breaking up. They were great together. I couldn't imagine those two single. I knew Kyle from way back as well. No, he'd be lost without her. I mean like now even with her gone … he's not himself."

"How so?"

"He comes down here once in a while but he seems so … so old and unhappy. I never see him smiling. He's always alone. It made me think about my wife. If she disappeared tomorrow, I would want to die too. I can't live without her. That's the thought that comes to my mind every time I see him."

"Can you think of anyone who might want to hurt her or have her out of the way?"

He laughed, "oh my I would say, there were a few who were

jealous of her. She was beautiful, brilliant and just amazing. She wasn't one of those people who were full of themselves. Linda was also kind. Let's face it … if you are asking, you must have someone in mind. I would say maybe her friend Jasmine Foster … they were friends for as long as I remember but whenever something bad happened to Linda, Jasmine would be smirking or was a little too happy about it. I heard she had been dating Kyle before Linda. Jasmine also thought Linda stole all her boyfriends but it was Linda. Guys just flocked to her. I never met a guy who didn't have a crush on her. That guy who worked in her department he ended up getting her promotion. He wasn't someone I would trust. That kid that accused her of coming on to him, I don't know what happened to him but he wasn't well liked after that. I'm sure he blames her for some of his issues. Di her assistant she was one weird kid. I didn't trust that one at all. Then Tracey O'Connor, now she is a freak that really scares me. She appears nice and Stepford wife on the outside but that woman is bat shit crazy if you ask me. Yeah, she would be on my list of suspects too."

"If you had to pick just one who would it be?"

"Well … my money would be on the crazy chick or Jasmine. Jasmine not because she turned me down several times in high school but I think she is evil."

Dice nodded, "did you notice anyone following Linda around before she disappeared?"

"Following her?" he pressed his lips together. "No, I never noticed anything like that."

"What were her hobbies, besides boating and tennis?"

"I heard she had a science geek group at the university. Oh and she had some kind of book club that met Tuesdays or Wednesday something like that."

Dice nodded. "Did you ever go to those?"

"Me, at a book club? No, that wasn't my thing." He laughed. "I love movies mafia and gangster movies. I have read biographies of real-life gangsters and accused mafia personalities."

"Well, thank you for your time. That wraps it up, here's my business card. If you can think of anything else please give me a call." She passed him her card with her cell phone number on the back. Then got up, shaking his hand he walked her out.

"Miss Maddox, I hope you find her." He looked so serious and sad.

"Me too," she gave him a small smile and nodded to Katie.

Back outside she went over to her car looking down at the boats floating softly in the water. Turning her mini recorder off, she pulled out her keys. Checking the time, she would just make her next appointment to Tracey O'Connor at 'Tea, Books and Candles' if she hurried. Getting in and strapping herself in, her radio came to life and she pulled out after checking her mirrors.

CHAPTER NINE

It was a quick drive across town she pulled into the visitor parking lot and got out. A couple people referred to Tracey O'Connor as the crazy one, she wondered what defined the woman as crazy … she was about to find out. If memory served correct, Dice had met her once before. Grabbing her bag, purse and flicking on the mini-recorder she walked into the 'Tea, Book and Candles' shop. She was here last month for her first case when she thought it had something to do with the supernatural. Mrs. Winters wasn't supernatural as it turned out. The tinkling of the chimes was like a familiar hello, as she pushed open the door. The scent of jasmine and lilacs greeted her as she walked in.

Looking around, the placed looked the same when you enter there was a counter to the left side behind the counter a wall full of brightly colored bottles and to right a couple of rows of bookshelves. Beyond the counter, there was a little area that resembled a small café with seats and tables. They were there for the card and tea readings.

Tracey O'Connor saw her coming in and waved at her like they were good friends. Dice walked around the bookshelves and was surprised that she spotted a couple new books on the shelves. A young woman came over and introduced herself.

"Hi I'm Molly are you looking for something in particular?"

"No, I'm here to see Tracey O'Connor, we have an appointment."

"Oh right, she is just finishing up with a client. Have you been here before?"

"Yes about a month ago."

"We are having a sale on books, if you buy two, you can get 15% off."

"Thank you," Dice smiled and nodded. Hoping the young woman would go away. She tried to look like she was interested in the books; Dice picked up one and pretended to read the back.

"Oh that is a good one, it's about this boy who dies and comes back ... it's about his death and the people he meets in heaven. I totally believe in heaven and angels."

Dice put it back on the shelf. "I'm just going to look around." She turned and took a few steps away from Molly.

"Sure no problem but if you want any help or if you have any questions please just give me a shout," she smiled. Then leaned over and pointed to another book, "That one is really good too. Angels they do exist," she grinned.

Dice smiled and nodded then slipped around the rack to the other side. Sighing she tried to look busy. Bigfoot is real, UFOs, Human First Contact Already Happened, The Watchers ... there was a strange collection of books. Peeking over the shelf, she could see Tracey getting up and shaking her client's hands. Then Tracey stopped at the counter and briefly spoke with Molly before making her way over to Dice.

"Hi we've met before. Miss Maddox is that right?"

"Yes, Tracey O'Connor, I'm Dice Maddox ... I am a private investigator hired by Kyle Barnett looking into the disappearance of Linda Barnett."

Her eyes widen a bit and she nodded. "Please come into my office."

Dice followed her down the hall and into the office. It was the same as before. The room was crowded.

"I am so glad you have decided to come see me finally. I have been talking to her."

"Talking to whom?" Dice paused as she pulled out her pen and note pad. Thankfully she already turned on the mini recorder.

"Linda, of course," Tracey looked at her as if she was crazy.

"I'm sorry Linda called you?" Dice was hopeful then remembered where she was and her excitement died down quickly like rainwater on a small campfire.

"Yes, she has contacted me on a number of occasions."

"Where is she now?"

"Here," Tracey nodded. "When she knew you were coming she said she wanted to meet you so she said she would be here today."

"Can you see her?"

"No, I can hear her when she speaks to me."

And there it was. So it was a psychic connection … feeling a little annoyed and disappointed, Dice continued, "in your many conversations with Linda did she mention where her body was?"

"No, I didn't ask her that."

"Did you ask her what happened?"

"Yes, of course, I had to."

"And?" Dice prompted.

"She said she was out with Kyle and they got into an argument. She didn't tell me what that was about either. Just that she left and when she was driving home she saw this bright light on the highway. Her car stopped and the next thing she knew she was just standing there. She was all alone in the middle of nowhere. She was standing beside her car. When Linda tried to get in to drive home she found that she was passing through objects. She couldn't get into her car. Then she saw Kyle show up and he was screaming her name and racing around. He couldn't hear her either."

"Was there anyone else in the area?"

"I don't know."

"Can you hear her now?"

"Linda? Linda?" Tracey got up and walked around her office. "Linda!" she called out.

Dice could hear nothing but just watched. Wondering how long Tracey could carry on with this charade. The woman walked around in circles calling out Linda's name. Dice said nothing and watched as if she was interested.

Dice began to make a little to do list in her head. After this visit with Tracey, she would pop by Divya Grayson's old address see if she left a forwarding address or if anyone knew her or remembered her. Then perhaps she would stop by the grocery store and pick up a few staples her kitchen was looking a little bare this morning … or maybe swing by the Red Dragon and then the grocery store? Decisions … decisions … suddenly Tracey's face was right in front of hers. Staring at her wide-eyed.

"Did you reach her?" Dice smiled politely.

"Yes, she is here," Tracey nodded.

"Great, ask her if she minds me asking a few questions."

Tracey nodded. "She can hear you and she said no that would be okay. Plus she likes your hair."

"My hair? Well, thank you," Dice thought that was peculiar … if she was on the other side … ghost like … someone's hair would be the last thing she would have noticed. "The night you disappeared do you remember that?"

She waited and watched Tracey's reaction. "Yes, a little bit … it's a bit foggy."

Nodding, Dice asked, "Were you having dinner with Kyle?"

"Yes, we were."

"Do you remember what you were talking about?"

Tracey nodded, "yes but it's personal."

"I see, was it about adoption?"

Tracey looked at Dice, "How did you know?"

"I was talking to Kyle … did you guys talk about getting a divorce."

Tracey shook her head no, then her eyes widen, "Really, dear? I had no idea." Then turned to Dice, "She says yes."

Dice wondered how much did Linda confined in Tracey. "This question is for you Tracey how close were you and Linda?"

"Well, before her disappearance I only knew her from the book group. Since she has come and talked to me a few times."

"I see," Dice jotted that down. "Linda, when you were driving in your car home, did you see anyone else on the road with you that night?"

Tracey waited … "the answer is no, it was dark and there was no one following her or coming towards her."

"Did you have the radio on?"

"The radio?" Tracey looked at Dice then waited. "No, she didn't. She says normally she does but that night she doesn't remember having it on."

"What was the last thing she remembers?"

"She says she was driving home, it was dark … it was really quiet … then there was a bright light. She woke up on the ground outside the car. There was no one around. The car was still on. The door was open. The light was on inside the car and the car was making a ding

ding dinging sound because the car was still on and the door was open."

"The light that you saw … was it a bright white like shaped like a door?"

"No."

"Was it in the sky or on the ground?"

"It was like a ball and then it got bigger until it swallowed me. I don't remember what happened next or how I ended up on the ground."

"I see, was there anyone else around you at that point."

Tracey walked over to her desk and sat down. "She says yes but it didn't seem like she could communicate with anyone. First Kyle was there when he found the car abandon he began freaking out. She tried to calm him down but that's when she realized he couldn't hear or see her. Linda says she tried to touch him and grab him by the shoulder several times but her hand just went right through him. She says she was freaking out and he was freaking out but they couldn't hear each other."

"Did she hang around until other people showed up?"

Tracey waited and nodded, "yes she did. Her words, 'it was a nightmare. No one could hear me. No matter how hard I screamed. My hands and body kept going through everything. I realized after the shock wore off that I had to be dead. But no one could find my body.'"

Dice looked at Tracey waiting for her to continue.

Tracey looked a little uncomfortable. "She's crying. I can hear her sobbing. Sorry Linda. That's why Dice is here. She's looking for you now … yes …I know." Tracey looked at Dice. "She just wants you to know Kyle isn't the one who did anything to her. He couldn't. I agree with her. The few times I met him I never got the impression that he would do anything to hurt her in any way. He really loves her."

"I got that impression too Linda," Dice talked to the room. "What about Jasmine Foster?"

Tracey waited, "They are best friends … Linda doesn't believe Jasmine would do anything to hurt her either."

"What about Ishia Wren?"

Tracey waited and frowned, "hold on she is upset about him. No, she doesn't think he would go to that length to kill her. He was a jerk but she doesn't think he would kill her."

"Another question for her, her assistant what was their relationship like?"

Tracey waited, "Divya was great ... always hanging on to her every word. Eager to help out, never had to ask her to stay she always was hanging around. So smart she was like the daughter she wished she had."

"So they were close then?"

"Yes," Tracey nodded. "She really liked her, she was very intelligent and fun to hang out with."

"Does she know where Divya is now?"

Tracey waited, "no, she hasn't seen her."

"Does she remember if Divya spoke of any family or friends?"

Tracey waited again, "no ... no she didn't speak of anyone like that."

"Do you remember seeing any personal pictures or if she took any personal calls while working for you?"

"No ... no she doesn't remember, she says she isn't feeling well and she needs to take a break."

"Okay, well Linda thank you for your time." Dice put her things away. Standing up, she nodded at Tracey. "Thank you so much for your time."

Dice showed herself out and turned her mini recorder off when she reached her car.

"Dice!" Tracey raced after her. "Dice if you have a moment. I know not everyone believes in what I do but I can speak to her. I want to help her pass on. It is so lonely for her being trapped in the middle like that."

"I appreciate your time and the information you gave me was very valuable I am going to do my best to find out where her body is and we will do everything we can to help her."

"If you need anything confirmed or any more information please call me."

"Yes, and here's my business card I almost forgot. Please call me if you or Linda can think of anything else that might help us out with this investigation," Dice passed her business card over to Tracey.

Smiling Tracey took it and put it in her pocket. "We will. Please find her body and then find out who did this to her. Be careful of the one eye metal horse."

"I'm sorry?" Dice blinked and looked at Tracey.

"Sorry, it was a warning from your spirit guide. He wants you to be careful of the one who owns the one eye metal horse, he is not to be trusted."

Forcing a smile on her lips, she nodded. "Thank you I will." Feeling a little shiver come over her, she got in her car and waved at Tracey. Well, that went well she thought. Pulling out her note pad, she flipped to the notes for Divya Grayson. Finding Divya's last known address, she pulled out from the Tea, Books and Candles shop.

The thought that Tracey O'Connor could have overheard or read those things and filled in the rest with her idea of what it would be like to cross over to the other side of life was a real possibility. Did Dice believe in life after death? No, not really. There were some things that she could not explain in life but that didn't mean anything either. Just because she couldn't explain it didn't mean that there wasn't a rational explanation for it. She was not someone who was all knowing nor did she feel the need to become all-knowing. It was something that just didn't interest her besides a person couldn't possibly know everything anyways.

Pulling up to the apartment building that was Divya Grayson's last known address, she parked and got out. Grabbing her purse, she flung it over her shoulder, grabbing her notepad and pen then reaching into her pocket she flicked on the mini-recorder. Looking for apartment 304 on the mailbox there was just D. Grayson on the label. Dice felt a little hopeful that maybe she was still here. There was no elevator just some stairs to the right. Climbing the stairs to the third floor, she found apartment 304. Knocking on the door, she waited ... no answer. She knocked again and waited. There was noise but it wasn't from apartment 304 across the hall she heard the door from apartment 308 creak open.

"If you are looking for David he's not home yet," the little old woman smiled at her.

Dice gave the woman her full and undivided attention. "No, I'm not looking for David. I'm looking for Divya Grayson, do you know where I might find her?"

"Oh dear. No she has moved out six months ago. You are not the first person to come looking for her though. There was a man that was Asian looking who wasn't very nice looking for her. It was right after that woman she worked for Linda Barnett disappeared."

"Oh really?" Dice was standing outside the woman's door listening eagerly.

"Please come in," the woman about in her sixties smiled and held the door open for her.

Dice nodded and graciously accepted the invitation. Inside the place was really neat and tidy the only thing Dice found alarming were the six cats that came to greet her. Each taking turns rubbing up against her pant legs.

"Okay fellas let the lady in," the woman shooed them back. They all ran to the living room to claim their places.

"Can I get you some tea?"

"Sure," Dice nodded knowing all too well this was a gold mine of information.

Within minutes the woman came back with a small serving tray carrying two cups and saucers some cookies and pretty pink and yellow flowered teapot. Dice watched as she pours them both some tea. "Do you want some sugar or milk?"

Dice nodded, "a little of both please."

The woman stirred a matching teacup picking it and its saucer up handing it to Dice.

"Thank you," Dice nodded. "The man that came to visit Divya, did he get to speak to her?"

"No not the first few times."

"How many times did he come here?" Dice sipped the tea.

"About six or seven times then he finally caught her."

"Did you hear what he wanted with her?"

"Not really. He seemed upset with her."

"Hmm, I wonder what that was about?" Dice said more to herself.

"I'm not sure but he was very handsome."

"Handsome?"

"Yes, he was tall, dark hair and looked a bit like a movie star."

"A movie star?"

"Yes, I wish I had taken a picture of him for you."

Dice laughed, "Well me too, if he was that cute. Hey I'm single."

The woman laughed, "me too."

Holding out her hand to the woman, "I'm Dice Maddox private investigator, I didn't catch your name."

"Silva Harris," she shook Dice's hand.

"How long have you lived here?"

"I've lived here for eight years. I like the neighborhood me and the kids don't make a bunch of noise so it's nice that it's a quiet place for us to live."

"Did Divya have a lot of visitors?"

"No, she was a quiet girl like us ... she kept to herself mostly. I never even saw her bring a guy back to her place. She must have and if she did she was very discreet."

Dice nodded. "Did you two ever get together?"

"She would come over here once in a while when she made too much food and we would eat together. I think I reminded her of her mother."

"Does her mother live nearby?"

"No, she had died when Divya was 15, hit and run. The woman didn't stand a chance."

Dice knew that pain all too well not having a parent to raise her. "Did she have any siblings that she spoke of?"

"Just a sister that lives in Sudbury, that's the last I heard."

"Oh that's not far from here."

"It is if you don't drive. She had mentioned her sister a couple of times."

"Did they get along?"

"Not really but it was the only family she had."

"What about her father?"

"He took off on them when they were kids. Her mother didn't tell them much about him."

Dice nodded. "Did she grow up here?"

"Yes, they both did. Her sister is eight years older than her and after her mum died her sister Dharma took care of her."

"Have you ever met Dharma?"

"Yes, I have she is a lovely young lady. Just a treat to talk to."

Dice nodded, "Do you think she went up to see her sister?"

"She may have but the last I heard they were on the outs."

"Do you know why?"

"No ... I didn't pry it wasn't my business."

Dice nodded, "did Divya talk about friends? Anyone she hung out with?"

"No, she was a private girl. She didn't have a lot of close friends and just her sister who she wasn't speaking to."

"What about her work?"

"She loved working for Mrs. Barnett. Divya could talk for hours about her boss and her job. It's so nice to see young people connecting on that level with something. But she really loved her work."

"Did she say what Linda Barnett and Divya were working on?"

"No ... those things never came up. She would talk about those people you see on TV all men ... that talked about the universe and our planet. That one in a wheel chair and that other one mainly, he was Asian too I think."

"Are you talking about," Dice paused and flipped through her notes, she had written something down about that. "Stephen Hawking and Michio Kaku?"

"Yes sounds like a sneeze," Silvia laughed. "Divya said that Mrs. Barnett was on the right track and if she kept it up she would be a name that people knew in that field. She would be the first competitor with those men. Whatever her project was that they were working on. Divya was excited about it but was very tight-lipped because she didn't want it to leak out."

Dice nodded. "The last time you saw her did she mention she was going anywhere?"

"No, we had dinner here ... she was concerned about the project since it didn't look like Mrs. Barnett was coming back."

"She was hoping that they would have found Linda Barnett?" Dice interrupted.

"Well, I guess ... whenever she talked about her work and her former boss it was like the woman was on vacation and would pop up at any time. I think it was because Mrs. Barnett was more like a mother figure to her and she was having trouble dealing with the loss. That's just my two cents worth."

Dice nodded, "Sounds reasonable. Did she work with anyone else since the time Mrs. Barnett disappeared to the last time you saw her?"

"She had been assigned to work with a man she didn't like much. He had a bird name, like Seagle or Eagle ... Owl ... no, that's not right either. I can't remember his name but it was a man that worked at the university with them. She didn't like him and thought he was after Mrs. Barnett's job."

"Could it be Ishia Wren?"

"Yes! That's it ... I think ...," she frowned. "It could be that. Anyways they assigned her to him. After Mrs. Barnett's disappearance and being stuck with a man she didn't respect or like she was always in a bad mood. Maybe sad is a better way to put. Sad or mad it didn't matter she was no fun to hang out with. When I invited her over she ignored the kids and that was unusual for her. Whenever I asked her about work she mumbled something and change the topic to the weather. I just got the impression that she was looking for work elsewhere."

"I see ... you don't happen to have her sister's address do you?"

Silvia pursed her lips and thought about that one. Then slowly shook her head no, "no I'm sorry I don't have that and I'm not exactly sure where about Dharma lives but I think it was Sudbury."

"No worries I can look that up. Do you know if they have the same last name?"

Nodding, "yes they do. Dharma was living with a guy. They have a beautiful daughter but they never got married."

"Did she move out?"

"No, our landlord Lenny was pretty upset about that. She just skipped out. He took all her things and had a yard sale. I tried to get the important stuff for her. Pictures and mementos that I thought she would have wanted."

"So she just up and disappeared?"

Silvia nodded. "That Asian man came looking for her and just you. No one else has. I called the police when she didn't come home. She didn't mention she was going to her sisters but I can only assume that's where she went. But why would she leave all her stuff here?"

"Yes, that does seem odd." Dice wondered what would make a young woman take off and leave her things behind. Was she being threatened? Was someone harassing her? Who was she running from was the question.

"I have two boxes of her things that I could sweet talk off of Lenny. Are you going to go to her sisters?"

"I am thinking about it, yes."

"Could you deliver the boxes to Dharma?"

"I could."

Silvia got up and disappeared to another room. Dice noticed that there were eight cats in the room. Sipping the last bit of tea, she felt something in her mouth and spit out a piece of cat fur, she noticed the cat fur was all over her. Trying not to let it bother her at least not while she was in Silvia's home, she sighed heavily and found a little gray and white cat bumping her hand with its head. Petting him, she smiled at it, "How are you doing?"

Looking around aside from all the fur the place was very neat and tidying and it didn't smell like eight cats lived here. There was a vanilla scent that clung to the air around her. Silva came back out carrying two big boxes. Placing them down on the chair, she smiled at Dice.

"Okay you have been a great help. One more thing did she get along with anyone else in this building?"

"Nope, I never saw her speaking to anyone else. Mary down the hall always thought Divya was stuck up. But that's not true. She is a little shy that is all."

"I have another appointment I need to get to. But thank you for your time, the information and the tea." Dice got up and started for the door stopping she pulled out her business card and wrote her cell phone number on the back of it. Then stuffed her notepad and pen into her purse before gathering up the boxes.

"If you hear from her or find out what happened to her can you please let me know," Silva jotted her number down on a sticky note and pressed on the top box outside flap.

"I will." Dice waited as Silvia opened the door for her.

"Good luck Miss Maddox it was nice talking with you."

"You too, please Silvia, call me Dice. Have a good day."

"Thank you Dice. Shoo, you boys get back inside."

Dice carefully went down the stairs and took the boxes out to her car and stuffed them in the trunk. Popping back inside, she stopped at the landlord's apartment. Knocking on the door, she waited.

A short chubby man wearing a white sleeveless undershirt answered the door. The shirt was white once, not anymore it had a yellow tinged to it. He probably put too much bleach in the washer Dice thought, while forcing a smile as she stuck out a hand. "Hi my name is Dice Maddox I am a private investigator. I was wondering if you could tell me anything about a past tenant."

"Who?" his eyes narrowed as, he watched her suspiciously.

"Divya Grayson," Dice smiled sweetly.

"That loser who skipped out on me? I wish I knew where she was. I wasn't happy. She left all her shit here and stuck me with her rent."

"Was she behind in her rent?"

"No, she always paid on time but she needed to give me two months' notice before she moved. Then she just left all her shit here I had to get rid of it."

"Did she leave behind her computer?" Dice wondered if Divya's leaving unexpectedly meant she left her work behind too.

"Yes, I reformatted it and it's like new. I kept it for myself as part of her rent for the missing month."

"Did you call the police?" A small part of her wondered if she should make the man an offer and see if Ronnie could retrieve anything. Something told her it would cost her more than it was worth.

"For what? They don't care if you lose money on rent. They are useless. I had another tenant who was a drug dealer. I called the police several times and nothing came of it."

"Really?" Dice wondered if the tenant was really a drug dealer or the drug dealing was just part of an over-active imagination and too much TV.

"They are useless around here. I think most of the cops in this city are on the take." Dice knew a few of the cops and this guy was way off base. She didn't like him at all.

"I wouldn't know about that." Dice nodded and gave him her best grim face expression. "Do you have a forwarding address or a contact name or number for Divya?"

"No forwarding address, … the crazy bitch just up and left. She has a sister but I don't have any information for her."

"Was Divya a friendly tenant?"

"No, she kept to herself I never got a complaint about her ever."

"How long did she live here before she disappeared?"

"A couple of years," he looked behind him the TV was blaring in the background.

"I can see that you are busy. Thank you for your time. Here is my business card if you can think of anything else please call me."

"Sure lady … wait …," he looked her up and down. "Are you single?"

"No," she answered a little too quickly.

"Whatever, you're not my type anyways. Too skinny, I like a woman with a little meat on her bones." He shut the door in her face.

"Well, you have a good day too." She said to the closed door and then chuckled to herself.

CHAPTER TEN

TUESDAY 6:02 PM

She was back in her car and heading to The Red Dragon. After today she needed a break. Wondering if she would see anyone she knew there as well. Parking in the back she walked around to the front door and went in. Gary was behind the counter and nodded at her as soon as he saw her come in. Looking around, she didn't see anyone she knew and found a seat in the corner.

Lily came over and placed a hot tea in front of her.

"Thanks Lily," she smiled.

"Are you hungry Dice?"

"A little, let me get you something good." She winked, smiled then turn and left.

Dice stirred her cup and smiled what a strange day. Well, a least she found out who her missing assistant was. Perhaps she would have to take a drive tomorrow after she got finished with her interviews to see if she could find Dharma and Divya Grayson. She wasn't sure what it was but she had a nagging feeling that the assistant might be able to assist her with this case.

Tracey O'Connor was she really a seer? Could the woman really speak to the dead? What were the woman's intentions ... that bother her. Maybe because she didn't really trust those who said they could talk to the dead. Why? Was it more her own hang ups about .... She couldn't pin it on any one thing. Tracey O'Connor felt she was really giving her a play by play.

"Hi Dice," a familiar voice greeted her.

Looking up, she smiled. "Chris how was your day?"

"Better now," he pulled up a chair. "Hey what have you been up to? I've been calling so we can all get together again."

"Chris I need to tell you something," she was about to tell him about Sean Larke kissing her and then his crazy girlfriend threatening her.

"Sure, what is it? You finally see the light and want me back?" he grinned at her.

Shaking her head no, "not quite. The other night when we were here ..."

"Hey look who's here!" Sean Larke came up to them.

Swallowing back her words, she forced a smile and watched as Chris pulled up an extra chair for him. He sat close to her. Staring at her with what she thought could be desire. He smiled and nodded then looked at Chris. "How's work?"

"Great no complaints, that client I was telling you about finally came clean it was great. I knew he was guilty. Doesn't matter either way I get paid. What about you did you close that new deal you were talking about?"

"Yes, I did. It is perfect just opened a couple more deals for my company."

"Hey I'm sorry Dice you were about to tell me something. Sorry go ahead."

Her eyes went wide then she laughed. "I completely forgot what I was going to say."

"Something about the last time we were here," Chris smiled and prompted.

Lily came over with a couple of drinks for Chris and Sean, and then placed a plate of steak and potatoes in front of Dice.

"That looks good," Chris eyed her plate. "I'll take one of those I am starving."

"Make that two more, I want one too. Thanks Lily."

"No problem fellas," she smiled and disappeared.

"How's the case going?" Sean asked.

She looked at him and shoved a bite of potato in her mouth. Chewing she watched as he watched her mouth and licked his lips. Swallowing she answered. "I've gotten a couple of leads and I'm checking them out."

"If anyone can figure it out I know my Dice can," Chris smiled at her and reached out grabbing her free hand giving it a squeeze.

All she wanted was a little peace? Or did she? Maybe she wanted to run into them she thought to herself. Why else would she be here? If she didn't she would have just gone to the store picked up a few things and went straight home.

Dice watched the two men as they continued to talk about their work. Then she overheard Chris asking Sean where Alisha was. Sean looked over at Dice a little nervously and wondered what he was thinking. Was he thinking about how he kissed her in the parking lot declaring that he was dumping his crazy girlfriend or was he thinking about the game of tongue hockey he displayed on his balcony not even two hours later? Who was he kidding? If Dice was smart, she would swear off men altogether. Then she remembered how wonderful he smelled. That and how his hands felt so good on her body. A little shiver went down her spine at that memory.

She felt someone watching her. Looking up, she saw Chris watching her. He noticed the look Sean gave her ... and he noticed that she was being quite. She silently prayed he wouldn't say anything out loud in front of Sean.

Sean changed the subject and continued to talk about sports. Chris watched them both with a keen interest. Knowing Chris all too well, she was sure he was getting some perverse kicks from this. Dice continued to eat as if her food was the best thing in the world, reminding herself, that if she finished eating before Sean's crazy girlfriend got there than she could avoid a scenario that would be even more uncomfortable. Chris lazily leaned over and helped himself to another bite off her plate. Waiting ... taunting her to open her mouth to say something. She studied the table and then the floor.

Sean's cell phone rang, he checked it and excused himself. He got up and walked away, she tried to excuse herself to run to the bathroom.

Chris grabbed her wrist. "Spill it, Dice."

"Spill what?"

"Don't play coy with me, tell me what's going on with you and Sean. Is it serious?" Chris watched her carefully.

"I don't know what you're talking about."

"Spill it, Maddox," Chris leaned so close she could feel his breath on her face.

Lily came back with the guys' orders. "Sorry it's starting to pick up in here. Enjoy, shout if you need anything."

"I need you to tell me what's going on. You like him don't you."

"I don't know what you are talking about," she couldn't look him in the eyes.

"Really?" he grinned. "Look me in the eyes and tell me you are not interested in Sean Larke."

"I really don't know what you are talking about," she looked at him and felt the guilt rising up in her stomach.

"Dice it's okay if you do. He's a great guy."

"Yeah but he's taken right now. So really not my type."

Chris laughed, "well, I can tell you he doesn't look at Alisha the way he looks at you. I think you have the home team advantage."

"The what?"

"Well, you know you practically live in the same building."

She snorted a laugh, "please don't say anything ... I don't think anything is going to happen in that department and really right now I don't think I need that kind of distraction anyways."

"What are you two talking about?" Sean asked.

Dice couldn't breathe ... she coughed and looked at Chris. Chris laughed, "we were discussing how I was going to sleep over at Dice's tonight."

"Oh," Sean looked like he had just been kicked in the ribs. Then smiled, "well you could do worse Dice."

Swallowing hard, she still couldn't find her voice. Maybe that look was a figment of her imagination. It was most likely her imagination she chastised herself for even thinking those thoughts.

She felt like a teenage girl. Deciding not to let this moment ruin her evening, she looked at Sean and then at Chris. "Well, guys it's been fun I should be getting home."

"I thought Chris was staying over?" Sean looked at her.

She laughed, "Well Chris?"

"I'll catch up with you later Dice. You're such a nag," he teased.

Rolling her eyes, she started to get up.

"Wait why don't you have one drink or some dessert before you leave."

Dice wasn't sure if she could stand being in this uncomfortable position any longer. Looking at these two men whom she liked and didn't like. Chris because she almost got married to him, but he cheated on her twice, she forgave him and they were friends now. He wanted to be more than just friends but she didn't have that on her agenda. Then Sean someone she met a few months ago, she constantly got his mail delivered to her address. It was only recently that it stopped coming altogether. They shared a few intimate moments but in the long run it didn't work out either. She ended up alone and he ended up with a pretty red head that was very crazy. Friends ... she wasn't even sure that she would call it that. Since he started dating the red head, she hardly ever saw him ... that and the hot and cold mixed signals he was giving her. They really didn't share any conversations that counted as good friends. Hell she had a better relationship with Silvia Harris than she did with Sean Larke.

"I guess I could have another cup of tea before I leave," she smiled at them both. Feeling like she recollected herself she sat back down and waved at Lily, pointing to her cup she motioned she wanted another one. Lily smiled and nodded.

Chris moved in closer to her, watching Sean's reaction. Dice was beginning to think maybe this wasn't such a good idea. Considering Chris was trying very hard to get back in her good graces this moment though was not helping his case in any way. She wanted to punch him in the arm and tell him to stop it and grow up but he continued by wrapping an arm around her shoulders.

"When do you want to get together again all four of us?" Chris asked them.

Dice kicked him under the table and smiled, "well I'm not sure when I'm going to be free. Tonight I need to follow up on a couple leads and then tomorrow I have a few more interviews following another lead I'll probably be leaving town for a day or two."

"Where are you going?" Chris asked looking at her suddenly full of interest.

"I'm going up north about a four-hour drive to Sudbury."

"Sudbury? Why would you want to go there?" Chris asked as if she said she was going to go have all her teeth pulled out.

"I told you I am following up on a lead. I am looking for someone who might know a thing or two about my missing lady."

"Do you want some company? I have some friends up that way, I could come along for the drive and we could hang out?" Sean offered.

A small part of her wanted to jump at the chance.

"What would Alisha say about that?" Chris grinned.

Dice elbowed him in the ribs, he really was asking for trouble.

"Well, I will tell Alisha the truth, of course, that I'm going to go visit some friends up north," he smiled at Dice.

"Okay fellas," Dice laughed this was not uncomfortable at all no, no not at all. "I thank you for your concern but I can handle this myself. You know I do know how to protect myself."

Chris looked at her and his smiled faded. "For the most part yes, I know you can but there are some things that you are not so good at. Like matters of the heart. Dice you are like a child when it comes to that."

She narrowed her eyes at him. "A child? Really?"

"I mean inexperienced with those sorts of things ... you are not as experienced as some people are," Chris looked at Sean. "I don't mean it in a bad way. It's just I'm a friend of yours and I know because I hurt you when we were dating it's something that I'll never forgive myself for. I am just so grateful you and I are still friends." He squeezed her and kissed her head. "I really care for you Dice. I don't want to see anyone hurting you," he looked back at Sean.

Dice felt this was more for Sean than for her. Shrugging out of Chris's grip, she looked at him and frowning. "Really?" rolling her eyes. "Okay, I don't know what you guys are up too, but I've had a long day and I'm heading home now. Alone," she glared at Chris.

"Hey, if you want me to come over later to check under the bed for creepy crawlies let me know," Chris winked at her.

"If you change your mind about the trip let me know," Sean smiled at her.

Alisha came sweeping in, glaring at her. "Trip? What trip?" Alisha sat in Sean's lap. "Hey baby," she kissed him in front of everyone.

"Have a good night," Dice walked away. Stopping at the bar, she went to pay for her dinner. Gary laughed and said her money was no good there. "Really Dice?"

"How are you and Aunt Sophie?"

"My god I can't thank you enough for reintroducing me to that woman. She is amazing but then you already know that."

Dice smiled. "She is pretty amazing I have to agree."

"She wanted me to ask you when you could get some free time to come over for dinner."

"I'll make some time this weekend if you want to do it then?"

"You know the answer to that keep your weekend evenings clear,"

Gary winked at her.

"Fair enough, I'm heading out."

"Guy trouble still?"

"Nope, I don't have a man in my life and for the record I don't need one." She smiled at him.

"Sean is a good guy."

"He's taken. Chris … well I've been down that road too. Not interested in history repeating itself in either case."

"Alright," he smiled at her. "Don't shoot the messenger."

"Tell Auntie Sophie that I am doing just fine on my own. That I am happy and content." She smiled at him.

"I know you are kid."

"Alright see you later," she headed for the door and kept going. Grateful that it didn't get any uglier in there when Alisha walked in. What did he see in her anyways? It's none of your business she reminded herself. Stopping on the way home, she decided to pick up a few grocery items.

Looking at the can of peas, she turned it over in her hands before she placed it in the shopping cart. Turning the corner, she ran into someone else' cart. "Sorry …," her eyes fell upon her victim. Chris Douglas … what was he doing here? Didn't she just leave him at the Red Dragon?

"Well, imagine meeting you here," he smiled.

"What are you doing?" she frowned at him. "Are you following me?"

"Do you need a stalker? My rates are cheap."

Shaking her head, "you know this is unhealthy right? We have broken up we are considered exes. Why are you following your ex around?"

"I was just worried about you," he dumped his things in her cart.

"What are you doing?" frowning she stared at him. "Alright, why are you stalking me for real?"

"I was just worried about you."

"You were?" she began pushing her cart around the corner. "Well, don't I am a big girl and can take care of myself."

"I know you can but even though we are no longer engaged. I still consider you my friend."

"Friend? Really? After you cheated on me not once but twice?" She snipped.

"Dice I am so sorry about that I truly intend to make that up to you any way I can. I have changed."

"What your underwear?"

"I'm not wearing those."

"Really?"

He grinned, "I am trying to be serious with you Dice."

"I am in a grocery store right now and I don't need this …," she looked around. Then hissed at him, "people are looking at us."

"It's because you are making such a scene."

"I am?" she growled.

"Dice you're getting angry. I think you need to relax."

"It's a free country to do what you want."

"I want to go shopping with you," he smiled at her.

"Fine whatever," she grumbled and pushed pass him. He was stealing the fun out of her shopping. Well, she wasn't someone who went crazy for shopping to begin with it was more like a chore than anything else.

Going through her list, she had everything checked off in the matter of minutes. He helped fill up her cart with things he was buying. Sharing a cart with her ex-fiancé was probably unusual for some people. For Dice it just was another thing that she couldn't get rid of. Did she want to? He wasn't a great boyfriend or fiancé but he wasn't a very bad friend. He was annoying and always popping up on her unexpectedly. Maybe, it was the distraction she needed.

Heading to the checkout with Chris in tow, she began pulling her items out of the cart and placing them on top on the conveyer.

"So what do you want to do tonight?" he asked her casually as he helped her with her purchases.

"I already told you."

He laughed, "that's what you said for Sean's benefit … I know you … you don't have any plans tonight. How about a movie?"

"I don't know," she wondered if she really wanted to go out. Then she caught herself. This was her ex, the little voice reminded her; do you really want to go on a date with him?

"How about we go and hang out at the tennis courts?"

He was really trying to reel her in. If she recalled correctly he didn't like tennis so much, looking at him with an annoyed look that said, 'Really? Really now?'

"Is it wrong for me to want to spend some time with you?" he asked with a devilish grin.

"I don't know, it depends on what your motives are."

"My motives are pure, I swear dear lady they are." He grinned.

She laughed. "Whatever, I'm not interested in knowing what you are up to. Why not go and do some miniature golfing."

"Now you're talking lady."

She paid for her purchases and popped her bags in the cart. Waiting for him, "maybe we should go home and put away our frozen first. Then you can come pick me up."

"Careful Dice that sounds like you are asking me out on a date."

"You wish," she laughed. "That ship has sailed, need I remind you?"

"Nope," he smiled at the lady and paid for his things.

Dice help put his things at the back of the cart. "Yours and mine, no fraternizing."

"You and your sexy words ... Dice Maddox you better not be trying to seduce me."

"Alright, if it's going to be like this all night I've suddenly have a headache and can't go out." She started pushing the cart out.

He nudged her with his hip and smiled at her, "why do you always have to be a party pooper? I was just teasing."

Rolling her eyes, she began to wonder if it was such a good idea to spend time with Chris alone. She didn't want to give him the wrong idea but at the same time she didn't mind his company, as long as he kept Alisha and Sean out of the picture. She couldn't deal with them and whatever they have going on.

They stopped at her car first and she put her things in the back seat. She waved as he took the cart one row over and emptied the cart. Waving at her as she pulled out, it was a short drive home. Parking downstairs she grabbed her groceries and headed for the elevator. Pressing the button, she waited for the elevator. There was a TV prompt set above the elevator, with news feed regarding the office hours, pool and workout room. The elevator doors slid open. The little hairs on the back of her neck stood on end. She began to feel like she was being watched ... paranoia much? She rolled her eyes and pressed the button for her floor.

A few minutes later she was in her kitchen putting things away. Glancing out across the balcony at her neighbor Sean Larke's condo, she wondered if they were still at the Red Dragon. It was none of her business she reminded herself. "None of your business," she repeated out loud just to hear the words.

Popping into the bathroom, she brushed her teeth, reapplied makeup and fixed her hair. Grabbing a jacket, she thought she would bring it just in case it got cold. Then her cell phone rang.

She noticed it was Chris, "hello?"

"Yeah I'm downstairs out front."

"Okay I'll be right down." She hung up.

Coming out the front door of her condo building, she saw Chris parked out front in the no-parking zone. He was standing outside his car waiting for her. Opening the passenger's side, he waited for her to get in and shut the door for her. Then came around and hopped in the driver's seat.

"Did you fix yourself up for me?"

"I just brushed my teeth … for me," she laughed.

"Well, excuse me," he chuckled. "Maddox you are so going down."

"We'll see Mr. Mouth, we'll see."

"Do you want to stop and get a coffee?"

"No, and you can't have one either because then when you start playing badly you'll have to go to the bathroom or something. Nope. We can stop and have a drink afterwards."

"Sure you just want to beat me, get me drunk then have your wicked way with me."

She laughed, "I'm sure it wouldn't take much if I wanted to do that. You're a man after all and most of the time your standards are not that high."

"Really now? I'm hanging out with you."

She laughed again, "my point exactly."

He laughed. "Whatever, fine we won't stop anywhere and we'll see who's the best at the mini-putt greens."

"I'm just hearing a bunch of meaningless words slip off those lips."

"You want to study my lips?" he winked at her.

"Really?"

"Really really," he grinned.

The Mini Putt Golf Course was a little busy. It took Chris a few minutes to find a putter that he liked. He had to try four of them out before he was satisfied. Getting their balls and score card, they headed out and waited in line for their turn at the first hole.

"Well, let's make this interesting shall we?"

"How so?"

"Friday night you have to double date with Sean and I if I win and if you win … let's see …"

"I could bring you to my Aunt Sophie dinner party she wants to have this weekend it will be Saturday or Sunday night."

"Hmmm," he thought about it. "Yes, that is a fair trade."

"I'm really not crazy about going out on a double date of any kind with Alisha around."

"Ohhh woman rivalry nice, Sean is so lucky a cat fight," Chris teased her.

She frowned, "really?"

He laughed, "a man can dream." Chris winked at her, "Don't worry babes my money is on you."

"Shut up."

"I'm serious, Alisha may be small and excitable but I know you can take care of yourself."

"How would you know that?"

"You took self-defense classes … see I pay attention even when you don't think I am."

"If only you had done that more when we were dating."

"Well, there are a lot of things I wish I did differently."

"Don't worry about it, we just weren't meant to be a couple."

"You really think so?" he looked at her, sounding a little hurt.

"Trust me you will find someone if that is what you want but you don't need anyone."

"I don't know I like sex, it's okay by myself," he laughed. "But so much better when there is someone else around to join in." Chris hugged her.

"Don't go getting any ideas," she pushed him away. They finally got onto the first hole. He motioned for her to go first. She set up her ball and lined it up then whacked it. The ball bounced off the left side of the wall and bounced across to the other side of the wall and then swirled around towards the first hole. Slowly it rolled over and fell in. "Hole in one!" Dice grinned at him. "Your turn big shot!"

He looked annoyed. Dice took a little pleasure in the fact that Chris was a very competitive person and this was going to get him going. She watched as he put his ball down, wiggled his butt, looked at the hole ... looked up at her and then winked. He hit the ball and it went sailing to the other end bounced once and swirled into the first pit.

The next three were much the same they were matched for points. The fourth one she beat him by a point then the fifth he beat her. The sixth was with a waterfall. Dice went first and it was a two-hitter. She got it halfway through. He took his turn and it went right through. Dice followed him behind the waterfall.

He waited for her to catch up. They got through the whole course and were at the last hole she was leading by three points. Hitting the ball it slid through the windmill spinning propellers and out to the bottom green area. Staring at the windmill, she flashed to her case. Linda Barnett ... one minute she was alive ... the next she was sitting on the other side unable to communicate to those she knew. Dead ... death was so final.

"Hey you okay?" Chris nudged her.

Looking up at him, she smiled. "I'm fine." Dice wondered why Linda popped into her mind. She wondered if Linda and Kyle Barnett ever went mini putting?

Chris was next. He hit the windmill and it bounced back to him. Growling under his breath, she watched in amusement. This was one of her favorite holes, she watched him try it again. It finally went through. They went down to the lower level.

Dice weighed the distance from the hole and her ball and set herself up gently hitting the ball it rolled over and went into the cup. It was Chris's turn. He did the same and missed. Tried it again and got it in.

"Looks like I win," she smirked at him.

"Don't look so smug," he laughed. "Alright come on let me buy you some ice cream and then a movie?"

She laughed, "Sure what did you have in mind?"

"It's a surprise," he took her golf club and headed back to the main counter. She waited for him to return then they walked down the block to the parking lot stopping just before they got there for ice cream. He went in and bought them both cones and they headed over to his car.

"I had fun tonight, Maddox."

"Maddox? Not Dice?" she smiled.

"No not when you beat the snot out of me at mini golf."

"You're such a baby," she teased. He came around to the passenger side and opened the door. Holding it open for her, it was part of his charm; he always held the door open for her.

When he got in the other side they sat there and listened to the radio with the windows down and talked about the songs that came on. It was fun and easy. Nothing serious, just enjoying each other's company. She reminded herself not to go beyond friendship with him. Just keep it strictly on a friend bases, the little voice reminded her a couple times. When they were living together they stop making that effort to hang out with each other. Being friends ... just friends ... there were no expectations and it was fun to hang out with Chris again. He was definitely a looker. Women liked him and she saw a couple slip him their number he smiled and nodded. Then she noticed that he threw them out. It didn't matter, the little voice reminded her. You should be at home resting up and working on this case instead of hanging out with your old boyfriend.

It was late when she finally got in; Chris dropped her off at her front door and wished her luck with her case saying that she didn't need it. Stopping at her mailbox, she checked there was just junk mail. Heading upstairs, she was grateful to enter her condo. Kicking her shoes off at the door and locking the door behind her. She went to the bathroom and had a quick shower, then changed into her pajamas and wrapped a robe around her. Slipping her slippers on, she went out to the kitchen and poured herself a glass of wine. Grabbing her throw blanket off the sofa, she stepped out onto her balcony. Going straight to her favorite seat, she wrapped the robe tight around her and then got comfy. Lying back in her lounge chair with her feet up, she sipped her wine, then pulled out her vanilla candle from the little box beside her and lit the candle then sighed heavily ... starring off into the night sky she wondered what had happened to Linda Barnett. What really happened to her? Could she be communicating through Tracey O'Connor? Was Tracey just making that up? Sipping her wine, she listened to the other tenants around her. Someone was playing soft classical music, they must have had a window open or their balcony door open a crack because she could hear the music waffle across the air molecules and grace her ears.

Trying to figure out what she wanted. Taking a chapter from Linda's book seems like she was a strong woman who didn't hold back. Dice wondered what really happened to her? Was she lying dead buried somewhere? Chances of her being alive were next to nil giving the circumstances. Sighing ... Dice wonder who could be behind it ... she had not met Ishia Wren yet. From the sounds of it, he could be a suspect. Or the kid who accused her of sexual advances then disappeared, she needed to find him and see what he knew. The assistant ... where did she run off? Was there something Dice was missing? Was the young woman just flaky or was she running from someone? Could she be running from Ishia Wren? It may not have anything to do with Linda Barnett, Dice reminded herself. It could be an old boyfriend or something else? Maybe she wasn't running away at all?

What caused her to pick up and to leave without any notice? She wasn't terribly attached to her things inside her condo and most of it was replaceable. Yet, she couldn't just pick up and disappear without a few staples ... clothes ... etc...

A young woman leaving without her laptop ... Dice wondered if Divya kept any of her files from the lab on her laptop? When she was taking her courses she had saved her files on her laptop. Even in high school she had saved her files and major projects on her laptop ... in fact she would email herself her important projects that was worth a lot just in case her computer crashed. Perhaps Divya did the same or used cloud computing? It was possible. If that was the case then maybe leaving behind her laptop wasn't a big deal?

The apartment building that Divya lived in didn't look that high end. Of course Dice had a couple boxes of Divya's personal things that she had stowed away in her trunk! Getting up Dice hurried through her condo slowing down briefly as she grabbed the keys on the way out.

Within minutes she was downstairs heading to her car in her robe and slippers. The underground parking was empty. It was really quiet and her footsteps as soft as they were ... were the only noise that greeted her. Reaching her car, she unlocked the trunk and was grateful for the bit of light that illuminated the area to a small degree. The trunk light came on and it helped a little more. Opening the first box she was greeted with some books and paper. Binders, a few photo albums and trinkets ... Dice pulled everything out. The trinkets were cute and all science-related. A few trophies for science fairs she had won first place. A couple of snow globes of weird-looking buildings that didn't make sense to Dice ... nor did she recognized them. Flipping the globes over, she looked for any telltale signs of a label. Nothing ... she turned them over and looked at them again. Something didn't feel right about them. Not sure what it was she left them out on the side of the box. There was a cup that had the periodic table on the side, in color.

"Cute," Dice mused. Looking back at the other contents, she found some Jules Verne books, nodding not bad. The scrapbooks contain many photos of a young woman and her friends and family. Linda Barnett was in a few of them. They looked like they were all having fun. There seemed to be lots of laughing. Several pictures contained Divya receiving awards and trophies. Dice assumed it was Divya. The young woman had brown mousey hair that was a short crop cut, her large green eyes always looking at the camera.

In a couple of the photos it looked like Divya tried different shades of hair dye. Lime green, then bright light purple. Each a short little bob, each picture with Divya grinning wildly ... had Dice wondering what was so funny. The next scrapbook was of the lab and the students in it. Linda Barnett was there ... some pictures the people all look so serious. One picture that caught Dice's eyes, Divya and Linda standing in front of a large square metal machine. There were hoses coming in and out of it from the sides to the top. A computer screen was attached to the front of the machine, rows and rows of letters and numbers filled the screen.

Dice wondered what the machine was for. Flipping through, she found another one with the strange snow globes Divya was holding them and grinning from ear to ear as she stood in front of the mysterious machine. Dice peeled back the plastic and pulled the picture out. Joe, with Linda and Divya, dated the day before Linda disappeared.

Dice's jaw dropped open. Wow, just one day ... less than twenty-four hours before Linda disappeared. Before she most likely met her death? Placing the picture aside with the weird snow globes. Fewer than twenty-four hours. Linda and Divya looked so happy, proud and indestructible. She wondered why the snow globes seemed so important.

There were no other pictures with Linda ... there were just four other ones at the back of the book with Divya celebrating a birthday of a small girl. It may have been her niece. The one who lived up north in Sudbury ... the next few pages were blank.

Dice found some more notes and schematic drawings … looking at the pictures Dice realized they were of the machine in the pictures. Putting them aside with the snow globes … Dice still rifled through what looked like some bills, a couple science magazines. Putting the rest of the things back into the box, they didn't seem to be of any interest.

Opening the second box, she didn't hear the footsteps sneaking up on her. She did feel the hands that grabbed her waist. Unfortunately, her reflects was spot on super speedy, without thinking she grabbed the person behind her by the wrist, stepping backwards, she flipped the intruder over her hip and pinned him to the payment beside her. Stepping on his face with her slipper and holding his arm back so he couldn't move.

"Who are you?" she snapped. Her grip loosens and she steps back slowly as she recognized the person beneath her.

"Oh my God Sean are you okay?" she tried to help him up but he scrambled and back peddled away from her.

Looking up at her wide eye, "wow," he gasped, rubbing his arm.

She knelt down beside him. "I'm so, so, so very sorry, I didn't hear you coming." Gently she reached out to him. "I'm sorry."

"If there was any doubt about whether or not you could take care of yourself I think you just put that at ease. Hey don't look at me like you're going to cry, I'm the one who is suffering from you trying to crush my skull into the payment."

Pausing she looked around. They were alone in the underground garage. "What were you doing down here?"

"I … I …," he looked uncomfortable and started to look away. "Help me up," he looked back at her.

Moving closer, she grabbed him by the elbow and around his back. He struggled to his feet with her help. "Wow, how did you know how to do that?"

"I studied a little karate, judo and self-defense classes when I was younger. It was a while ago, but I guess I still remember a thing or two."

"I'd say," he nodded.

"So what are you doing down here? How did you know I was here?" she looked at him watching him carefully.

"Truth?"

"That would be preferred."

"I was sitting out on my balcony and saw you sitting there. I was kind of watching you."

"Watching me?"

"Yes," he blushed. "I'm sorry. I was sitting out there first in my defense. It's not my fault that you came out too."

"No, I never said that it was."

"I saw you run through your apartment and out into the hall, with your robe on." He reached out and grabbed the tie that was hanging loosely at her side. "I was worried about you."

"Worried about me? Why?"

"I can't say. I just miss hanging out with you. When I saw you tearing out of your condo like that I just came down here thinking I might catch you alone."

"What would your girlfriend say about that?"

"Don't ask me about her. I just wanted to talk to you."

"I see," she turned back to her trunk and continued with the search.

He bent over and picked up a flashlight. "I have some light," he stood by her and turned on the flashlight.

"That's fine."

"What are we looking at?"

She looked at him and wondered what he was really doing down there. If his crazy girlfriend found out, she would probably have a cow. Maybe then Alisha would piss off, probably not … Dice grumbled to herself quietly. Sighing, she looked back at the box. "These are the only things left to a lead I'm following." Grabbing up one of the snow globes. "You're into construction, what building is this?"

His eyebrows furrowed as he took the snow globe from her. Turning it over in his hand, he examined it with the flashlight. Shaking his head, "I have no idea. I have never seen this before. You got me babe."

Babe? Hmmm. She took back the globe and grabbed his flashlight peering at the globe closely she examined the underside first. Looking for a name or who created it … even a made in Taiwan would have set her mind at ease but there was nothing there. Peering into the snow globe, she studied the painted plastic but it just didn't look like anything she could place … biting her bottom lip she held the piece of plastic, which was really beginning to irritate her. Something just didn't feel right about it.

Sean reached out and rubbed her arm. Pausing she looked over at him.

"Dice you are not making this easy for me."

"I am so sorry Sean. Let's see for months I got your mail delivered to my address, thank you for having that finally corrected. We date a couple times, we have sex, you get all girly on me and begin with … this can't happen again I want more. Then I see you with someone else. You look happy so I don't bother and we seem to be just friends again. Then you kiss me when no one else is around not once but a couple times!" her voice echoed and bounced off the walls.

"Dice lower your voice," he hissed.

"Sure," she growled. Leaning close to him, she wanted to shout at him but looking into his deep brown caring eyes. She couldn't. She felt her eyes burn with tears threatening to spill out. Swallowing hard while looking away … staring at the dim light up in the corner by her parking number.

"I just don't know what you want from me," she heard herself stammer with emotion. Tears spilled. He grabbed her in his arms and hugged her.

"I know, I am so sorry. I am sorry Dice please don't cry." She felt him hug her tight. He smelled like fresh soap and mints. One hand held her close to him the other stroke her hair. "I am so sorry."

Berating herself for breaking down in front of him, she shoved him away. "Don't … just don't come near me anymore please." She stared at the things in her trunk. Scooping up the work that looked like the machine and the odd snow globes, she slammed her trunk shut and hurried away.

"Dice," he called to her.

She was almost at the elevators when he caught her. Standing in front of her, she pulled away from him took a couple steps backwards.

"Dice, I know I haven't been very good to you."

"Don't …," she shook her head. "Please Sean I like you more than I should but you know it's kind of wearing off." She looked around and refused to look at him.

"Dice please … give me just a few minutes. Let's go upstairs and talk about it. Over tea?"

Gnawing on her bottom lip, she shook her head no. "I can't do

this with you anymore. The truth is Chris and I are back together."
She lied.

"What?" he sounded hurt.

She nodded, "we were going to tell you the good news the next time we saw you and Alisha."

"I didn't see that one coming. What about your friend Ty?"

She looked at him and he looked angry. Dice never saw Sean Larke looking so angry. "What are you two seeing each other too?"

"Ty is my friend."

"Yeah, I saw that at the hospital … friends with benefits … how many of those friends do you have?"

"Excuse me?"

"You know what … you're right we aren't meant to be together."

"I never said that."

"No but I am," he turned and stormed off.

Sighing she let him walk away. Reminding herself it would be easier that way. She liked him but she wasn't about to be the one who interrupted his relationship with Alisha. She knew how it felt to be on the other end of that and she wasn't going to play that other woman role. Looking around her, she was grateful no one was around to witness that outburst.

Heading back to the elevator, she pressed the button and was grateful when it quickly dings open. Stepping on, she pressed her floor number. The door swooshed shut. Keying in the security number the elevator began to move. Getting off and heading back inside her home she locked the door behind her. Sighing she took the paper and the mystery snow globe over to the kitchen counter. Placing them on the counter, she spread the drawings and schematics out. They were diagrams for the inner workings of the mystery machine. She wondered what it did. Why would she leave these things behind? Wouldn't they be of some importance? It brought on other questions. What made her hurry off to leave these behind if they were of any value?

They looked important. But then again so did the papers that came with her toaster. Getting up, she went to the office and grabbed her laptop. Returning to the kitchen, she powered it on and waited for it to load the icons on the desktop and connect to her wireless Internet connection. A couple minutes later she pulled up her browser and Googled 'tourist sites around the world', then clicked on the images option. Several pictures loaded into the search window. Greece, England, Rome, Toronto, Paris … buildings and monuments that were very familiar popped up. Scrolling down slowly, she looked for anything that resembled the snow globe that rested beside her on the counter. Dice found herself scrolling a little more slowly, there were so many amazing sites … reminded her that she wanted to travel a little bit before she died, which was a long way off. After twenty minutes of stopping and looking at a couple sites. She changed the search field to 'tourist sites around the world not so popular'. Some less popular attractions came up mingled with popular attractions. Nothing resembled the snow globe.

How weird. Picking up the snow globe, she rolled it back and forth in her hands. "Where are you from?" she asked it. Then waited as if it was going to answer, the only answer she got was more silence. Placing it back on her counter, Dice stretched. Walking back out to the balcony, she looked across to Sean Larke's home. His balcony was empty … lonely and empty. Catching her breath, she paused. Then moved over to her seat, easing into her seat she stared up at the stars. Grabbing the throw blanket, she covered herself and mulled over her case for a little longer. The music stopped. Someone was fighting down below. It reminded her of her encounter with Sean downstairs in the garage. What was that about? Deciding as much as she liked him, she needed to put some space between them. It wasn't healthy. She wanted more than he could offer at this time. He was dating someone else. Dice hoped the conversation wouldn't come up in front of Chris. She didn't want to have to explain that and she didn't want to give him false hope. They were just friends and she didn't want to interrupt that friendship that they had. A light moved swiftly across the sky … a shooting star? Or was it something else? Last month she would have shrugged it off and not bothered. Now … not so much so… looking back inside her kitchen she saw the snow globe on the counter. Was it alien? Could it be from another planet?

She laughed at the thought … alien snow globes … time for bed she got up and went inside closing her balcony door and locking it. Heading straight to the bedroom, she didn't even stop at the kitchen counter.

Chapter Eleven

Wednesday 6:32 am

It was a fitful sleep she kept dreaming of weird-looking buildings, snow globes and weird diagrams. Dragging herself out of bed, Dice slipped into her running clothes and stretched in the hallway. Grabbing her iPod, she slipped on her shoes and grabbed her keys. Heading downstairs, she felt a little tired and achy. Rubbing her eyes, she got off and crossed the lobby … stepping outside the air nipped her exposed skin. It was a little cold out. Stretching again, she loosens up and turned her tunes on. Her mind automatically went over her day's agenda. First she was heading over to the University for nine-thirty to meet with Danielle Poulin in Human Resources. Then it was Sammy Whyte, she wasn't sure how Sammy fit in other than he was a colleague that was interviewed. The notes were vague, just that Sammy was a colleague and had no information. Dice thought if two people interview Sammy then she was going to interview him as well. Then there was Dale Stein. Caroline Riker thought Linda was having an affair with Dale, Dice wondered if Caroline saw something that no one else did or if she was just assuming because Dale and Linda were good friends. Dice wanted to find out what their relationship entailed. Then the mysterious Ishia Wren, most people thought of him when asked if there was anyone who could hurt Linda. He was the guy that was behind all the dirty pictures and Milton Hunter accusation. Could he have done that just to get a promotion? It was said that Linda also thought Ishia was behind it as well.

However Kyle Barnett said he knew him well enough to believe he would not hurt Linda. So who was right? Dice wanted to meet Ishia and see what kind of man he was for herself. See if she got any vibes that he may be behind the indiscretions that cause Linda problems.

She had time she could swing by the office and see if she could pin down an address for Divya's sister Dharma Grayson in Sudbury. While she was at it ... looking up Milton Hunter and seeing what he had to say about his accusations would also be interesting. There was something there ... out there ... in this world that would help Dice find Linda's body. She just had to find it. It could be related to those diagrams and that strange snow globe. It was possible. Dice felt like she was getting closer ... zeroing in on something. She just had to keep at it. There just had to be something that would be a good indicator. A clue ... a clue ... a clue ... she had some but she wasn't sure what they added up to. She wasn't sure if the globe was related to Linda's disappearance. Nor the diagrams for that machine ... there was something or someone knew something that would help her find Linda Barnett. It was just a matter of time. Dice knew if she kept at it ... kept looking ... kept hunting ... She would find Linda's body. Hopefully she would piece together Linda's last night here on earth and provide some closure for her husband Kyle Barnett. As far as Dice was concerned everyone deserved closure. It didn't matter who they were.

A quick shower and a bite to eat and she was feeling wide awake and back to normal. Emerging from her bedroom, she grabbed her purse and briefcase. Scooping up the diagrams and shoving them in her briefcase, she wasn't leaving without them or the strange globe. Not wanting it to get broken she shoved the globe in her purse.

There were no interruptions as she headed into the office. It was just after eight am, parking outside in her favorite spot. Dice checked the time and knew she was on a tight schedule. Unlocking the door and slipping inside, she headed right into her inner office. Booting up her computer Dice found the left over coffee cake in her drawer. Breakfast! Getting her pen and pad out, she first searched for Milton Hunter. Most of his information was private or unlisted. Dice using her magic fingers found his address and jotted it down. Then she checked on Dharma Grayson who was listed. Dice were able to find a few pictures online of Dharma, her boyfriend, their daughter and her sister Divya. Bingo ... right people found. Jotting down the address and phone number Dice shut down her computer, stuffed her pen and pad back in her purse.

Turning off the lights, she started for the front door. Aunt Sophie was in the outer office.

"Hey there," Dice smiled at her aunt.

"Gary says you were looking tired. Have you been sleeping?" Aunt Sophie eyed her carefully taking in her whole appearance.

"I am better than fine. Look at me," Dice put on her best smile for Aunt Sophie.

"Dice maybe this case is too much for you. Kyle said you went by to see him the other morning and asking questions. Do you think he's behind Linda's disappearance."

"Okay I am fine ... I was just asking him a few questions it wasn't anything serious. I don't think he did anything. You're making me late for an appointment. I'll see you this weekend."

Aunt Sophie grabbed her by the shoulders and eyed her suspiciously. Then smiled, nodding she said, "alright, just remember to get some sleep don't stay up all night mulling over this case."

Dice smiled and put an arm around her aunt's waist, "lock up on your way out. See you later."

Fortunately for her the drive to the University wasn't too far and traffic was unusually light. Finding a parking spot in the visitor's parking area, she put some coins in the parking meter. Pulling out her note pad, she found the directions to Human Resources and headed over to the administration office. Danielle Poulin's office was on the third floor. Once inside the main doors Dice found the elevator easily and was on her way up before she knew it. Getting off on the third floor, the office was down the hall and to the left. Her name was engraved on a plate and mounted to the wall beside the door. Knocking on the closed door, Dice heard a 'hello, come on in."

Opening the door, she pushed it forward and found a reception area. A young man was sitting behind the desk.

"Miss Poulin has a 9:30 appointment but if you write down your name and what your problem is I'll see if I can squeeze you in," he handed her a clip board and pen.

"Thank you but I am Miss Poulin's 9:30 appointment."

"No, you're not," he looked at her and raised an eyebrow.

"Alright," Dice looked at him and the door behind him

wondering if she should just knock him off his chair and check to see if Miss Poulin was ready to see her. "I'm Dice Maddox and I do have an appointment with Miss Poulin for 9:30 if you can double-check that I would certainly appreciate it." Dice put on her nice smile.

"You are a private investigator?" he looked at her with disbelief as if she told him she was a super model.

"Yes, I am," she smiled. "Now if you could let Miss Poulin know I'm here I won't shoot you in the leg." She grinned as his face turned to shock and he closed his gaping mouth. Nodding, he picked up the phone and mumbled into it, "you're 9:30 is here."

Dice looked around the office it was boring and had posters mounted up on the wall which was supposed to be encouraging and support equal rights.

"You can go in now," he nodded to the door behind him.

"Thank you," Dice headed into the inner office.

"Miss Maddox?" a middle age woman smiled and stood up as she entered the office. "Please have a seat, how can I help you?"

"Thank you," Dice took a chair across from Miss Poulin. Turning the mini recorder on in her pocket, she pulled out her note pad and pen. "I am Dice Maddox, a private investigator who was hired by Kyle Barnett to find out what happened to his wife."

"You're the sixth person that has been to see me. What makes you so special?"

Dice forced a smile, "I was hired to look into Linda's disappearance. I just have a few questions for you."

"Fine, how can I help?"

"Well, I was curious to know if Linda made any complaints to you about any of her co-workers?"

"No, she didn't. She did have a student that said some things that weren't true. I'm sure you already know that."

"I do Milton Hunter. What happened to him?"

"He transferred to another campus."

"I see, and the photos did you or Linda suspect anyone here?"

"We had our suspicions but nothing came of it."

"May I ask whom you suspected?"

"I can't say it wouldn't be right since nothing came of it." She smiled at Dice.

Dice could tell the woman was not going to be forth coming with anything or be helpful. "Did you and Linda get along?"

"I never had a problem with Linda."

"Were you two friends?"

"No, I wouldn't say that."

Dice nodded, "I see." She jotted a couple things down glancing up at Miss Poulin briefly. Then asked, "Was there anyone that didn't get along with Linda?"

"No everyone loved Linda."

"Do you have an address for her assistant Divya Grayson?"

"I can get Marc to pull that up for you." She grabbed the phone and pressed a button. "Can you get Divya Grayson's address."

"And her sister's address if you have it on file, it would probably be her next of kin," Dice smiled politely.

Looking a little annoyed, "and her sister's address too."

"Is there anything you could tell me about Linda that you may not have mentioned to the previous investigators?"

Danielle Poulin pursed her lips together and stared at Dice with annoyance. "No."

"I see and where were you the night that Linda disappeared?"

"What?" she snapped, leaning forward. "Surely you don't think I had anything to do with this?"

"It's just a question Danielle, I like to make sure everyone I talk to has an alibi … think of it as me just crossing my t's and dotting my i's." Dice smiled.

Danielle Poulin looked like she wanted to kick Dice out of her office but she gritted her teeth and said. "I was at a meeting that ran late, I stopped on the way home for gas and fast food. I arrived home around eleven pm, my ex-fiancé can confirm this since he was with me the whole time."

"His name is?"

"You don't have that already?" she glared at Dice. Dice wondered where this angry was coming from but figure it had nothing really to do with her. "Sammy Whyte."

"Oh," Dice smiled. "Perfect he's next on my list."

"Well, I have things to do Miss Maddox, if we are done. You can pick up Divya's information on the way out."

"Thank you for your time." Dice got up and handed Danielle Poulin her business card, "in case you think of anything else. Please give me a call, have a nice day."

Dice left the office, stopping at Marc's desk on the way out. He handed her a slip of paper with Divya's last known address, which she was no longer at. And her sister's address, which Dice already had on a purple lined note pad.

Heading down the hallway, she found Sammy Whyte's office and the door was open. No one was sitting at the desk in the outer office.

"Hello?" Dice called.

"In here," a male's voice called out.

Dice walked around the desk and found an older man, somewhere in his late forties or fifties. Either that or time wasn't too kind to him. He looked up and smiled at her as soon as she came in.

"Hi Mr. Sammy Whyte?"

"Yes," he beamed.

"My name is Dice Maddox, I'm a private investigator working for Kyle Barnett. We talked on the phone. I'm here to ask you a few questions."

"Why yes, come in my dear. Have a seat. You look so young."

She smiled, "I won't take up too much of your time. I'll keep it brief."

"Not at all on the contrary I am intrigued how did you get into this line of work?"

"I've been doing this for years. How did you meet Linda Barnett?"

"We worked together. She was an angel."

"We're you two good friends?"

"I would like to think so."

"Did Linda have any enemies that you know of?"

"Most of the women who worked with her, Linda had it all, brains, beauty and to top it off she was so damn nice. Some of the women here didn't like her much because of that. But she was a great gal."

"Did she ever mention anyone that she had a problem with her specifically?"

"Well, let's see … my ex, Danielle Poulin didn't like her much. Danny saw Linda as a threat, even though Linda didn't work over here. Plus Linda was happily married."

"Did Linda confide in you?"

"A few times, she came to me because Danny was threatening to suspend her because of the student accusations."

"Oh, she didn't mention that."

"No, she wouldn't. When it came down to it though, the student was of age. In fact they were two consenting adults, if anything had happened it wouldn't have been the end of the world. It happens all the time. More often you hear women making the complaints against male professors. If you know Linda, you know she wouldn't even think in those terms, she viewed her students as kids. Even her assistant was a student who put her in the kid category. Linda wasn't condescending or anything to them it was just she thought of them as kids."

"I heard she did get suspended."

"No she took a couple days off but it was her choice."

"How was her relationship with her assistant?"

"Miss Grayson kept to herself. Very watchful, she shadowed Linda everywhere. Sometimes I have to admit I went down to speak to Linda and I didn't even notice that Miss Grayson was in the room, this is going to sound weird but it felt like she was always lurking."

"Linda's assistant who is supposed to be there ... lurking?" Dice wondered if he was a bit of a drama queen. Lurking? Hmm.

"Like I said it doesn't sound right but that's what it felt like."

"Did you notice if Linda felt that way around her assistant?"

"Twice Linda and I were downstairs talking about her work when we saw Miss Grayson just lurking in the corner not saying anything ... ease dropping. Linda made light of the situation but I could tell she felt a little awkward by Miss Grayson's presence."

"Isn't her assistant supposed to be there?"

"Well, one time Linda had sent Miss Grayson on an errand so we could have some privacy. The young girl came back quickly and just stood there, listening in."

"Was Linda working on anything top secret?"

"Not really," he hesitated. "We all have our projects or papers that we work on for special funding. So it is in your best interest to kind of keep it to yourself if it is anything good so the others won't scoop you on it."

"Is there a lot of competition?"

He laughed, "well it just depends on what department you're in."

"How did Linda fair compared to the others? Science, physics it's not like you get to discover anything new. Most of that stuff has been discovered already," Dice wasn't sure what the big deal was.

He laughed again. "Oh dear girl ... you are just like the rest of the population when it comes to these things. So ignorant."

Ignorant? Frowning Dice's eyes narrowed as she watched him. "Enlighten me then."

"We are always working on something … trying to disprove someone's theory, amend others. Create theories of our own and test them. Funding for extra projects depends on what you come up with. There are a few that just don't care and then there are others who are in a league of their own, Linda happened to be one of them in a league of her own."

"Do you know what she was working on?"

He laughed again, "good heavens no!"

Dice was thinking at least I can amuse this one. The last interviewee wanted to light me on fire. This one thinks I'm funny. "Is there anyone who might know?"

"Her husband maybe … I guess Miss Grayson would, after all she was Linda's assistant."

"The pictures and the accusations that were made against Linda, who do you think was behind them?"

"Probably disgruntled students," he replied.

"You don't think it could have been a colleague maybe to distract her? Or throw her off her game? Discredit her?"

His eyes widen at the thought, "no I hadn't considered that. I just assumed it was a disgruntled student. No harm came to it. The student thing well like I said it wasn't the end of the world as for the pictures it turned out that wasn't even her body. Anyone who knows Linda would know that wasn't her thing."

"I heard Linda was pretty upset over those things."

"Yes, she was," he looked thoughtful. "You know I guess someone could have done it just to mess with her considering the time of year. Submissions for next year funding was coming up. With that kind of distraction yes she may have lost focus on her project."

"What about Ishia Wren?"

"Ishia?" he looked at her like she just grew another head. "There is no way. I know Linda and Ishia didn't see eye to eye on a lot of things but they did respect each other greatly. I would even go so far to say they were friends as well as colleagues."

"I'm sorry did you say friends?"

"Yes, I did. They were like family, supporting each other by pushing the other one to be better. There wasn't anything going on there that I would have thought otherwise. They would often have lunch together. Now you wouldn't do that with someone you couldn't stand … would you Miss Maddox?"

"No, I guess I wouldn't," she replied then immediately thought of Alisha. Yes she didn't like her too much, yet she was seen eating out with her.

"Did Linda have any enemies?"

"No … not that I know of, except for like I said a few of the ladies didn't like her but not enough to kill her or hurt her in any way. If she tripped and fell on her face, they may not stop to help her up. If she was seriously injured I would like to think they would have stopped then. Well, you're a woman you must know what I am talking about. Women can be hateful beings to each other."

"What about her relationship with her husband?" Dice shifted the conversation before she felt the need to kick him in the shins and blame it on being a woman thing.

"I think they were a great couple. I can't see Kyle hurting Linda. From what I heard he was very dependent on her. When she disappeared he suffered a breakdown. It was fortunate that her friend Jasmine stepped in and helped him through it." Well, that was the first she heard about that. Interesting, Dice wondered how true it was. Getting up, she pulled out her business card, "here is my card if you happen to think of anything else please feel free to call me. Day or night, thank you for your time." She nodded and left his office. Turning the recording device off, she went in search of the English department her next appointment was with Dale Stein.

After asking a few people, she got directions to the English department it was across campus. The building looked a little older than the other buildings on the campus, stepping inside the hallway felt really steamy. There was a heavy smell of sweat and books that lingered in every crevice. Dale Stein's office was on the second floor, the elevator had a sign on it that it was out of order. Finding his office was easy. Knocking on the door, she waited for an answer. There wasn't one. She knocked again and waited. A woman popped her head out from her office across the hall.

"Hey Dale just went downstairs to get a coffee he'll be right back up in a few minutes. You're welcome to wait in here."

Dice peeked in the woman's office. Just a single room, it looked like a truck carrying a load of books stopped by and threw up all over this little room.

"Don't mind the mess. I got a book-signing coming out, next month. I am just preparing."

"Congratulations, what is your book about?"

"It's a romance ... historical romance to be precise."

Dice smiled and nodded. "Your family must be proud."

"For the most part," she giggled. "It doesn't matter, I did it. I published my first book and I have a book signing party here next month. I would never have gotten this far if it wasn't for a friend of mine who encouraged me to keep at it."

"Friends are very good for things like that."

"I just wish she was here to see it."

"We'll give her a call," Dice heard someone coming down the hall.

"I wish I could. It's not that easy. She's gone ... disappeared."

Dice whipped her head around and studied the woman a little more carefully. "Who was your friend? The one who encouraged you to do this?"

"Linda Barnett, you probably heard of her. She used to work here but disappeared last year. Most likely dead."

"I'm sorry I didn't catch your name."

"Catherine Jones," she smiled at Dice.

"Do you have any ideas who might be you know behind her disappearance?"

"No ... everyone loved Linda."

"Hi there," a tall man with a goatee grinned at them, it was the only hair on his head except for his eyebrows and a stray one that came out of his left ear.

"Dale," Catherine smiled. "This young woman is waiting for you."

"Thanks Cat, Miss?"

"Dice Maddox," Dice got up and shook his hand. "I'm a private investigator hired by Kyle Barnett."

"Yes, please come into my office."

"A private investigator oh my I thought you were a student. You look so young."

Dice smiled and nodded. "Thank you for your hospitality. Good luck with your book signing."

"Why thank you young lady," Catherine beamed.

Dice followed Dale across the hall. He opened his door and gestured for Dice to go in first. She found a seat and was pleased this room was more neat and tidy. It didn't feel at stuffy. He had a tiny window cracked open and was lucky to be on the side of the building that the breeze was blowing through. She waited for him to come around his desk, sit down and get comfortable. She had slipped her hand in her pocket and turned on the mini recorder. Then pulled out a pen and pad of paper she was making notes on.

"How can I help you Miss Maddox?"

"I just have a few questions for you." She noticed a picture of Dale Stein and another man that looked about the same age as him, they were always smiling and hugging in the pictures. Perhaps, his brother? She wasn't sure.

"Ask away," he smiled.

"Were you and Linda close?"

"I would like to think so, we were best friends. I know Jasmine wouldn't like to hear that but I understood Linda more and I wasn't after her husband like someone else was."

"So you think Jasmine was after Kyle Barnett?"

"Oh yes it was obvious, she took pleasure in every unfortunate mishap that Linda endured."

"Such as?" Dice looked at him.

"Well, two years ago Linda didn't get the funding she wanted but her husband helped out with a private donation. It's nice to have a rich man around. Then the photo situation, there were some scandalous photos that went around causing Linda some trouble, even though it goes on merit for funding there is a public image we must up hold. I think just before that ... that student Milton made accusations against Linda she was very upset about it. Some people will do anything to make others miserable. I don't know I kept telling Linda those who knew her wouldn't think that about her. Even the photos come on, I love Linda to death but she was in her forties, those photos clearly had no cellulite on those bones, they were not the body of an older woman. It was just foolish to think that Linda would do that at her age or even when she was younger that was not Linda's style."

"We're you and Linda an item?"

He laughed so hard he almost fell off his chair, "oh honey, no, no," he wiped the tears from his eyes. "No, my boyfriend Jack wouldn't have appreciated that. My mother, on the other hand, would have been thrilled ... only for the grandbaby option but that ship has sailed as far as I'm concern. Besides mummy loves Jack, and to answer your question no, we were just friends … great friends but only friends."

Dice smiled and nodded. "What about her relationship with Ishia Wren?"

"Oh as far as I know they were friends, they collaborated on a few projects a few years ago."

"Do you think he was behind the photos and the student that came forward with the accusations?"

"Ishia?" he looked at her as if she was crazy. "God no he wouldn't do that. Ishia can be a little cold at times but he has standards."

"I heard he took a little pleasure in her misfortunes?"

"No, whoever said that didn't know him. When it happened he was the first one there supporting Linda. He told her not to take it personally."

Dice nodded. "What about her relationship with her husband?"

"Kyle? Well, I can't imagine a happier couple."

"What if I told you someone said they might be getting a divorce?"

He laughed again, "no way. Not in this lifetime. I know she wanted a baby but they wouldn't have split over that. Even if they separated it wouldn't have lasted for long. They were very much in love and I couldn't imagine one without the other. They were like peanut butter and jam, coffee and cream, cookies and milk… you get the idea. Nope, they wouldn't have survived without the other one. I really don't know how Kyle has managed over this last year without her. Grace of God I tell you. That and perhaps that little tart Jasmine."

"How about her relationship with her assistant Divya Grayson."

"Oh that girl was peculiar. You know I think she was dating Milton the kid that accused Linda of coming on to him."

"Really?" this was the first.

"Yes, there was something about her that didn't seem right. Linda professed the young thing was brilliant and just misunderstood. I thought she reminded me more of a grim reaper at a senior's birthday party."

Dice chuckled at the image. "I heard someone referred to it as lurking in the background. Did you notice any of that?"

"Oh God yes that is it precisely. I stopped by Linda's lab a few times and she did … lurk I mean. I'm telling you the girl is creepy."

"What do you think happened to Linda?"

"Had to have been a stranger ... anyone who knows Linda would never have been able to hurt her. As frustrating as it is to see her and hear her ... she was still the nicest person in the world."

"Did she ever mention wanting to travel anywhere?"

"She wouldn't leave without Kyle."

"Is there anything you can think of that you may not have mentioned to the other detectives that interviewed you previously?"

"Well, I think I told you everything. They never asked about that kid, or the creepy assistant."

She pulled out her card and passed it over to him. "If you think of anything please don't hesitate to call me. My cell phone number is on the back. Thank you so much for your time."

"Anytime ... I hope you find out what happened to her. We really miss her and it would be nice just to know." He looked so sad.

"I'm sure you will hear about it." She smiled and nodded. Getting up, she shook his hand again and headed back outside.

Interesting ... she thought, a couple people thought Divya Grayson was a lurking creeper. Dice couldn't wait to find her and see for herself. Stepping back outside, she located the science building. Ishia Wren was next on her list. Crossing over to the science building, she thought this building was one of the newer ones. Stepping inside it had a lobby that was lined with plaques and trophy cases that were filled with several first-place winners. Pictures lined the upper wall near the ceiling of all the professors that were current and who taught in the past. Linda Barnett's smiling face was among them. There were three hallways taking the first one she found class rooms on either side. Classes were going on. She tried not to make any noise. All the way down she came to another hallway that connected with another one. The entrance for a very large lecture hall that was empty, quiet and inviting. Going down the other hallway, she found a number of labs, two of which, contained cadavers lying on cold metal tables with students' milling around. Not peeking into any more of the rooms she noticed there was one labeled freezer, another labeled supply. Coming to the end of the hallway, she found herself in front of the very large lecture hall. Was it the same one? Yes it was. The third hallway had to be offices. A student came around the corner.

"Excuse me," Dice called to him.

He turned. Looking her over smiled and gave her his undivided attention. "How can I help you?"

"I'm looking for Professor Wren's office, how do I get to it?"

"Oh, go down any one of these hallways until you get to main lecture room, there you will find an elevator and all the offices are on the third floor. Are you new here?"

"Thank you," she smiled at him.

"No problem my name is Harry and I'm always around if you want to get a bite or a drink later," he called after her.

She followed the hallway she just came up all the way down and found the large lecture hall again right next to it the elevator. Before she knew it, she was stepping off the third floor and looking for Ishia Wren's office. He was no longer just a professor here he was the Dean of the Department.

His name was engraved on a gold shiny plate. With Dean of Science under it, the door was open a crack and she knocked on it.

"Come in," a man called.

She pressed the door open and walked in. "Hello? Mr. Wren?"

"Yes," he smiled up at her. "How can I help you?"

"I'm a little early, but we have an appointment scheduled."

"Dice Maddox?" he looked at her surprised and a little amused. "I'm sorry I was expecting someone a little older and quite frankly a male."

She laughed, "Well surprise. Can we talk now?"

"Absolutely, pull up a chair."

She grabbed the chair in front of his desk, "I am a private investigator hired by Kyle Barnett looking into Linda Barnett's disappearance."

"Please tell me how I can help," he gave her his undivided attention.

She searched her pocket for her pen and turned on the mini recorder. Then pulled out a pen and pad from her purse, "I am curious what was your relationship like with Linda?"

"We were colleagues."

"Colleagues … hmmm, would you also consider her a friend?"

"Well, yes I would."

"Did you and Linda get along?"

"For the most part, we had opposing positions on a few theories and she was fantastic to debate things with. Brilliant I would describe her as brilliant."

"Did you two compete for funding?"

"Of course, she was competition at times. But it wasn't like that was all it was here. We looked out for each other too."

"Were you behind the photos and Milton Hunter's accusations?"

"No," he looked hurt and annoyed. "I kept telling her not to pay any attention to that. It was most likely a student that disagreed with her marking system or felt she had wronged them. Anyone who knew Linda would know that wasn't her. I know it bothered her those pictures kept showing up in labs and lecture rooms. It upset her greatly. I kept telling her she couldn't let the students see that. She had to pretend it didn't bother her. But she didn't. Whoever was behind it got under her skin. It wasn't right. They were cowards."

"What about her assistant Divya Grayson?"

"Bright girl, not very sociable, she was assigned to me after Linda's disappearance. I don't think we were a good fit. I caught her trying to steal some of my work one night and told her that I was going to report her."

"What happens next?"

"I reported her, and she disappeared I never saw her after that."

"What was she trying to steal?"

"Some of my equations on worm holes, she never got away with anything. I think it was the first time she tried it. Linda was so trusting. Had Miss Grayson stolen anything from her Linda would have been furious had she found out. Yet, who knows right?"

"Do you know where Miss Grayson is now?"

"Nope she disappeared. I found out she dropped out of school as well. Had someone come looking for her a while ago, but I assumed it was one of Kyle's detectives."

"Did he say he was working for Kyle Barnett?"

"No, he didn't. I didn't think to ask. The only one who has ever come around here looking for Linda or information about Miss Grayson was an employee of Kyle's."

"Did all the investigators ask about Divya Grayson?"

"No, it was just the two detectives that wore dark suits and asked a lot of questions like you're doing to me now." He smiled.

Dice thought the man had a very nice smile. "Alright, what did you tell them?"

"Same thing I just told you."

"Anything else?"

"No, I don't know anything else."

"Did you see Divya Grayson hanging out with anyone?"

"Nope, she was a bit of a loner from what I saw."

"Do you think she was jealous of Linda?"

"Jealous? No ... well you never know right."

"True," Dice agreed she didn't get the impression that Ishia Wren held any ill feelings for Linda.

"Was Linda fooling around on her husband?"

He looked at Dice blankly. "I ... I wouldn't know. I don't think so. I mean I knew her, and would consider her a friend but I don't think she would have confided in me for that. I've been to their home a few times I never saw anything that would indicate that she and her husband were anything but happy."

"The detectives that came the one that had a partner did they leave you a business card?"

Ishia Wren paused thinking about it and then slowly shaking his head no. "I really don't think they did." He pulled open a draw and pulled out a few business cards. She recognized the other investigators names but saw nothing that stood out. "No, I don't see anything and I don't remember them leaving me anything."

"Do you know what Linda was working on?"

"No, my guess would be time, space maybe dark matter."

"Would anyone want to hurt her over her research?"

"No, I can't imagine that."

"Did she have any other competitors that would want her out of the way?"

"No, not at all."

"No problem, I really want to thank you for your time. Here's my card, if you remember anything else please call me." She got up and shook his hand.

"May I ask you something?" he asked.

She was at the door and paused, "yes?" she turned to look at him.

"How old are you?"

"I just turned 27 I know I look young."

"I have another question how long have you been doing this?"

"Started eight years ago."

"Really? What made you get into this line of business."

"I love puzzles. How about you?"

He laughed, "I love puzzles too."
She smiled. "Again thank you for your time."
"Anytime young lady."

CHAPTER TWELVE

WEDNESDAY 12:48 PM

Dice headed down the hall and was moving across the campus to the visitor's parking lot when the young guy who helped her find her way in the science building came running up to her.

"Hey good looking where are you running off to?"

"Thanks but not interested." Dice kept moving.

"Come on I'll buy you a drink," he matched her pace.

"Really I'm not interested kid."

"Kid? Really? Come on I'm forty years old."

She paused and rolled her eyes. "Really unless you know someone I'm looking for then I'm not interested." Dice continued to head towards the parking lot she could see her car in sight.

"Who are you looking for?"

"Di Grayson and Milton Hunter," she kept moving.

"They use to date you know," he said jogging to keep up with her.

She came to a dead stop and he jogged past her. "I'm sorry what did you say?"

"I'm not saying another word until I have a drink in my hand," he grinned at her.

Biting back the urge to knock him on his ass she grinned, "okay you win. What is your name again?"

"Harry Frost and your name pretty lady?" he took a couple steps towards her invading her space.

"Dice Maddox," she stepped back. "Where's the pub?"

He grinned, "Over this way, come on. Dice Maddox … I like

that."

Following this college student, she hoped something would pan out of this drink. The campus pub was behind the science building and right beside the gym. How fitting you could go and work out and when you were done pack on some calories with a few drinks. Inside the place was dimly lit. It didn't make her feel any more comfortable. Harry Frost led her over to a table. She slipped her hand into her pocket and turned on the recorder.

He disappeared over to the bar and returned with a couple of beers. She took one and placed it in front of her. "So are you friends with Divya or Milton?"

"Neither I just know them."

"What are they like?"

"Why are you asking?"

"It's my job. What are they like?"

"What are you a cop? Fuck that is so sexy, do you have handcuffs? I would be so into that if you do."

"Okay listen if you don't want to answer my questions you're wasting my time," she started to get up.

He grabbed her hand, "no, no wait. I'll tell you whatever you want to know."

Looking down at him, he reminded her of a kid pleading in the store for a new toy that he didn't need. Slowly sitting back down in her chair she looked at him and tilted her head a little. He suddenly felt a little uncomfortable.

"How well did you know them?"

"Divya was in my class a couple of times, she's really smart but you can't get anything out of her. I mean I tried to get her to come here with me a couple times but she wouldn't. Milton was in the science club that Professor Barnett held after school hours."

"What did you think of Professor Barnett? We're you in any of her classes?"

"Yeah I did get into a couple of her class for a chick she really knew her shit. I mean I think she was the smartest person in the world. That's one of the reasons I joined the club she had going on. She had this theory about parallel universes I have never seen anything like it."

"Did you hear about the pictures of her?"

"Yeah I did," his smile faded. "Whoever did that … well they are so lucky we didn't find out. Don't get me wrong Professor Barnett was smoking hot, god I wished she came on to me but that's wasn't her style. She was married to some old guy too. Plus I think she was old herself like my mom's age. That would have been weird. Milton was a loser for saying those things and no one really believed him. I mean maybe the admin department but hell they have nothing better to do. Milton switched schools because no one liked him much before that happened but after that happen no one wanted him around. And his girlfriend she was all weird like."

"Weird like how?"

"She kept to herself and rarely talked to anyone. I mean I think she was just really shy or something."

"Has anyone come by here and asked your students about Professor Barnett or about Divya Grayson?"

He shook his head no slowly. "So do you have a boyfriend?" She nodded.

"Figures, is he a student?"

She shook her head no, "he's a lawyer. I'm much older than I look. I could be your older sister."

"You look like your twenty."

"I'm twenty-seven."

"Holy shit really? Yeah you're my sister's age. She has some hot-looking friends but none like you. You know I am very experimental and love older women."

She laughed, "Yeah that's not helping."

"I really mean it I am eager to please," he moved closer to her. "I have a lot of energy and I can go for hours."

She shook her head. "Okay, listen if you think of anything or if anyone else comes looking for Milton Hunter or Divya Grayson, let me know." She handed him her business card.

"So, I can call you?" he grinned.

"Only if it is related to my case, do you know where Divya Grayson went to?"

"No, she just disappeared."

"What about if I want to hire you for a couple of hours? What do you charge?"

She got up, "for you? Too much."

"Awe Dice you don't play fair, but you know what I know where you work now." She looked at him and shook her head, "not really scared. Have a nice day, Harry. Good luck with school."

"Hey you didn't touch your drink," he called after her.

She turned and looked at him, "consider it my gift to you." She gave him a wink and left. Back outside she turned her recorder off. How interesting Milton and Divya were definitely a couple. She wondered if they were still seeing each other.

Within minutes she was back at her car and noticed that she had a flat tire. Checking her tires the other three looked okay but it was only the one. Opening her car, she dumped her purse and briefcase inside and popped the trunk. Rolling up her sleeves, she moved the boxes of Divya's out of her trunk and hauled out her spare. It took her twenty minutes, one of her all-time fastest. But she had the spare on and was putting the flat in the trunk when she noticed it was slashed. Pausing she looked around her but no one stood out. Someone had slashed her tire. Noticing the security cameras in the parking lot, she put her flat in the car and the boxes back in slamming the trunk shut she grabbed her purse and locked her car up. Heading back to the main building, she remembered seeing the security office there. No one was there. Looking around, she knocked on the counter. A middle age man came around the corner and smiled at her friendly. "How can I help you miss?"

"Someone just slashed one of my tires. Can you check and see who did it?"

"Oh I can't do that."

"I'm sorry what?"

"Well, they are on disks and we ...," he began.

"Wait who takes care of your security?"

"Rowsen and Gyerse."

Dice turned and called her friend Ronnie. Within minutes the man behind the counter was on the phone with someone else. He looked over at Dice and glared at her. Within ten minutes on the fax machine a picture came through with what looked like some skinny kid taking a knife to her tire, and it looked like it was when she was approaching her car with Harry in tow. The time was stamped on the picture. Dice didn't recognize the person. They were dressed in black and kept their face turned away from the camera.

"Thank you," she left the security office and headed back to her car. Checking the tires before she got in. Who would have done that? Stuffing the print out in her bag, she wondered who would slash a tire. It was someone who looked small. They wore a hoodie and jogging clothes extra baggie by the looks of things. Pulling out her notebook, she looked up his address.

It was a little out of the way but she found it about thirty-five minutes later. A townhouse on the other side of town, it was one of those new ones. This area was an area that had been developing over the last couple years. Parking in the driveway she got out and went up to the door. Ringing the bell, she wondered if anyone was home. She rang the bell again and a young boy opened the door. "We're not interested."

"I'm sorry I'm looking for Milton Hunter, are you Milton?"

"Who are you?"

"Someone who has a few questions for you."

"I have nothing to say."

She put her foot in the doorway so he couldn't close it. "I'm not leaving without asking you a few questions."

"Fine," he grumbled eyeing her suspiciously. "What do you want to know?"

"First you are Milton Hunter is that right?"

He nodded.

"I'm Dice Maddox, I'm a private investigator hired by Kyle Barnett."

"What do you want to know," he didn't look any less suspicious. "Professor Barnett didn't make any advances towards me I made it up."

"Why?"

"Because I didn't like her."

"Really? Why?"

"What do you mean why I don't need a reason. I just didn't like her."

"So you accuse all older women whom you don't like of raping you?"

"What?" he gasped. "No, well …," his eyes narrowed. "She gave me some bad grades."

"And?"

"And nothing that's it. She gave me a bad grade and I got even. End of story."

"Hmm, I see, what's your relationship with Divya Grayson?"

"Why what did she say?"

"I'm asking you," Dice grinned. "I have already talked to her."

"Have you? Can you give me her address or phone number please?" he opened the door wider. Looking around outside, he grabbed Dice by the wrist and pulled her inside. "If you know where Di is I need to talk to her."

"Tell me why you accused Professor Barnett?"

"I told you already."

"You didn't really tell me anything."

"Fine I did it because … someone asked me to."

"Why?"

"I can't say."

"Was it Divya?"

He looked at her and his mouth dropped open.

"Why did Divya want you to do that?"

"I don't know. She just asked me to do it and I did. Professor Barnett was really hurt and I felt bad. I wanted to come clean right away but I didn't want Di to get into trouble. She told me if I said I was lying then she wouldn't speak to me anymore. That and everyone really didn't believe me anyways. Professor Barnett was really good looking for an old lady. But she reminded me of my mom."

"How did your parents take it?"

"They were pissed and went after the school. When I couldn't take it anymore I told them that I had lied and someone paid me to do it but I didn't know who it was."

"Have you told anyone else this?"

He looked like he was five years old and got caught stealing a cookie before dinner. "I never told anyone this."

"Alright, so when's the last time you saw Divya?"

"About six months ago she was scared and wouldn't tell me why. Just that something was going on at the university. Some guys in suits came asking a few of us if we knew anything about Di. Of course as far as I know no one said anything."

"Do you know what Divya was working on?"

"What do you mean?"

"At school? Was she working on anything special? A project or something?"

"No, she was always shadowing Professor Barnett before she disappeared."

"Think back before Professor Barnett disappeared was Divya

doing anything different? Did she act differently?"

"No," he paused sighing heavily he began to bite his lower lip. "Well … well … yeah she stopped talking to me. I mean we would talk on the phone every night. But it was a little over two months before Professor Barnett disappeared that she stopped calling me. In fact, I started to get worried and thinking she was seeing someone else. There was this guy that seemed interested in her at school and I thought maybe she decided she got tired of me and wanted to date Harry."

"So what happened?"

"I went to her place a few times to see if she would speak to me."

"So what was she doing?"

"I don't know my best guess from what I overheard … she was working with Professor Barnett on a project."

"Do you know what they were working on?"

"No, it was top secret. When I did corner her outside the lab she was really excited about the project but she told me she couldn't hang out with me anymore she was just too busy. I had asked her if she was seeing someone else she said no, she didn't have time."

"She was excited about the project, and she gave you no indication what kind of project?"

"No, I just got dumped by the only girl I ever loved. It sucked. I didn't care about her project. I thought it sucked."

"Okay, did you notice anyone else taking an interest in the project?"

"Anyone else?" he looked at her and shook his head. "No, I really didn't notice anyone."

"And you didn't see or overhear anything about it?"

"No," he shook his head.

"Alright, so what happened to you … did you switch campuses on your own or was it suggested by someone else?"

"My dad made me do it. He didn't want me to be associated with that lie I told and thought switching campuses would give me a fresh start."

"Did it?"

"I guess … I just miss everyone though especially Di."

"I can understand that."

"Do you have Dharma's address in Sudbury?"

"Yeah, I can get it for you." He turned and went into the living room sitting down at a computer he pulled up an email. And then grabbed a pen and a pad of paper, Dice watched as he jotted it down. He came back and handed her the sheet. "Do you think she's at her sister's home?"

"Have you stopped by her place recently?"

He nodded, "yeah there is some other guy living there. He didn't know who she was and said I was the second person to come looking for her. When I asked who was the first. He said two police detectives were looking for her about a month ago."

"Interesting … what is she like?"

"Di?"

Dice nodded.

"She is amazing, so smart and beautiful. I just miss her so much. If you see her again, can you tell her that I am still thinking about her."

Dice nodded, "sure. Alright, thanks for your time."

Leaving she had the feeling of someone watching her again. It was an uneasy feeling in the pit of her stomach, a warning. Looking up and down the street, she didn't see anyone who stood out. Nor anyone she recognized.

Dice checked her car again just to be on the safe side; slipping into the driver's seat she wondered what made her think of that. Then thought, Dice don't question those urges. Checking the time, she knew she could make it to Sudbury before it got dark if she left now. Reaching for her iPod, she noticed she didn't bring it. Frowning she sighed and put her car into reverse it would take a few minutes to head back over to her place to pick it up but traveling four hours was not her idea of fun without some of her favorite tunes. Checking the balcony lock, she made sure everything was locked and grabbed her iPod and slipped it into her pocket. Heading back down to the garage, she had that feeling again that someone was watching her. Standing still, she looked around. Not a single soul … she didn't see anyone. It was a little creepy. Heading over to her car, she checked the tires and got in. Checking her mirrors and looking around her … there were no signs of anyone lurking in the dark corners.

Slipping it into gear, she slowly backed out. Dice kept her eyes peeled. Popping her iPod in, she turned up her tunes and then pointed her car towards highway 400 North. Traffic was heavy, and bumper-to-bumper what should have taken her twenty-five minutes took her two hours. When she finally got past Barrie and the turn off loomed ahead, the traffic finally began to thin a bit. Signaling she got over for her turn off.

Highway four hundred slashes sixty-nine ... the sun was starting to go down. Dice decided she would just check into a hotel and pop by Dharma Grayson in the morning. The traffic wasn't too bad until she got closer to Perry Sound. Not in a rush at this point Dice just drove the speed limit and chilled to her tunes. Keeping an eye on the traffic, she didn't have that feeling any more of someone watching her ... which was good. She didn't like that feeling and it made her get a little nervous. Perhaps she was on the right track. She did find out a lot more today. Like for one, Ishia Wren wasn't the creep everyone thought he was. He was a little awkward but not a creep. Linda and him were friends at least on a professional basis.

Plus, it would seem that Milton was working for Divya Grayson ... he was in love with her. Dice remembered her first crush it was a guy name Victor ... she would have done almost anything for him. Except lie, or cheat, or accuse someone of doing something that they didn't do. She had standards and wasn't going to cash in on them in the name of love. No, she did that later, in a sense. When she met Chris Douglas while on a case. Handsome a little older, professional lawyer who had it all going on ... very handsome Chris Douglas ... he's only flaw ... he couldn't stay loyal to her. She remembered the first time she found out he had cheated on her. It was a day that was burned into her mind forever. She just told him they were done and she didn't want anything to do with him. Then her aunt called and told her that her Uncle Eric and partner ... Eric Lawson of Lawson Investigations was in a car accident. Dice didn't hear anything else. She raced to the hospital. It was Chris that drove her there only to find out Eric died on impact. Her world capsized and she felt like she was five years old ... alone and no one wanted her. Pushing the thought out of her mind, she knew everyone made mistakes but it's what you learned from them that counted. If you went through life and didn't learn anything then you weren't really living.

Divya had stopped seeing Milton. She didn't have time for him anymore. She was too busy helping her professor out on a project. That's what Milton had said. Dice wondered what could they have been working on. Everything had been discovered ... they wrote theories. Theories on things that they couldn't really test. Theories on black holes ... worm holes and other dimensions. Dice chuckled to herself. If they had discovered something new that could be tested scientists around the world would be all over it. No ... if it was something new ... it would be newsworthy. They had a shuttle going out to the far reaches of the Milky Way Galaxy, she saw it on the NASA website. Any little tidbit of information showed up.

Then again ... not everything was exposed for what it was ... through Ty a close friend of hers, she met a man named Muffin and his lady companion named Charlotte. Those two were quite the characters ... who would have thought there were people like them living so close. Muffin and Charlotte were alien experts, partly because one of them was an alien and the other was the alien's companion. She wondered how many people knew about their story? Dice thought they were fascinating and was great in a sense for being introduced to them. Yet, they did say that alien first contact on earth had happened centuries ago. The mere thought of aliens living on Earth walking among humans. Living and working beside humans on a regular basis was a little creepy. Then again why not? She asked herself. It would be very foolish to think we were the only intelligent beings in the vast universe ... there had to be other intelligent beings out there. So why not visit Earth and blend in ... what better way to understand humans, their motives, how we think and react to things. It made sense. If she was an alien, and could get away with it and wanted to know more about a species ... blending in as best you could be the ideal way of understanding the species ... the enemy? She grinned to herself yes she did think 'enemies'. Not that it mattered.

Charlotte had confided to Dice that she was the alien ... Ty thought Muffin was ... Dice wondered if they were both humans just pulling everyone's leg. It would be a fun joke to have on your friends and people you meet. It's not like she could tell anyone that she met an alien ... it wouldn't go over so well. People would think she was just plain crazy. Some people thought she was crazy for opening up a private investigation business by herself, being a woman and all. Yes, that was just so crazy, she thought sarcastically. Then she remembered while she was at Muffin's and Charlotte's fortress ... Charlotte had kissed her and Dice could have sworn she felt a forked tongue poking in her mouth. Snake-like ... she remembers telling Ty and he laughed. It wasn't funny. Maybe Charlotte was an alien. ...

which brought her back to the little business of maybe there were new discoveries happening all the time that just were not trickling down to the masses via the media. It was quite possible that there were things that the general public didn't know about and had no right to knowing about it.

If that was so, what happen to Linda Barnett? Was she kidnapped, tortured and killed lying beneath dirt somewhere ... becoming worm food or plant food? It would be the logical consensus. Yet, it still nagged at her that she hadn't heard of any other woman go missing back then. There were no warnings that women needed to be extra careful coming home from school or work. Thinking hard, she didn't remember anything like that ending up in the news. If that was the case then what else could it be? A single murder? A crime of passion? Someone taking a liking to her and she didn't reciprocate the admiration? There should have been some kind of trail. She saw the police report there was nothing at the scene of the crime to indicate that there was any foul play. In fact ... if it had been a crime of passion chances were there would have been some kind of indication ... some kind of clue should have been left behind.

Talking to Divya would hopefully give Dice some insight on what was going on with Linda Barnett at work. Her assistant was like a right arm ... couldn't leave home without it.

The rest of the drive was boring nothing exciting occurred in fact, Dice drove into Sudbury pulling over at the first gas station she found and asked for directions to the closest hotel. It was one she had stayed at before when she was there last time. It had been awhile. It was back when Uncle Eric was around and they had tracked down a guy who had skipped town on his wife who put up bail for him. In turn, mortgaging their home that their three kids lived in. They got into town in the early evening, catching the guy by midnight and was back in Toronto before noon the next day for his court appearance saving the woman's home. She was so grateful ... Dice couldn't blame her. But she remembered this rocky little town.

Pulling into the hotel parking lot, she grabbed her bag and headed inside to the front desk to check in. The young man behind the counter took her information and slipped her a card to access room 315. Heading over to the elevator, she pressed the button. Dice felt that weird feeling of being watched again. Thinking it was the night clerk she ignored it and got on the elevator. Pressing 3 for the third floor, it was a short ride and she got off at the third floor. Finding room 315 was easy opening the door she flicked on the light and dumped her bag on the spare bed. Slipping her laptop out of her bag, she plugged it in and turned it on. Grabbing the phone, she ordered a pizza and some ice tea. Turned on the TV, she liked having the noise in the background since she really didn't watch much of it.

Checking on the address again in comparison to where she was staying she found the quickest way to Dharma's address. Checking her email, she then checked her voice mail. Plugging in her cell phone, she checked her voice mail. Rick Li was on there, 'checked it out for you Dice, just remember I'm not your secretary. No there were no other missing people at that time matching her description. Not a serial kidnapping or killing. There was nothing linking her to anyone else. Good luck and you owe me a dinner for this, I'm not cheap.' He laughed and hung up. Smiling she appreciated his help.

The next message was Chris wanting to know if she was still in town or if she took off up north. If she did take off, he was looking forward to hearing from her when she got back. If only he had been this attentive when they were living together, they still might have been together. Get that thought out of your mind Maddox she told herself. Instead, she busied herself with jotting her case notes up.

Before she knew it, the pizza guy was knocking at her door. Paying him and giving him a tip, she saved her files and slipped into some pajamas. Crawling into bed, she fluffed up the pillows and flicked through the channels. It was not having to worry about what you look like. Chilling out by yourself and slobbing out on food that you normally didn't eat but it was a treat.

A couple slices later she was into the murder mystery on TV and then the people upstairs started. Looking over at the clock, she couldn't believe her eyes it was going on midnight and the bed in the room above her head was creaking ... sighing she turned up the volume and tried to ignore the noises. She could do this. They just got louder. Frowning Dice got up and packed her pizza over on the desk went to the bathroom and brushed her teeth and washed her face. Then came back in and started another TV show. The noise lasted for only another fifteen minutes she smirked to herself as her neighbors upstairs became quite. Turning down her own TV, she lowered her pillows and watched mindless TV as her mind raced about on the case she was working on. Milton and Divya were a couple. Hmm ... that made Dice wonder why Divya would do that to her mentor. From the stories she heard Divya looked up to Linda, she was not only her boss but her mentor. Dice could never imagine doing anything to hurt her mentor who had been her Uncle Eric. So why would Divya do that? What was Divya Grayson thinking? Was she really behind the student accusations and the pictures? Dice always thought whoever was behind putting Milton Hunter up to accusing Linda Barnett of coming on to him and making advances it would also be the same person behind the dirty pictures of Linda ... which Dice reminded herself were not Linda's body it was just her head cropped onto someone else's body. Who would do that? Divya Grayson? According to Milton it was his girlfriend Divya who put him up to do that. It was embarrassing and had Linda upset for months. She was distracted ... sitting up in the dark room. With those accusations going on Linda Barnett was distracted. So why would Divya Grayson want Linda Barnett to be distracted? Did Linda discover something new or was she on the precipice of discovering something new? If she was why would her assistant want her distracted?

"Think Dice ... think ... if Divya was working for someone else? It seems like a far stretch. Yet, it was possible. Wasn't it?" Yes ... yes it was ... if Divya was double-crossing Linda then it was plausible, whomever she was running from she may have double-crossed them as well? Her brain was in over load. Turning the TV off, she rolled over and stared at the wall in the dark. It would be assuming Linda did something or came up with something that someone else would have wanted to steal. Sighing what did Sammy or Dale say ... chances of something new being discovered was next to nil.

Drifting off to sleep, she found herself dreaming of hanging out in the park. Lying on a blanket staring up at the clouds. She felt like a kid watching those fluffy white mounds lazily drift through the blue sea. Birds flew overhead dipping down and soaring high. It was so amazing to watch. A cool breeze tugged at her hair and danced across the soft velvet green blades of grass. Staring at the clouds as they moved and shifted. Changing their shapes and appearance it was like watching a ballet in slow motion. Everyone merged together to create a magical show. Gazing at one fluffy piece, she felt like the world was turning slowly. It was exhilarating.

'Hey beautiful," a tall shadowy figure stood above her. She smiled back and said nothing. The person leaned over and looked at her. The sun blotted out everything. It was just a dark blur, the sun was so warm and bright. Inhaling deeply the air smelled fresh and invigorating. She couldn't get enough of it. The sun felt warm on her skin. When she was younger she would sit in the window at home as the sun shone in ... she saw a cat doing it a couple of times and tried it herself. The warm sun felt like angels hugging her. She would close her eyes and she could swear her mother and father were there, reaching out caressing her skin and hugging her. It was the warmest feeling ever, both spiritually and physically. Lying in the sun was therapeutic in every way possible.

Dice felt the man she knew sit down beside her. She loved how he smelled fresh and inviting. Not looking over at him she kept her eyes on the prize the beautiful clouds were putting on a show and it was such a show. His warm hand found hers as he entwined their fingers locking into a gentle embrace.

"I see a dinosaur," he whispered in her ear.

She giggled, "No you don't. Where?"

She watches as he used his left-hand points above them and outlining a dinosaur. Giggling again she shook her head. "I see it now."

"I was looking for you, where did you go?"

He was interrupting her cloud party, feeling a little annoyed that he wanted to get serious now when all she wanted to do was be five years old and lay in the sun and cloud watch. Then it occurred to her. This is something her dad and she did when she was a kid. Tears welled up in her eyes and the fluffy white mounds began to blur. Blinking back the tears, she tried not to think about it. But she couldn't help remembering those times with her dad. It was so long ago. How she wishes he was still alive. A picture of her mother etched into the clouds as they floated above her. Her pretty face, large eyes and that warm smile she always gave her. Even when she was doing something bad, her mother always smiled and laughed. They had been so happy ... it was only when she was dreaming that her parents would come and visit her. Looking over at the man lying down beside her the tears slide down her face and she felt tears dripping into her left ear. It was her dad.

"Daddy?"

He smiled and nodded, "hey baby."

"Daddy," she snuggled into his shoulder. "I miss you and mom."

"We're always with you Dice. Don't cry baby." He wiped the tears away. Closing her eyes tight, she breathed in his smell, it was a combination of vanilla, jasmine and cinnamon. Her aunt told her that was because her mother was always burning candles or incenses that smelled of those scents.

Rolling over, she found herself awake and hugging a pillow. Alone in the dark … alone with just her ghosts of memories. Were they even real? Sighing she hugged her pillow tighter not wanting to let go of the illusion.

CHAPTER THIRTEEN

THURSDAY 6:43 AM

Waking up, she stretched and yawned, then stretched some more. It took her a couple minutes to realize where she was. Getting out of bed, she slipped into her running outfit. Grabbed her key card for her room and her iPod for her tunes.

Stepping out into the morning crisp air, it held a promise that it would be another beautiful day. With that thought in mind, she gave a few more stretches and then headed off. The city was alive with people getting off work and others going in. She liked this time of morning because the city seemed to be waking up, rubbing the sleep from their eyes and preparing itself for the day for it to all come to an end

Dice wondered what Divya had been up to. Why would she betray her mentor's trust? If Milton Hunter was telling the truth, which Dice had a feeling he was. Then how could Divya Grayson justify her actions? Did Linda Barnett do something to Divya that warranted retaliation? The only people who knew the answers were Divya Grayson and Linda Barnett. Since Linda was most likely dead, she would be of no help in solving this matter. Did Divya murder Linda? It left Divya Grayson to answer these loose ends that Dice came to.

Dice took her time and made her way around a few blocks then returned to the hotel. After having a quick shower, getting dress and ready for her day she stopped at her computer and had leftover pizza for breakfast. Checking on a couple things, she began packing up her things and cleaned up after herself.

Dice carried her bags downstairs and checked out. It was a short drive over to LaSalle street, finding the address for Dharma's apartment wasn't hard. Finding a parking spot in the visitor parking Dice grabbed her purse and left everything else in the car. Checking the time it was eight-thirty hoping she was catching the woman before she went out anywhere. Finding D Grayson in the list on the wall Dice pushed the button to ring Dharma's home. She could have called and gave her the heads up but catching them off guard was what she wanted at this point. No one answered. Then someone was coming out. Dice slip in and located Dharma's door. Knocking on the door, she waited. The door cracked open a bit.

A man who looked like he was in his thirties, with dark circles under his eyes opened the door and gave Dice a deadpan look. Smiling broadly, she asked, "Is Dharma Grayson in?"

"How did you get in? You know ... whatever," he held the door open for her and motioned for her to enter. "What now?"

Dice wasn't sure who he thought she was but was grateful to be let in. "I'm Dice Maddox, I am a private investigator. I think Divya Grayson may be in danger and I'm looking for her."

"Yeah you and everyone else," he slammed the door behind her then trudged over to the sofa grabbing a cigarette he lit up one, scratching his crotch and then sitting down. "What else is new? With Dee Dee it's always something." He rolled his eyes. "We call her Dee Dee."

Dice kind of figured that out. "When's the last time you saw Dee Dee?"

"She came and stayed with us about three months ago. I hate when she comes by she almost got me kicked out of here the last time. I mean what goes on between Dharma and me is between Dharma and me. I mean who does she think she is? It's not like she even has her own shit together ... no she comes over and starts crap up. Stirs the pot until Dharma is after me for every little thing."

"Do you happen to know where Dee Dee is now?"

"Not far enough away from me, that's what." He grumbled some more. Then poured himself a shot from the nearly empty bottle of Jack Daniels sitting on the table in front of him. "I don't know she hooked up with some guy named Adam something or other and they took off to Wawa or Sault Ste. Marie. I don't know who cares ... they probably have bears in their backyards there. Some place rural. I hear they marry their cousins up there."

"Have you ever been there?"

"Oh god no, that's more Dee Dee's kind of place."

"Has she ever been in trouble before with anyone?"

"If I could I would tell you stories ... she always manages to get out of trouble. I mean ...," he took a gulp of liquor and grinned up at her. "Who are you again?"

"I am looking for Dee Dee she might be in trouble," Dice wondered where Dharma was.

"Oh yeah, you said that already. I don't know where she is... I just hope she doesn't find her way back here. Just because some people think she is a genius doesn't give her the right to ruin other people's lives. I mean like mind your own business bitch."

Dice nodded, "yup, I hear you. Hey, do you know where Dharma is?"

"Yeah." He took another long puff and stared at the ceiling as he lay on the sofa.

"May I speak with her?" Dice pursued it.

"I guess."

"Is she here?" Dice tried a different tactic.

"Huh?" he half-looked over at her and took another puff.

"Is Dharma home ... here ... is she here?"

"No, she took our daughter to school, she'll be back in a few minutes you can help yourself to a drink. Do you like Jack?" he chuckled to himself.

Dice smiled, "no I'm fine, thank you."

"Why, yes you are fine lady," he gave her an approving look.

She sat in the chair that was the furthest away from him as possible. "When Dee Dee was here last did she come with Milton Hunter or was she dating someone else?"

"Milton? Nah she had someone else. I didn't really like Milton he was such a pussy. Constantly ... Di let me do that for you ... Di I think you are amazing," he mimicked in a girly voice. "Yeah he needs to grow a pair."

"Did she mention anything about school? Or working with Professor Linda Barnett?"

"I don't know ... she might have. When she came by she was

crying over something. I have no idea what she was bawling for. I let Dharma take care of that and I took off bowling with the guys."

A woman that was in her mid-thirties came barging in looking a little worse for wear and was in mid conversation, "really? Come on can't you just get off your ass to do anyth …" her voice trailed off as she saw Dice sitting in the chair. "Who the hell are you?" She snapped. Turning to her boyfriend, "just great you just let anyone in here."

"Excuse me, I am Dice Maddox I'm an investigator looking for your sister I think she may be in trouble."

"What?" her eyes narrowed. "What kind of trouble?"

"There are some people looking for her and I'm not sure why. The woman she worked for disappeared. I am a little concern she might be next."

"Has to be related to that idiot she was dating. Well, I'm not sure where she is. She took off west either Sault Ste. Marie or Wawa with her new boyfriend. I don't trust him either."

Dice glanced at Dharma's main squeeze and decided she may not have the best judgment regarding men.

Dharma looked at her boyfriend and frowned. Perhaps she was thinking the same thing. "Can you go and find something to do, if you can't help me clean up in here."

He gave her and sulky look reminding Dice of a disgruntled kid who was just asked to pick up his toys and thought the task might just kill him. Reluctantly he dragged himself out of the sofa and dragged his ass down the hall disappearing out of Dice's line of sight.

"Are you here really trying to help Dee Dee?"

Dice nodded, "that is my intention. I understand a couple people came by here a couple months looking for her. Can you describe what they look like?"

Frowning and pursing her lips, she started to pick up the clothes absently as she began, "they were both in black suits, said they were working for the government." She looked sad. "They said she had information that didn't belong to her. Told me that they would find her if I agreed to help them or not, but then threatened me."

"They threatened you? How?"

"Accusing me of being in on it too, suggesting that I was a co-conspirator."

"In on what?"

"That was just it, they never said. What she was supposed to have stolen, so I never knew exactly what they were after. They just kept telling me if I was lying or if they had to come back I would be trapped in jail until my daughter graduated from college. In all honesty, they kind of freaked me out."

"So they claimed she stole something? From who? Or where? Did they say?"

"Nope, when I asked they just started threatening me and telling me that I knew and not to play coy with them because they knew that I knew."

Dice shook her head, "no that doesn't sound suspicious at all."

"See that's what I thought. Andy was telling them everything he knew … which thankfully was nothing. I mean just because you flash a badge at me doesn't mean I'm going to just roll over and spill my guts to you."

"You're absolutely right. So what did they find out from Andy?"

"Just that she was here for a couple weeks met a new guy and they were supposed to go north or north-west. He told them Wawa. I don't think they went that far. I wouldn't be surprised if she was somewhere between here and Sault Ste. Marie. I don't know where her new boyfriend is from."

"Do you have a name?"

"Who are you working for again?"

"I am a private investigator working for Kyle Barnett, while investigating his wife's disappearance, Linda Barnett I have uncovered some information that your sister might be in danger." She wasn't completely lying, after hearing about the guys in suits she very well may be in trouble.

"Oh, Linda Barnett, Dee Dee loved working for her. It was the best job she ever had. I still can't believe that woman just disappeared like that. I warned Dee Dee to be careful."

"Did you catch her boyfriend's name?"

"Yes, it was Don Fennelly, I don't know where he's from originally. He did mention he worked out in Calgary for a bit."

She jotted down the name. "Did Dee Dee ever mention the project that she was working on with Linda?"

Dharma looked nervously over her shoulder and then moved closer to Dice, "I feel like I can trust you. That doesn't happen often. Promise me you will not say a word of this to anyone … promise me please," she begged.

Dice nodded, "sure what is it?"

"One night when she was staying with us we went out Trevi's, a girls' night out. It was one of my only days off from work so it was nice to get away. We were sitting there, she left Don somewhere or he took off I don't know where he was. We were sitting there having a couple drinks just the two of us." Dharma paused. Glancing over her shoulder, she leaned closer and whispered, "she told me that Linda and her travelled to another world. They were in another place that looked like this Earth but it was different somehow. She was really excited about it and said they brought stuff back. The only problem was that they brought someone else back too."

"What?" Dice lowered her voice, "sorry, what?"

"I know it's really creepy. I didn't believe her at first but then she showed me this weird snow globe and told me it was from this other world."

"Did she say how they got there?"

"Yes, but I couldn't follow her. My sister is a genius and she has a tendency to talk over people sometimes. We were drinking ... she was excited and she wanted to tell someone. She said her and Linda swore not to mention to anyone and it was just their secret until they could map it out and whatever. They wanted to patent something ... anyways she told me that they went to this place twice. The third time Linda went by herself but never came back."

"How did she go?"

"Well, my sister looked pretty guilty and started crying at this point telling me it was all her fault."

"So, wait your sister told you that she and Linda were working on something and that Linda is trapped in another world somewhere?"

Dharma nodded, "mmhmm, you can't tell anyone."

"Okay that might be what these people are looking for."

Dharma nodded again and looked like she was about to cry. "Please ... you are planning on helping my sister right?"

Dice nodded, "I am. If I can find her, I will do my best. That means Linda Barnett might still be alive?" The thought seemed so foreign to Dice. She honestly thought that Linda was gone for good. That finding her decomposing body was her mission. Tracey was talking to her from the spirit world.

"That's what Dee Dee thought too."

"Why didn't she just open the door or whatever they did in the first place so she could come back?"

"Dee Dee was crying like a baby and wasn't making any sense. I don't know why. You need to find Dee Dee to find out."

"Does she have any friends or family in Sault Ste. Marie or Wawa?"

"No … wait … no I think my cousin married an American and moved south. We did have a cousin who lived in the Sault but I don't know if she is still there."

"What's her name?"

"Darlene Grayson, same last name as us unless she got married."

"Okay." Dice wrote the name down. "Do you remember anything else?"

Dharma shook her head no, "I really don't. Please help my sister." Dharma grabbed her arm.

Dice nodded and patted Dharma's hand. "I will do my best. Here's my card with my cell phone number on the back of it. If you hear from her call me." Dice handed Dharma her card. "What number can I reach you at so I can check in with you?"

Dharma took the pen and wrote her cell number on Dice's pad.

Leaving Dharma Grayson's home, she got into her car and headed over to the nearest donut shop, taking her laptop and purse inside with her. Ordering a coffee, she sat where she could see the road and her car. If what Dharma Grayson said was true then Linda Barnett may still be alive! Linda could be a live living somewhere in another world? It seemed far-fetched. Divya thought they brought someone male back with them. Dice wasn't sure what that really meant. Pulling the snow globe out of her purse, she tilted it in her hand. The building in the snow globe didn't look like it was from here. She had Googled attractions, snow globes and strange building in snow globes nothing came up that resembled this particular peculiar snow globe. Stuffing it back in her purse, she pulled up Google on the free Wi-Fi and looked up Divya's cousin Darlene Grayson. There was one living in Sault Ste. Marie. Jotting down the address, Dice then Googled map the address compared to where she was now. Nodding she looked at the clock on the wall not even ten yet. She could be there before dinnertime and maybe she could meet this Darlene and see if Divya stopped by. The goal now was to find Divya Grayson and find out what this contraption that Linda Barnett and she was working on. Plus, could they really travel to another world? What did that even mean? Was it in outer space somewhere? Was it a different planet? She chided herself at the thought it wasn't likely that aliens made snow globes for local attractions. Enjoying her coffee, she waited a few more minutes before realizing the sooner she got on the road the sooner she could find Darlene. With that thought still fresh in her mind she packed up her laptop, grabbing her bag, purse and coffee. Heading out to the parking lot, she got that feeling that she was being watched again. Reaching her car, she took her time pulling out the keys as she surveyed the area looking for anyone who had an eye for her. No one seemed to stick out, nor did anyone look like they were taking a particular interest in her … no … she was being paranoid again. Shrugging it off, she got in her car and headed for highway 17. She had never traveled to Sault Ste. Marie before. She couldn't remember but she thought Eric had come up this way once or twice. Eric had Dice working on other cases at the time.

She stopped once to fill up her tank and empty her bladder then grabbed another coffee for the road. Dice put her iPod music on shuffle and had the sun high in the sky as she made her way into Sault Ste. Marie. It looked like Sudbury to some degree. Lots of greens and blues, driving she took the path that Google maps gave her and found Darlene's address. Parking down the street but where she could see the house she waited. She watched the neighbors and waited until she noticed an old couple take an interest in her sitting in her car. No one came or left Darlene's house. Dice decided she would just take the direct approach. Driving into the driveway of Darlene Grayson, Dice knocked on the door.

A woman came to the door and peeked outside. "What do you want?"

"I am looking for Darlene Grayson."

"Why?"

"Because I am hoping she can help me find Divya."

"Well, you're wrong go away."

Dice put her foot in the door and was grateful she didn't wear her soft sneakers. "I have just come from Dharma Grayson and we are concerned for Dee Dee's safety."

"Well, she's safe."

"Is she here?"

"No, no she's not."

"Listen I just need a couple of minutes of your time. Please."

The woman glared at Dice. "Dharma sent you here?"

Dice nodded.

She opened the door a little wider. "Fine come in." Darlene peeked outside looking up and down the street. Grabbing Dice by the arm Darlene pulled her inside. "They are watching."

"Who?" Dice tried to peek out the door as Darlene closed the door.

"The people that are after Dee Dee, it wasn't safe for her here anymore. I have a friend that lives about 45 minutes outside of the city in a little town. You passed it as you came into the Sault."

"I see. When was she here last?"

"Dee Dee was here a couple weeks ago but then two guys showed up on my door in suits asking a lot of questions. I let on that I didn't know anything and that I hadn't seen her. They asked my neighbors and a couple of them nosey bodies spilled their guts. I want to kick them in the ass … no one can mind their own business around here. Hell, if I need help shoveling my driveway, I can't get anyone to see me out there struggling with that. My cousin comes for a visit and I'm like some Hollywood diva. I tell you I am so sick of some of them."

"Dharma mentioned that you may have gotten married and moved south."

"Ha! I met that guy online and he was nothing like his profile. He came up here and moved in with me. I couldn't get rid of his ass until I started inviting some of my biker friends over. Seriously they ride motorcycles and dress in leather. He thought they were a gang and couldn't get out of here fast enough. I met them online too." She laughed. Her laughter bounced off the walls. Dice couldn't help but smile.

"That's certainly one way to get rid of unwanted house guests."

"Oh yes, he complained that I kept that off my profile. The funny thing is most of these people are working professionals that just like to take their bikes out for a ride every once in a while. We started a book club, Nancy is a great baker so it was so worth that woman bringing over her scones."

"Did Dee Dee talk to you at all about Linda Barnett?"

Darlene suddenly looked a little uncomfortable she gave a little nod. Dice almost missed it. "Can you tell me what she said?"

"About four weeks ago we were sitting in the back yard, having some beers and barbequing some burgers and sausages. It was later in the evening. Her idiot boyfriend went with a friend to get more beer. While they were gone, I think she had one too many to drink, to begin with. She started bawling her face off that she basically killed her boss. When I asked her what was she talking about she blubber on about how the two of them were working on this project. It was mainly Linda's baby Dee Dee was still the student. But they went somewhere a couple times, not sure where. She was sobbing pretty hard and I could just make out a word or two, something about a globe, and another place, they traveled there twice and the last time she sent Linda there without telling her. Now she was trapped there."

"Did you find out where there was?"

"No … she wasn't making any sense. I don't know I think she said at some point they ate worms. Dee Dee is really quite brilliant you know half the time when she is sober you don't know what the hell she is talking about. When she was drunk it was even worse. Especially lately, I thought I could protect her. I don't know if she's still there. But I can give you the address."

"I would appreciate that. What can you tell me about what she did?"

"Oh I really don't know she worked for that lady Linda Barnett she was in the news a while ago. She had disappeared. I don't think Dee Dee was behind it. She couldn't have hurt her. Don't get me wrong, I just have a feeling that she is involved somehow and that is scary for us all. I know Dee Dee feels responsible somehow but if you knew Dee Dee you would know that is nothing new. She always takes on other people's burdens."

"So she may not have anything to do with Linda Barnett's disappearance then?" Dice knew Darlene needed to hear that, even if she was beginning to wonder how much Divya was involved in Linda's disappearance.

"You know," she paused and looked at Dice hopefully. "You could be right."

"Alright thank you so much for your help," Dice got up and took the address down and then gave Darlene her business card. "If someone comes here looking for her, or if you hear from her, call me."

Darlene grabbed Dice in a hug, and a tear slipped down her face.

"Please help her, she's family. The girls are the only family I have left. We don't get together as much as I would like to, but I would be ...," her voice caught in her throat.

"I understand," Dice hugged the woman back. "I will do everything I can to help Dee Dee out. I'll have her call you when we get this sorted out."

"Thanks Dice."

"You're welcome." Leaving Darlene Grayson's home Dice couldn't help having that feeling creep up her spine of being watched it could be just the neighbors, she warned herself. The question was should she go directly to Divya's current address? Deciding to stop for a bite, she would decide after that. It was getting on about five or six. The sun was still up but she was bothered by the sense of feeling like she was being followed. Driving around she found a restaurant called Wacky Wings and pulled in. She wasn't familiar with this one, she wasn't sure if they had one down south or not. Taking her purse and laptop bag with her, she went inside and grabbed a table. Checking for Wi-Fi, they had it. Dice ordered chicken wings and a salad off the menu.

Finding the friends' location where Divya was staying at Dice was pleased to note that it wasn't that far away and it was on the way back to where she wanted to be. If she went after eating, she could catch Diyva and then maybe they could drive overnight back to Toronto. The food was good she couldn't complain. Finally, she shook off that feeling of being watched. Could it have been just Darlene's nosy neighbors? Enjoying a cup of Earl Grey tea, Dice checked her email and then the weather website. No rain or bad weather ... perfect for driving. She suddenly thought of Muffin and Charlotte quite the odd couple, she had met just over a month ago, when she was working on her first case. Dice wondered if things didn't pan out with Divya Grayson perhaps she could take a swing by and see if Muffin and Charlotte had any options for her. She smirked to herself as she thought about telling them, hey don't know if you can help me but I have this client and his wife is trapped in another world. Not sure where it is or what it is, but look here's a snow globe. They would think she was off her rocker. No, that wasn't an option. Besides they were a strange couple ... Dice sighed and pondered the case. This was definitely turning out to be a weird one. Like one of those strange X-Files cases her Uncle Eric and Ty use to look into. Which made her think of her parents … she had found a file of her parents in that mess of weird cases. Dice wondered why Uncle Eric had a file of her parents. How long did he have that? Why couldn't she just have a regular case? One where someone goes missing and they are found dead or alive … but no aliens or weird crap … unless it's strange human stuff. She wasn't making any sense she thought maybe she was feeling tired? Decisions … decisions …should she continue on and just get this done one way or another or grab a room? Packing up her laptop, she grabbed up her belongings and paid for her meal.

"I hoped you enjoyed your dinner," the young woman smiled at her.

"Yes, I did, thank you. Do you know if you guys have a location in Southern Ontario?"

"Yes, we do, there are currently seven locations in Ontario, two here in the Sault, Timmins, Sudbury, North Bay, Brantford and Mississauga," she smiled cheerily.

"Thank you," Dice took the receipt and tucked it in a special envelope since it was an expense she had while working on this case. Dice stepped outside. The sun was shining brightly it was still early evening. If she checked into a hotel, she would be up for hours driving herself crazy with thoughts about this case. The need to know and to find Divya Grayson outweighed anything else.

Checking her car over there were no flats or slashed tires. She still wondered who would do that. If someone wanted her off a case there would be the slashing of the tires or threat of some kind and usually a note went with it, just to make sure she didn't misunderstand. Chuckling to herself, she got in and plugged her iPod back in adjusting the sound and then checking her mirrors. She didn't have that feeling of being followed or watched. Just the anticipation of finding Divya and asking her questions hopefully getting a better understanding of what that woman did or think she did and how it all tied into Linda Barnett's disappearance.

Dice headed for Highway 17 heading back in the direction of Sudbury. It wasn't long before she found the turn off for Pumpkin Point Road West. There were a lot of trees, Dice wondered what she was driving into. The road was much smaller at least it was paved with asphalt, the homes were so far apart, if felt like she fell into another world, she thought with a smirk. Trees over hung the roadway creating a green canopy that reminded Dice of going to her Uncle's cabin. Then she came out to a clearing of farmland, passing a road that was less developed looking than the one she was on, called Lakeview Road, she kept heading south on Pumpkin Road. She came to a cross roads and looked at her notes turning right on to Point Drive, finding 228 Point Drive was easy and she was grateful the sun was still up since there didn't seem to be a whole lot of street lamps around. Pulling into the gravel driveway, Dice turned off her music and listened as the stone crunched under her tires. Parking, she turned her car off and grabbed her purse and laptop bag. Heading over to the front steps, the house was a one-storey bungalow, with chipped weathered paint. It was a faded blue and white as she stepped up to the three steps each one creaking under her weight, she crossed over to the front door in two steps, knocking on the door she looked around. It looked like the grass was recently mowed and there was a patch of flowers surrounded by a bed of blue and white painted rocks. She could hear the water lapping up against the shore. It was really quite quiet. It reminded her of her uncle's cabin. A cool breeze swept in from the lake playing with the chimes causing them to swayed creating music to keep her company.

The door opened a crack. Divya Grayson peeked out at her, her soft grey eyes and pale face looked tired, worried and alone.

"Sorry Lee is not here right now she went to town because her daughter is having a baby. She'll be back sometime tomorrow evening," she said in a small voice.

"I'm not here to see Lee, Divya Grayson I am here to see you."

Her face dropped and Dice wasn't sure how much more this girl could pale. "Please don't hurt me."

"I'm not here to hurt you I need to speak with you. Please let me in so we can sit down and talk about Linda Barnett."

"Who are you?" she backed up a little as Dice moved forward.

"I'm Dice Maddox, I am a private investigator working for Kyle Barnett. Darlene told me where to find you."

She moved aside, "Darlene sent you here?"

Dice nodded as she ducked inside. Taking her shoes off at the door, the little house was carpeted from wall to wall, a lush dark gray.

Divya closed the door behind her. "I didn't kill her."

"I know. So who's after you?"

"I don't know they said they were with the government but I'm not sure."

"So let's talk."

"How about some tea?"

"Sure that would be fine," Dice followed Divya out to the kitchen. "Do you prefer Divya or Dee Dee?"

"You can call me Dee Dee, the only people that call me that is my family but if Darlene told you I was here, you are like family." Dee Dee went over to the counter and filled up the kettle then put it on the stove, turning the burner on she got out a couple of mugs and tea bags. "Do you like milk or sugar?"

"A little of both please," Dice turned on her mini recorder. "Were you and Linda close?"

Dee Dee nodded turning and looking at Dice her eyes were welled up with tears. "That's the worst part of this. Yes, we were, she was like a mother to me. Linda is amazing. I feel so bad for Kyle. I know how much he loves her. I wanted to tell him the truth but I couldn't. I knew how crazy it all sounded. No one would believe me I would be sent to the psych ward for sure." Tears tumbled down her face as she wiped them away with the back of her hand she shook her head. "I still can't believe we did the things we did."

The kettle started whistling, she sniffled and poured them some hot water. Bringing the mugs over, she grabbed a little milk carton and a small bowl of sugar. She didn't speak again until she got them a couple spoons and sugar cookies. Sitting down, she looked at Dice. Dice noticed how young this girl was. She was only 19, still full of hope and wonder.

"It was my fault."

"How?"

She heaved a sigh. "I saw Linda earlier that day and we agreed that we needed to patent the project. I was so mean to her. Before she disappeared I was upset because I didn't think I was going to get any credit on the project. I mean I worked hard and yes it was mainly Linda's idea. She would have gotten there eventually even without my help. It was my mind and my eyes that got her there faster. I got mad at her and had those pictures made up of her. I posted them everywhere. I also had Mil accuse her of trying to rape him. Then I found out she had put my name on the preliminary work and intended to give me credit as well for helping her with the project. I felt like such an ass. I should never have doubted her. I told her she was really hurt, I felt so bad but she hugged me and told me it didn't change anything. That was our meeting that we had before she disappeared. I was supposed to catch the bus to go to my sister's house. It was her birthday and I hadn't seen her in a while. Since I missed the bus, I went back to the university it was just a few blocks away. I stopped in intending to just get a picture of myself with the machine and the paper work with my name added to the project. I wanted to show my sister."

"Makes sense," Dice nodded.

"I shouldn't have gone there."

"Why? What happen? How did Linda disappear?"

"Wait," Dee Dee got up and went to her bag that was in the living room. Picking through it, she pulled out her cell phone. "This," she said as she walked back to the kitchen. Showing Dice a picture of herself and a large machine it was about eight feet by six, a computer was mounted to the side of it attached to a console that had wires and hoses running from the computer to the box and God only knows where else they went. Then she flipped to another one of just the machine, a couple more of Linda who was holding a necklace in her hand that looked like an odd shaped with a crystal mounted on to it. "That is how."

"What is it?"

"It's a Dexto …," she paused looking at Dice. "It is the key so to speak. Well, more like a homing device. Linda designed that. I had helped her with the programming and the calculations she was off by a bit that's why it hadn't worked before."

"Is this what you worked on in the science club?"

Dee Dee laughed and shook her head, "no way, no one knew about this. No one." Her eyes lit up. "What we did was open a doorway to another world. Another dimension. We not only proved that there are indeed different layers of reality but we went there and came back. No one has ever done what we did, no one."

Dice looked at the picture of the necklace Linda was holding in her hand. She was smiling at the camera, at Divya, her eyes were all bright and shining her face lit up like a Christmas tree. She looked like Divya did when she talked about their project. So excited so happy and yet she had no idea what was going to happen to her. Dice wondered if she would have continued with the project if someone told her not to … warning her of what was going to happen.

"Linda and I crossed over to another Earth reality. We stayed there for lunch and bought a couple of snow globes. Then came back here, it was amazing. Everything looked the same to a certain extent. There were some weird-looking buildings but everyone dressed the same as we do here. There were differences but they were so small." Dee Dee drifted off as she stared at her cup on the table. "I mean the cars were slightly different looking and people they looked so sad all the time. It was the same as here."

"You went back to that place twice?"

"We did," she smiled and nodded at Dice. "Linda wanted to go back again. "Kyle was being whiny and was talking about how Linda spent too much of her time at the university."

"Did he ever drop by?"

Dee Dee nodded, "all the time. He was so needy. Linda used to joke that she didn't need a real kid she had her husband to take care of. I knew she wanted a kid. Kyle couldn't give her one you know. She would have been the best mom ever. I mean it. She really would have. I don't think she will now. If I can find a way to get her back here I think she will be just happy to be back."

"So this other Earth-like place was it Earth?"

Dee Dee nodded, "yes it was … it was like being here but we weren't here there were definite differences. Even the air felt and smelled different there that sounds crazy I know but that is what it is."

"What happens next?"

"Well, I missed the bus, and I stopped at the lab to get a picture of myself with the machine. While I was there, I started cleaning up from the afternoon's science project. Some of the club members left a bit of a mess behind. I thought I would just help out. Professor Wren saw me there and stopped in. He asked me what I was doing there I told him I was just trying to clean up a bit because I know how Linda doesn't like a mess there. He wandered around and stopped at our machine. He was drinking a can of soda, coke or something. He rested it on the console, and started pressing the buttons. I had asked him not to do it. He then went on about how when he became Dean of the Science department he was going to get rid of the club. I told him that he could if he was lucky to get the position. Linda was a sure win for it. Everyone was talking about that even with the shit I stirred up for her she was still the front runner."

She paused and took a sip of tea, her face got sad, "If I had just caught the bus or waited at the bus station. We shouldn't have been there it was late. The sun had already gone down. Then he wouldn't have walked in there. He powered on the machine and it was kicked into high gear. I raced over and screamed at him, he just laughed. The machine flashed he jumped and knocked over his soda. The machine began to spark and catch on fire. Professor Wren grabbed the fire extinguisher and put the fire out. I thought it was done and gone for good. I thought when Linda saw that we were goners. Professor Wren told me I could go and catch my bus he would log the fire and let Linda know."

Dee Dee began to tear up again. "If I had just stayed at the bus station or caught that god damn bus, Linda would still be here."

Dice reached out and patted her on the shoulder. "So how do you know what happened to her?"

"I left and let Professor Wren take care of it and headed back over to the bus station. I caught the next bus and it was while I was at my sisters that I heard on the news about Linda's disappearance. They thought Kyle was responsible. I didn't connect it right away I'll have to admit it I really didn't. When I came back the lab was cleaned up all right but the machine was gone. I went to Professor Wren and he said it was broken so he let the cleaning crew take it out. Then when they didn't find Linda at all everyone was devastated. It was a couple months later when I thought about it. Then I realized that I might have sent her to that other Earth. I went to Professor Wren, he thought I was crazy and was just grieving over Linda being gone. He even offered to take me under his wing. It was okay for a while but then these guys saying they work with the government showed up. They noticed a surged here at the university ... a power surge. Yeah like the government really gives a shit if we get a power surge, when I asked them questions about that ... they arrested me and took me to some weird jail cell, or at least I thought I was at jail. They kept me there asking all kinds of questions and I told them I didn't know anything. They wanted to know what Linda and I were working on ... I lied. I did ... I lied and I stuck to my lie story. I wasn't telling them anything else but I overheard them talking in the hallway, they thought they had closed the door and that's when I heard there was atmospheric fluctuations just like the other two times. They knew I knew something. It was at the university in the lab and where Linda's abandon car was found. That confirmed it. It sealed the deal. I had unwittingly gotten rid of Professor Linda Barnett. She is the only friend I have, the only person in this world that understands me and I basically ... lack of a better word zapped her to a parallel universe. We have never been over there that long. I didn't think it would be possible for us to stay there I told you the air is different, they are different. I basically killed her."

"You don't know she's dead."

"Think about it every day. The probability that she survived in another atmosphere is not likely. I killed her."

"You don't know if she's dead."

"I don't."

"Alright, and you are certain she is over there? Or wherever?" Dice looked at Dee Dee.

She wiped the tears off her face and nodded mutely.

"Why didn't you build another machine?"

"I don't know how. Linda had made most of it. I just helped her with the programming of it. Her calculations were off a little, and when I say a little it was fractional. But enough to keep it from working properly, like I said I think she would have gotten it in time without my help."

"Hmm," Dice got up and walked over to the living room window the sun had gone down really fast. It was twilight and dark outside. As Dice thought not a lot of streetlights since no one was coming back here grabbing a few hours of sleep might be a good idea. "There just has to be something we can do."

"I have racked my brain over and over again but I just don't know how ...," Dee Dee's red eyes started to well up again.

"Okay, well you need to stop crying ... there just has to be a way."

"I'm open to suggestions," Dee Dee sniffed.

"I don't know. So we are quite sure she is off in this other dimension that you two went to already, not once but twice. What do we know? We know it can be done and has been done. Plus, it wasn't a fluke, because you did it on purpose twice."

She nodded. Dice walked over to the sofa and sat down. Dee Dee crossed over and sat down beside her. "We got to help her."

"I agree," Dice felt a headache coming on. "Wait how did you escape the government suits?"

Dee Dee looked at her and shook her head, "they just let me go.

When they arrested me I thought that was it. I am going to be held responsible for Linda's disappearance. After they badgered me for hours one guy came in … he was wearing a police uniform unhand-cuffed me from the table and re-cuffed my hands together then he took me for a ride in the back of a white van. He stopped two blocks from the university and let me out. Took the cuffs off and told me if I was smart I would disappear."

Dice couldn't believe her ears. "What did you do?"

"I went directly to the nearest bank machine grabbed some money and left town. I didn't even go back to my apartment. I just left and ever since I have been hiding out here and there. I don't think that cop was friends with the other ones. I don't know who he was."

"Could you pick him out in a line up or have a sketch artist give it a go?"

She shook her head no. "It was really strange, he stood in the light and I couldn't really see his face the whole time. When he dropped me off outside on the street it was dark. Again it is odd when you think about it but he may have known that … or was it just luck for him? I don't know but I couldn't tell you what he looked like. He had a deep voice that sounded really nice. It's funny but I bet he has a really great singing voice. I just don't know what he looks like."

"It was a long shot anyways." Something about that story felt unsettling to Dice. Last month she had met a police officer at the hospital, but no one knew who he was. Could it be the same guy? There were a few things that didn't sit well with her.

"You should stay here tonight. I can sleep on the sofa and you can sleep in the spare room," Dee Dee offered.

Dice shook her head. "No, I'll take the sofa. In the morning will you come back with me?"

"Where to?"

"Toronto, if we both go to Ishia Wren with this maybe we can all sit down and think this out."

"But I don't have any of the blue prints for the machine."

"Maybe you don't but I do."

"You? How did you get them?"

"I went by your apartment and met your neighbor when Larry your landlord sold all your stuff she grabbed up as much as she could."

"He sold my stuff! That asshole," she ranted and began to pace back and forth.

"I have some of it in my trunk for you but it wasn't much." Dice got up and went over to her bags. Opening the bag, she pulled out the schematics and blue prints. "Do you think this will help us?"

"Yes," Dee Dee's eyes went wide. "Oh my God Dice I can't believe you have this."

"Don't thank me, it was your neighbor Silva Harris."

"Oh I have always liked Silva. She is such a great person."

Dice pulled out the snow globe and showed Dee Dee. She reached out and couldn't take her eyes off it. Gently she took it and turned it over in her hands. "We had to bring something back we just had to. Something just to let us know, that we weren't dreaming about the other place. Look at this thing. Isn't it amazing? This is a replica of a famous art gallery in the other universe. So amazing ... I don't know what they built it out of but it was the strangest material I have ever seen. Linda has one too. It was something. Maybe, we shouldn't have brought it back ... it doesn't belong here and yet here it is. Perhaps, that's why she was sent there? Do you think?" she looked up at Dice wide-eyed. "We shouldn't have played God ... displacement of energy and space, it's like ... karma, bad ... very bad karma coming back to bite us in the ass for doing what we did. We had no right to disrupt their atmosphere and by doing so, we have created a displacement overlap ... we could have even created a temporal paradox. This is very bad."

"I get some of what you're saying, but when you say bad once we can get her back that will correct it won't it?"

"No, it won't and it could have serious repercussion in the future. What if the person that is Linda in that universe hasn't been working on anything like our project what if she did something else for a living but then our Linda ends up over there and starts working on the project to get back here. Yet, when she starts working on that project she is creating a displacement overlap, because now over there, someone else was supposed to be working on this project. She shouldn't be over there, it disrupts everything the longer she is there the more trouble we could be creating for their universe and ours. It starts out on a miniature scale that escalates, it's like a small snowball starting at the top of a big mountain, and once it starts down the mountain it starts to build ... and builds until you have this really large snowball."

"So what are you saying we're going to get run over by this snowball?"

"Yes quite possibly so, as long as you are speaking figuratively."

"Well, of course," the thought of a large snowball coming out of nowhere and mowing them down created a nice image for Dice. "Okay wait do you think by opening up this doorway to get Linda back it's going to cause a chain reaction of some kind?"

"I honestly don't know. We never really thought about it before. We were too busy thinking about if we could do it. Not really thinking about should we do this," Dee Dee handed the snow globe back to Dice and looked at it as if it was something poisonous. Dice stuffed it back into her purse and then turned back to Dee Dee, who was handing her back the diagrams for the machine. Dice took them and put them back in her bag.

"Alright, I had a long day, why don't we get some rest and sleep on it? When we get up in the morning we can try to figure out a plan, does that sound okay to you?"

Dee Dee looked at Dice and nodded, "Thank you for finding me."

"Well, I'm happy you wanted to be found. There has to be something we can do. But for now let's get some rest."

Dee Dee nodded, "I'll get you some pillows and blanket. If you want to change there is a bathroom down the hall."

"Maybe I will," Dice grabbed her keys and headed back outside. It was quiet and very dark just the light from the open doorway. Dice went over and grabbed her overnight bag, then locked up the car tight. She didn't get the feeling of anyone watching her this time. From where she parked no one would see her from the road anyways. That and it was so dark she couldn't see in front of herself. The moon wasn't out, just a bunch of glittery stars that laid out in the night sky. Crickets chirped, an owl hooted there were other nighttime animal noises that were very distracting. Heading back inside, she hurried so she wouldn't let all the mosquitoes in.

Closing the door behind her, she locked it then headed down the hall to the bathroom where she changed her clothes, brushed her hair and pulled it back, then washed her makeup off and brushed her teeth. Coming out of the bathroom, she found Dee Dee had made up the sofa for her and was sitting in the chair beside it waiting.

"Wow you look so young like me."

"I'm pushing thirty," she shrugged.

"How long have you been a detective?"

"Started when I was eighteen," Dice sat down on the sofa.

"Really that is amazing. Are you married?"

Dice laughed and shook her head, "No came close to it once but I really like being single."

"I see guy problems," Dee Dee smiled.

Dice laughed, "yeah, something like that. The guy that I like is with someone else, my ex would like another shot but he's an ex for a reason right. So yeah … better off without."

"But you're so pretty."

Dice looked at her and frowned. "No looks have nothing to do with it. Being in my kind of work it takes someone special to date me. I may look cute and cuddle on the outside but like everyone else I got my own demons I have to deal with. So what happened to your boyfriend?"

"Milton, I don't know when I left I didn't say anything to him."

"No, the other one?"

"The other one?" Dee Dee looked at her as if she was crazy.

"Yeah, your sister and cousin said you had another one."

"Oh no, it was just a guy I was hanging out with. He wasn't boyfriend material or anything."

"Oh I see, well you're young yet there really is no rush."

"Sure, you sound like Dharma now."

"She's right." Dice laid back and tucked her feet up under her on the sofa. "So how bad is this? I mean with the objects and people jumping from one universe to another parallel universe?"

"Well, there is one theory where nothing really happens. Then in others there is a balance of energy and a theory that we all resonate and vibrate at a certain level, traipsing off to another parallel universe. If they don't have the same or similar or even in the same range of vibration then it's like saying butterflies flapping their wings all at the same time creates a typhoon in another part of the world."

"I don't get it."

"Okay, have you ever been at a pond or lake?"

Dice nodded.

"Well, it's like visiting a still pond of water and then dropping a rock in it. The rock sinks down to the bottom of the pond and mingles with the dirt but the surface of the water has ripples of water spreading out from where the rock entered the water."

"Is Linda the rock or the ripples?"

"She's both ... she's causing a displacement of molecules wherever she is. She is the ripples, everything she does is creating more ripples in the water."

"Okay so I see even getting her back can't stop the ripples but it will eventually die away."

"In theory yes, if she is still alive."

"It's been a year. How many ripples could she have made."

"It is endless."

"If we leave her there it causes more problems, if we bring her back ... oh this is confusing I am so tired. I heard you thought something came back with you?"

"I thought so."

"What was it?"

"I don't know."

"How do you know then if something came back?"

"I really don't know. Tell me about your guy friend, who is dating someone else? What is he like?"

Dice yawned and stretched out, "he's a hot mess. I shouldn't be telling you this ... I haven't told anyone this ... one minute he's telling me he's breaking it off with his new girlfriend and the next, he wants to go on a double date with me and my ex. Like how is that conducive to anything? I mean you are dating someone else. End of story. Quit kissing me."

"Oh he kissed you. Is he cute?"

"Does it matter if he's cute or not ... I just wish he would get it right. Pick a side and stick to it. I'm only human," her mind felt cloudy as sleep began to take its toll.

"You guys slept together didn't you?"

"Yeah, but that's before he started dating this whack job. She's crazy, she came to my office and threaten me." Stretching her whole body Dice felt her eye lids get really heavy, she mumbled, "I wouldn't be surprised if it was her, who slash my tire."

"She sounds crazy. Good night Dice," Dee Dee turned the light off. Dice felt a blanket get pulled up over her shoulder and she was grateful for the tuck in. Sean Larke was the last thing she wanted to think about before she went to sleep but thanks to Dee Dee that's who was lurking in the dark recesses of her mind.

CHAPTER FOURTEEN

Dice woke up feeling a little disoriented; looking around she couldn't remember where she was at first. Sitting up, she saw her purse lying on the kitchen table and remembered she was at Darlene's friend home where Dee Dee was staying. Stretching and rubbing her eyes, she listened for any sounds of life in the home. Dee Dee was probably still sleeping. Getting up, she stretched. Folded up the blankets and tucked them at the end of the sofa with the pillows piled on them. Walking over to the window, she peeked out and saw her car still sitting there. Checking the rest of the home out, she found Dee Dee sleeping quietly in one room and decided to go for a quick run. Stretch the legs and get some fresh air into the lungs. They had a busy day ahead of them. Quickly changing into her running clothes Dice was standing outside on the porch filling her lungs with fresh clean air and stretching. She started off down the road.

What a weird case this was. First Linda Barnett who they thought was dead may very well be alive somewhere. How crazy was that thought. The machine to bring her back was broken and dismantled. The only person who could create or recreate the machine was trapped in a parallel universe or so we think. Could be way off, she could be dead in a parallel universe and being or have been dissected by their morticians. That thought sent a shiver down her spine. What a horrible way to go, she thought.

They had to get back to Toronto and find Ishia Wren he was the only one who could help … or was he? Ty introduced her to a pair of individuals that were quite unique. Muffin and Charlotte ... why hadn't she thought of going to them first? They were on the way. Plus, if they didn't know how to fix this maybe they might know someone who could help them. It was a possibility. Feeling really good about her decision she started heading back to Dee Dee's. Coming into the yard Dice noticed the lake it was crystal blue and lapped up against the shore invitingly.

Entering the house it was still quiet. Dice packed up everything and had the car ready to go as Dee Dee came out of the spare room rubbing her eyes. "Wow you get up early," she mumbled.

"I do and it's a good thing ... I have a couple friends that might help us with our Linda problem."

"You?" Dee Dee looked at her suspiciously. "Have friends that can help us out by getting Linda back from another dimension?"

Dice laughed, "Don't be so intellectually snobbish. I have friends in high and low places." Dice winked at her. "Get ready I want to hit the road in five minutes."

"Five minutes?" She squeaked.

"Yes five minutes," Dice nodded. "I'll buy us some breakfast once we hit the road."

Dee Dee disappeared into the spare room and re-emerge fifteen minutes later. Dice sat in the chair waiting not so patiently.

"Sorry, I just wanted to make sure I got everything. And then I realized I didn't come here with much."

"Well, let's see what we can do about that today." Dee Dee wrote a note for the owner of the bungalow thanking her for her hospitality and then followed Dice out to the car.

Dice followed the road out to Highway 17 then headed for Sudbury. The first Tim Horton's they came to they went through drive through and each got a breakfast sandwich and a coffee for the road.

In between bites, Dice asked, "How did you get interested in Science?"

"I always loved science. In grade school I entered my first science fair in grade one it was a volcano. Then I was hooked. I entered every science show; I had a little science area in the kitchen and drove my family crazy. I read everything I could by the time I hit high school. It was just something that I understood a little better than other things and I went with it. What about you?"

"What about me? I wasn't really into science," Dice played the evasive card.

"No, I mean detective work?"

"I don't know I guess I like solving puzzles, it was something that kind of fell into my lap."

"That's amazing, so who do you work for?"

"My clients, I am the sole proprietor of my own business."

"That really is amazing. I think that guy Sean is crazy," Dee Dee looked out the window.

Dice was sure she didn't mention his name to Dee Dee and she was pretty sure she didn't talk in her sleep. How did she know about him? They drove in silence for some time. Dice stopped for gas, and to use the bathroom, she grabbed another coffee, and plugged in her iPod.

Within a half hour they were on the other side of Sudbury, Dice's curiosity couldn't take it anymore. "How did you know Sean?"

"Last night you were really tired as you were falling asleep I heard you mention his name. You were really upset with him. For someone you said you weren't that interested in, you certainly sounded like he means a little more than you are willing to admit."

"Please don't bring him up again. I'm not that fond of him at the moment," Dice felt slightly irritated.

Dice felt herself get lost in her own thoughts. Sean Larke was haunting the back of her mind. She really needed to call an exterminator to rid herself of him. Forget it Dice Maddox he's got a girlfriend, he's not that into you, the little voice in her mind taunted her.

Passing Perry Sound, she couldn't believe she was close to her Uncle Eric's cabin. Muffin and Charlotte lived close by. Dice wasn't sure how welcome she would be bringing an outsider with her. But she found the farmhouse and pulled into the driveway, which was empty.

"Your friend lives here?" Dee Dee looked at the place skeptically. "I don't think they are home."

Dice grabbed her bag and purse. "Come on," she nudged Dee Dee.

Getting out of her car, she walked over to the door and pressed the buzzer. Dee Dee reluctantly got out and dragged her feet across the gravel. "This feels weird."

"Dice Maddox, while I live and breathe, is that really you?" a familiar voice popped over the intercom.

"Hi Muffin, I hope I am not catching you at a bad time."

Dee Dee's eyebrows narrowed as she mouthed the word, "Muffin?"

"Who's your friend?"

"Divya Grayson she's a scientist," Dice looked over at Dee Dee.

"Really? Chemical or otherwise?"

"Otherwise ... physics."

"Really? Do come in."

The door opened. Dice proceeded down the long white hallway with Dee Dee in tow. Glancing back, she loved the confused and bewildered look that Dee Dee was sporting and thought back to when Ty brought her here. She must have had a very similar look on her face.

"What is this place?"

"Oh wait it gets better," they reached the end of the hall and the door was open a crack. Coming out the other side. It was just as Dice remembered it. Muffin stood by to greet her.

Grinning from ear to ear his eyes seemed to sparkle. "I knew it ... I knew you would be back." He hugged her. "So Miss Dice Maddox ... private investigator ... would you care for a drink?"

"I think we will need something stronger than tea this time."

His eyes went wide and seemed to glitter with excitement, "I knew you were a keeper," he grinned at her.

"That is debatable." Within minutes they were seated in the living room Charlotte brought out some drinks and sat down next to Dice. "Dice it's so lovely to see you."

"Wow, what are you guys some kind of rock stars?" Dee Dee asked.

Charlotte looked at Muffin and they both laughed. "Oh my baby can be anything she wants to be," Muffin winked at Charlotte.

"Right back at you my love Muffin," she grinned then turned to Dice leaning in close. "What can we do for you sweetie?"

"This might sound crazy but I was hired by my client to find his missing wife. She has been missing for just over a year now. Presumed dead, but we aren't sure. Dee Dee, or Divya was telling me about a project that she and Mrs. Linda Barnett were working on, also known as Professor Linda Barnett. She was a teacher at one of the universities in Toronto. Anyways Divya and Linda discovered a way to travel through to another dimension." Dice pulled out the schematics and blue prints passing them to Muffin who looked at them and nodded. "They built this machine and tested it out on themselves twice. Bringing back this," Dice pulled out the snow globe, and passed it to Charlotte who looked a little more interested in the snow globe. She was wearing this necklace that acts like a receptor or a key when this machine is activated. The night she went missing the machine was unwittingly turned on and activated. She was gone. The machine also got destroyed and we can't get her back."

"So she's been in this other dimension for how long? A year?"

"A little over a year," Dice corrected.

"I see. And you want me to what … zap her back here?"

Dice wanted to say yes but what were the odds that he was capable of doing that? "Can you?"

He grinned. "Tell me more … start from the beginning."

Dee Dee began from where she and Linda were working on their project, to getting it working. Muffin asked her some point-blank questions about the project that only Dee Dee knew how to answer. Even listening in to their conversation Dice felt like they were talking another language.

Afterwards, Dee Dee was wrapping up the story ending it with them standing outside their barn house. Muffin nodded. He held the papers that had the drawings and the strange snow globe. "Come with me," he had a twinkle in his eye.

Dee Dee looked at Dice who got up and began to follow Muffin. Dee Dee followed her lead and Charlotte smirked as she brought up the rear. Muffin led down a small hallway and they stopped at a door. He placed his hand on the door and where his hand was and only where his hand was on the door glowed blue. Then he pulled it back and the door slid open to an elevator. Dice had to know where it led. Stepping on, no one needed encouragement at this point. Dice watched as once everyone was on he did it again, there was a small square box and he placed his hand over it. Only the spots where his hand rested lit up blue. A keypad appeared he punched in a couple of numbers Dice thought it was 15. The doors closed and they began to descend.

"How many floors do you have here?" Dee Dee asked.

"A few," Muffin grinned.

Dice noticed that Charlotte was giving him the eye and didn't seem to be amused. He just smiled back at her ... like I got this don't worry babe.

The doors slide open to another hallway. The lights began to turn on row by row and the hallway that didn't look so big was illuminated to reveal something else. The white walls were wider than Dice had thought and it went on for a bit. Muffin stepped off, followed by Dice, Dee Dee and then, Charlotte. They walked until they came to the end again there was a muted doorway. No handles no indication that it was a doorway, it looked like a wall panel. He placed his hand on the door. It lit up blue only where his hand was. Then the door slid open. Inside there was a large table in the middle of the room that was a console, it had buttons, switches, dials and it looked like something that you would expect to find on a spaceship in a movie. Muffin went over to it and pressed a few buttons things started to light up on it. He pulled the sheets of paper out that Dice had given him, scanning each one and shuffling to the next he frown and looked up at them.

"Young lady I hope you remember the numbers for the entry point you and Professor Barnett used."

Dice looked at Dee Dee who mutely nodded staring wide eyes at the console.

"Well, come here then," Muffin coaxed.

Dice stood planted where she had entered the room watching in awe. Charlotte stepped closer to her. "He really shouldn't have shown you ladies this room. I have nothing against you Dice, I am concerned that we don't know her."

Dice glanced at Charlotte who watched Muffin and Dee Dee enter numbers into a machine that Dice didn't think should exist on any universal plane. They were at it for a bit, at least an hour and then they nodded at each other looking over at Dice and Charlotte who watched, Dice watched with suspicion and Charlotte watch with little interest. This surely couldn't bring Linda back it was absurd. Wasn't it?

Muffin grinned and pressed a button. A small platform rose up out of the floor and a glass cylinder there was large enough to cover the platform came from the ceiling the platform stopped when it rose about a foot up. The cylinder came down over it. The platform's floor lit up a bright green. There was bright flash of light that filled the room and then as it died down inside the glass cylinder was Professor Linda Barnett, looking as shock as Dice staring back with her jaw gaping open. Muffin pressed a few more buttons and the glass cylinder began to lift up and the platform began to slowly lower.

"How? Where am I? Dee Dee is that you?" her attention focused on Dee Dee. "Is that really you?"

Dee Dee looked like she had just won the lottery she raced around the console and flung her arms around Linda's neck. "I didn't think I was ever going to see you again!"

"Am I really home?" she looked around the room at the others.

Charlotte hugged Dice, "Oh I love happy endings. Come on let's go make some lunch and have some tea."

Dice nodded and allowed Charlotte to nudge her into action. They headed down the long hallway until they reached the elevators this time Charlotte placed her hand on the door and it slid open. Linda and Dee Dee were in tow behind them. Dee Dee was explaining what happened in the lab with Ishia Wren. Getting on the elevator all four of them. Charlotte didn't wait for Muffin, she put her hand on the console and it lit up blue then she pressed 1 on the keypad. The doors slid shut and they rose up to the main floor.

"So who are you two then?" Linda turned to Dice and Charlotte.

"I am a private investigator hired by your husband to find you."

"I'm a friend of Muffin's and Dice," Charlotte smiled sweetly.

"Who's Muffin? Who's Dice?" Linda looked a little confused.

"I'm Dice, the man downstairs is Muffin." The doors slid open and they entered the little hallway again. Everyone followed Charlotte to the kitchen.

Linda began telling them about how she was in another parallel universe and that it was amazing once she adjusted to it.

"Did you meet yourself there?"

"No, the version of me, was killed in a car accident a few years ago. She was a scientist too and married to Kyle in that world. He was so different there." Linda sat down at the counter and watched as Charlotte began washing and then cutting strips of chicken.

"Different how?" Dee Dee asked

"You were right the air was different I can feel the difference again now that I am back it's not as sweet as it was over there."

"What did you do?"

"After Kyle chased me down and confronted me and I explained what happened, he never questioned me. It was so strange. He kept me safe. He was different not as needy. It was refreshing."

"Did you meet me there?" Dee asked.

"Yes, I did," she turned to Dice. "I met you there too."

Dice didn't want to know she felt a little uncomfortable talking about herself from another world.

"I became a teacher at the university. There were some social differences that I managed to pick up on. I don't know if it was better there or if here is better. I never thought I would get back here though."

"Were you trying to get back here?"

"In all honesty I was at first but gave up about a month ago. I had built the machine and was entering the coordinates. Then I just stopped. I have to admit I changed my mind. Kyle made me change my mind. I have never felt so safe in my life."

"Sorry, it was a one way trip we can't send you back," Charlotte sprinkled season over the chicken and threw it in large frying pan, turning on the stove she put it on the burner as she gathered some fresh veggies and began washing and cutting them up she threw them in with the chicken.

Dice wondered how true that was. It seems relevant that if they could just pull her out of another universe they could send her back with the same machine. Then again she was no expert in that field she reminded herself. Watching Linda, she seemed to be glowing, so radiant and alive. There had to be something in the air over there.

While the chicken was cooking Dice watch Charlotte who didn't seem bothered by the fact that her boyfriend just pulled a human being from another universe and that person was now sitting in her kitchen like nothing was weird about it. She just pulled out some premixed salad and filled up five plates then threw the chicken mixture on top of the salad for each of the plates. She turned off the stove and set the table placing the plates there. Muffin came in and turned on the kettle. He got out five mugs and proceeded to make them drinks.

Dee Dee and Linda headed over to the table, Linda was discussing some of the things there, and Dee Dee was very engaged in the conversation. Dice, on the other hand, watched as Muffin made tea. Three of the cups he used a different kind of tea bag than the other two. He poured the hot water and brought the cups to the table. Dee Dee, Linda and herself all shared the same tea.

"This is a special tea I want to share with you ladies, I know you will love it." He sat down and they began to eat. As they ate Dice watched as Linda and Dee Dee became quieter with every sip of tea. Dice lifted her cup and smelled it, she wasn't sure what was in it but she was pretty sure she didn't want it.

"You don't like the tea?" Charlotte asked.

Reluctantly she took a sip and it was truly delicious, she took another sip and watched the others drink, suddenly forgetting why she didn't want to drink it in the first place.

"Well, it was really lucky for you that Dee Dee and Dice came along and found you this morning Linda," Muffin said.

"Found me?" she seemed a little lost.

Dice wasn't sure what he was talking about either.

"Yes. Outside down the road, when she showed up here we were more than happy to let you in and have lunch with you ladies but it was Dice with her keen eye that spotted you wandering around."

Dice nodded, wait that wasn't right, she told herself. No, I didn't find her. Did I?"

"Lunch was wonderful," Dee Dee smiled.

"Yes, didn't you say Dee Dee was asleep in the back seat?"

"Yes, I was," Dee Dee smiled and slugged back the tea. "Oh, that was delicious can I have some more."

"We have company dear," Charlotte nodded to Muffin.

"I'll go take care of that," Muffin got up and disappeared.

"Yes, I was driving down the highway I found Dee Dee and we were going to go back to town to tell Kyle something … I forget."

"It doesn't matter," Linda waved her hand away. "I don't know how I got out there … I don't really remember too much. I have a bit of a headache, though."

"I think it must have happened when you fell and hit your head," Charlotte offered her.

"You know something I think you are right," she nodded at Charlotte.

"Well, Dice Maddox you solved another case. How brilliant you are," Charlotte smiled at her.

Dice wanted to remember something but it was … it was a blank. It couldn't have been that important, she chided to herself.

Muffin reappeared with two men wearing black suits and looked very much like government agents of some kind. They looked a little disorientated and confused. "Honey, I found some new friends."

Muffin helped them over to the stools by the counter. They took the seats and were grateful. Muffin was pouring them some tea and they slug the cups back. Dice helped Charlotte clear the table. She was going to help her with the dishes but Charlotte refused. On the shelf in the kitchen near the sink there were some cookbooks that looked like they have never been used and some unusual trinkets. Dice couldn't help being drawn to the strange snow globe, picking it up she turned it over in her hand, there were no markings to indicate where the building that was inside it was from, nor where the snow globe was made. The building looked a little alien, Dice couldn't fathom that alien worlds would create snow globes for tourists it seem absurd. Putting it back on the shelf next to the metal horse, or was it pewter? Her fingers grazed the horse and it felt hot to the touch, it felt like it was vibrating as well. It had to be her imagination she pulled her hand back not wanting to know the origins of it. Muffin and Charlotte were a strange pair, she couldn't remember why she stopped by today. After finding Linda wandering around on the side of the road, it was strange to stop here. Looking over at Muffin, he was in deep conversations with a couple of his friends. They looked like accountants or businessmen.

"Well, we should get going, I need to get Linda back to her husband," Dice smiled.

"Take the quick way out," Muffin smiled and there was a back door that she hadn't noticed before, it must have been there ... doors just didn't appear out of nowhere. Dee Dee and Linda followed Dice out to her car.

Linda hugged Dice, "I can't thank you enough for stopping when you did and finding me out here. God only knows where I would have ended up."

"You've been gone for over a year ... are you telling me you don't know where you were?"

Linda's eyebrows furrowed in heavy thought and she shook her head slowly. "No, no I don't ... it is the strangest thing but I have no memories except that we had a book club meeting and we were discussing 'To Kill A Mockingbird,' by Harper Lee."

"My god Linda that was a month before you disappeared. You

don't remember anything else?" Dee Dee looked at her wide eyed.

"No," she shook her head.

Dice was about to get in her car when Charlotte came out, "Dice wait!"

Dice walked over to her, "yes?"

"You were all drugged. Muffin didn't give you as much as the others. But I can't tell you why. Just that you did a good job today and remember we are always here for you. We are your friends."

"Did I really find Linda on the side of the road?"

Charlotte shook her head no, "but stick to that story. Also Dee Dee doesn't have a home to go back to so, she will have to stay with Linda."

"Charlotte who were the guys in the kitchen?"

"They were agents following you. Don't worry Muffin is taking good care of them. They won't be bothering you again."

"I don't want to know do I?"

"I just couldn't let you go thinking you found her on the side of the road because I know you … you wouldn't settle for that. You would have been back out here trying to figure it out."

"A lot you know … I don't care … I found her and she's going home."

"Oh Dice," Charlotte grinned. "I know you really think that at this moment, but I think I know you well enough to know that wouldn't have worked.

"Why did I come here to you?"

"For us to help you find Linda, silly girl."

Dice turned and started for her car.

"See you later," Charlotte called after her.

"No, you won't," Dice grumbled under her breath. Getting in she was grateful that she found Linda and headed back to town. It was getting late in the evening and the sun had set when she showed up on Kyle Barnett's front door. Dice rang the bell and it took a few minutes before he came to the door. When he did he almost fell over.

"Linda?" he gasped. He took a step towards her and held out a shaking hand. "Linda, is that really you?"

She grinned from ear to ear and nodded. Linda was in his arms with her arms wrapped around his neck. They were kissing and crying. He was mumbling that he didn't think he would have ever seen her again. They all went inside. He wanted to know what had happened to her. He was just so grateful to have her back he wouldn't let her go, he kept her close by and was constantly touching her or holding her hand. Linda didn't seem to mind. After telling him their stories about finding her, they sat there in awe. It was such a good feeling to close this case. Dice was about to leave when Dee Dee got up with her. Then she remembered that Dee Dee didn't have an apartment to go back to.

"Dee Dee your landlord threw you out and I have a couple boxes with your stuff in my trunk," Dice told her.

"What? I'm homeless?" Dee Dee looked at Dice bewildered.

"You can stay with us Dee Dee," Linda was in earshot.

"Oh wow," Dee Dee looked like she was kicked in the stomach.

"Don't worry we will take care of you," Linda gave her a hug. "Let's get your things."

Dice led them out to her car and opened the trunk where the two boxes sat neatly tucked away. Linda took one and Dee Dee took the other one, they headed into Linda's home. Kyle hovered not leaving Linda's side.

"Wait!" Kyle Barnett came over to her as she was about to get in her car. "I can't thank you enough. I don't even care what the real story is. I am so happy to have my wife back." He hugged Dice, catching her off guard. Feeling a little uncomfortable, she smiled and patted him on the back.

"I'll send you the report and the final bill," she stepped back.

"Thank you so much," he was so happy he was crying.

"It's what I do."

He shook her hand, "your Aunt Sophie did a hell of a job raising you."

Dice smiled and nodded, it was great that she brought his wife back but there was something that had happened while out at Muffin and Charlotte's farm that she couldn't put her finger on. There was more to the story than she knew ... than any of them knew. After a few more thank you's and some more praising Dice finally escaped the Barnett's home.

Parking downstairs she grabbed her laptop bag, purse and bag. Crossing over to the elevator, she pressed the call button. The door slide open and she stepped on. Pressing the code, she waited for it to lift her to her floor. Stepping off, she was so happy to see her home, Unlocking the door she slipped inside. Dropping her keys in the dish, kicking her shoes off, she left the bag with her clothes by the door and dumped her purse and laptop bag on the counter. Grabbing the clothes bag, she headed down the hall where she left it to be laundered. Taking a quick shower and changing into some pajamas, she made her way back out to the kitchen in her robe. Turning the kettle on, she made herself a sandwich and then a cup of tea. Stepping outside the night air felt cool and welcoming. Parking herself in her favorite lounge she lit a candle and watched the stars as she ate her sandwich and drank her tea. It was relaxing and so good to be home. Tomorrow she would go into the office and finish off her notes pack up this case, drop the report and final bill off to Kyle Barnett.

Starring up at the stars she felt insignificant in the grand scheme of things. There were things in this universe she didn't understand. Aliens … women disappearing and reappearing out of the blue. Where was Linda for over a year? She dozed off in her lounge. Waking up a couple hours later, she outted the candle and headed back inside crawling into bed, it never felt so good.

CHAPTER FIFTEEN

SATURDAY 7:34 AM

Stretching she rolled out of bed and slipped into her running gear, stopping at the bathroom she brushed her teeth and brushed her hair pulling it back. Stopping in the kitchen, she grabbed her iPod and ear buds, grabbing the keys on the way out the door. The morning cool air was refreshing.

Running her usual route, Dice stopped at a bench and looked out over Lake Ontario. It was so beautiful the way the sun sparkled on the wave peaks. Birds flew lazily above.

Sitting there, she breathed in the fresh air and wondered what really happened.

"Hey kiddo, what's up?" a familiar voice interrupted her moment of solace.

"Sean Larke, I thought you were avoiding me," she didn't look at him. Instead she watched a boat speed across the water.

"Dice, I'm really sorry for how I treated you."

She nodded and said nothing. He came and sat down beside her. Then shifted himself closer to her. Sean reached out and grabbed her hand. "I am going through some things with Alisha now and I just need time. I really like you more than I should. I think I am in love with you and it's driving me crazy. Crazy to think you are angry with me."

She didn't turn to look at him. She couldn't look into his eyes. If she did she would melt and let it go. "You should be. I may still be considered young to some people but I'm old enough to know you don't treat people you care about like crap. You don't play with their emotions and you don't pretend to like them and then date other people. I stayed with a man for four years because I thought I needed to have someone in my life to help me through and be my rock. He cheated on me twice. I'm getting too old to play games." She pulled her hand back from him. "What I realized is that I am more stronger than I thought I was. I am my own rock and I don't need anyone to be there for me. I am sorry we slept together and you wanted more … something I couldn't offer you at the time. I'm glad you found it with someone else," she turned and looked at him. "I'm not here for your amusement. I can only offer you friendship. Take it or leave it, that is up to you."

"Dice didn't you hear me? I love you."

"I heard you but I don't think you heard me. I am not here for you to toy with." She got up and put her ear buds back in and continued with her run. She got a few feet away when he came up behind her and grabbed her shoulder pulling her to a stop. She turned around to give him a piece of her mind when he hugged her. Catching her off guard, she found herself sinking into the warm embrace. Her ear buds slips out. He kissed her on the lips and she pushed him back.

Looking her in the eyes, he promised, "I'll make it up to you. I'll make you believe me."

She wanted to snip a reply back but a part of her cheered and hope he meant it. Dice wanted to crush that inner cheerleader to bits. He turned and took off running in the opposite direction she was going.

An hour later she was showered, dress and sitting in her office at her desk with a coffee in hand. Pulling out her mini recording devices, she plugged it in and looked for the files. It was wiped clean. Nothing was there. Thank God she had a great memory and she had taken notes. Digging out her notes, she got her receipts and anything else related to the case out spreading it out on top of her desk. Then she went to it. It was three hours later she had her notes entered, the official report for Kyle Barnett done, which included a list of people she interviewed, notes on each day's investigation she had worked on the case. Dice gathered copies of receipts and stapled them to the financial expenses, the final bill minus the down payment in on top of the report. Dice put everything in a small paper box. She grabbed the files he had given her in the elastic band wrapped envelope. Grabbing her briefcase, she put the box and envelop in there. Then saved all the files, getting up she walked around the room and took down all the papers and pics she had taped up all over the walls. Peeling the tape off, she stuffed them in a folder and along with the copies, she made of the official report, she stuff the papers including the original receipts and financials in the folder. Filing it away in the filing cabinet under B for Barnett, Kyle, Dice grabbed her briefcase and purse and headed out. She called Kyle who said he was working from home today and he was pleased that she was so prompt.

Pulling up into the driveway, she parked and gathered up her bag and purse. Tucking her keys into her pants pocket, as she stepped up to the front door. It opened before she could knock. Kyle Barnett was standing there with a big smile on his face. "Come in, come in. Did you see the news this morning?"

"I heard Linda is no longer a missing person report."

"That's all thanks to you young lady." He hugged her and closed the door behind her. "Come this way into my office." She followed him through the house and into the back yard to the patio. He offered her a drink she accepted coffee. They sat down and she pulled out the documents. They went through them and she looked around, "where is Linda?"

"She went out to visit old friends and to see about getting her job back at the university."

"Oh that's great."

"I know she will drive me nuts if they don't take her back. I am prepared to make a large donation if I have to," he laughed. Looking down at her report that she brought over, he shook his head. "Wow you are really thorough. I can offer you ten times the amount you make working for yourself if you want a staple security job."

She laughed, "ten times the amount, yeah."

"Is that a yes?"

"I'm sorry are you seriously offering me a full-time job?"

"Yes, as head of my security detail. If you are interested, the job is yours."

"Ah," she stammered. "Thank you but I love doing what I am doing now."

"For you the job will always be open. You just need to ask for it."

Smiling she nodded, "well, thank you."

He pulled out his checkbook and filled it out, then passed it over to her. She looked at it and passed it back to him. "I think you made a mistake that's not what I am asking for."

"No, I know I gave you a bonus."

"Even if that is including a bonus that is way too much," she wasn't sure if he just made a mistake or what.

He shoved it back to her, "I know what I gave you and I included a bonus. You're the first person to question me like this. I am very serious about that job, you just say the word it's yours anytime."

She took the check and shoved it into her briefcase with the signed document that the contract was completed. "Well, thank you for your time Mr. Barnett. If you ever need my services again don't hesitate to call."

"I won't, you can call me Kyle. Thank you again for bringing my wife home to me," he walked her to the front door and gave her a big hug again. "I can never repay you for this."

"I was just doing my job I am so happy it worked out like this. Have a great day."

"I will," he waved to her as she got into the car.

Dice stopped off at the bank and deposited her check. Then headed over to the Red Dragon for a celebratory drink, grabbing a seat, Lily came over and asked her what she wanted. Dice ordered herself dinner and a glass of red wine. Just as Lily disappeared, Chris came in and smiled as soon as he saw her there.

He came over and gave her a hug and kiss on the lips. "Congratulations Maddox! You're all over the news."

She laughed, "I hadn't seen it, but heard about it when I stopped for coffee on my way over to my client's home."

He pulled a chair over and sat down beside her. "Everyone is talking about it. I wouldn't be surprised if this nets you more jobs."

"I did get offer with an obscene amount of money from Kyle Barnett to be head of his security detail."

"I'm not surprised the man is thrilled to death to have his wife back. Heard she got her job back at the university too," he waved at Lily and signaled her to bring him a drink. She nodded.

"I hadn't heard that, I couldn't imagine them not doing that though."

"Have you heard the news Alisha and Sean broke up? How do you feel about that?"

"I'm not interested."

He laughed, "yeah right."

"I'm not."

"Alright, don't let your stubborn pride get in the way of something amazing Maddox," Chris gave her a half hug.

"I just want to eat and enjoy my celebratory drink, another case wrapped up. If you want to talk about him go sit at a table by yourself."

"Your aunt called me about dinner tomorrow night."

"Ah yes … almost forgot."

"I told her we would be there."

"Great," she laughed.

"Alright, Maddox don't get so excited. After dinner you want to go play a game of mini putt?"

She laughed, "You are on."

To be continued ….

Keep a look out for **Book 3** in the Maddox Files Series

Maddox Files Down the Rabbit Hole

ABOUT THE AUTHOR

R. J. Davies is a Canadian author who was born in Sault Ste. Marie, Ontario and has lived in Toronto for a few years. She is currently residing in her home town and has been writing since she was 8 years of age. Attended Sault College where she started out in Police Foundations and then graduated from Computer Engineering. Also has a diploma in Accounting and Office Administration and Private Investigation.

You can find her constantly researching and jotting down story ideas, conversations and scenes in ratty notebooks, on napkins and slips of coffee stained torn envelopes. She loves reading theoretical physics books, science fiction and books by her friends. Another favorite past time is hanging out with her son, Denziel Mornix (Denziel the Best!).

Learn more about R. J. at Amazon

Or visit her website! http://www.rjdavies.ca

Other Books by the Author

Dice Maddox Series (Novellas)

Dice Maddox: Web of Lies
Dice Maddox: The Mad Hatter
Dice Maddox: The Hunt for Jackie Sparrow (coming soon)

Maddox Files Series (Novels)

Maddox Files: Back to Business
Maddox Files: Blurred Lines (this book)
Maddox Files: Down the Rabbit Hole (coming soon)

www.ingramcontent.com/pod-product-compliance
Lightning Source LLC
Chambersburg PA
CBHW071330250626
47159CB00004B/1539